THE ACE OF HEARTS

Philip Denham never *could* resist a wager. Which was, he reflected glumly, how he had come to this fix. As the lovely Augusta Glendenning whirled past him in the dance, the handsome gambler began to wonder if some wagers weren't better lost . . .

Berkley books by Elizabeth Mansfield

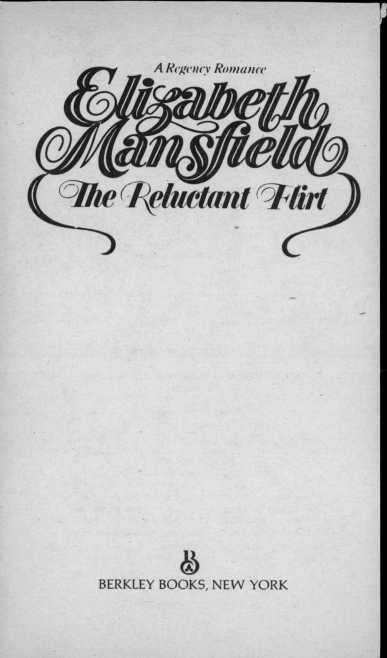

A Regency Romance

Elizabeth Mansfield

The Reluctant Flirt

BERKLEY BOOKS, NEW YORK

THE RELUCTANT FLIRT

A Berkley Book / published by arrangement with
the author

PRINTING HISTORY
Berkley edition / November 1981

ISBN: 0-425-05088-2

A BERKLEY BOOK® TM 757,375

PRINTED IN THE UNITED STATES OF AMERICA

Prologue

THE SOUND OF one malicious chuckle could be heard above the chorus of groans which issued from the throats of the onlookers surrounding the card table in the largest and most smoky room of Watier's Gambling Club. Philip Denham, the favorite, had lost another rubber to Marmaduke Shackleford, and Shackleford lacked the sportsmanship to restrain his glee. "Damnation, Shackleford," the elderly Lord Lytton rebuked, "can't you learn to win like a gentleman?"

Shackleford merely cackled again and rubbed his pudgy hands together in self-satisfaction. With only a flick of his eyes toward Lord Lytton, and ignoring the expressions of distaste on the faces of the other onlookers, he leered triumphantly at his opponent. "If you're too badly dipped to continue to play, old fellow," he chortled again as he swept up the guineas from the center of the table and stacked them in front of him in neat, impressively high piles, "I'd be happy to advance you a monkey or two. Your vowels are always good."

Vowels. Philip Denham, leaning back in his chair with a nonchalance that belied the tension in his stomach, was growing to hate the sound of that word. In this, its gambling usage, the word 'vowels' had been coined to permit the speaker to avoid the more vulgar term I.O.U. The word had once struck him

1

as a rather witty pun, but it only irritated him now. Whatever one called that little scrap of paper, it was an "I owe you" all the same. And of late Philip had signed many too many of them.

But there was nothing in the glint of his cool blue eyes as they roamed over the florid face of the man seated opposite him to reveal his inner turmoil. "Very generous of you, Shackleford," he responded with noncommittal lightness, a slight smile on his lips. "Very generous."

The gentlemen surrounding the table held their breaths. They were all aware of Denham's precarious situation. A prime favorite among the members of Watier's for his daring, his cool elegance, his calm deliberation under stress and his prowess at all gentlemanly sports, Philip Denham had been causing them all to shake their heads in concern over his sudden onslaught of rotten luck at the gaming tables. Whether at basset, faro or piquet (the game in which he'd just indulged), Denham, who for years had seemed to be Fortune's darling, had suddenly found out how fickle the Lady Chance could be. The cards and dice had turned against him. No matter how skilled his play, no matter what daring he exhibited, his luck was out. Night after night, Dame Fortune continued to show her back to him.

There was no doubt in the minds of his many friends that his luck would soon turn. Bad luck, they knew, was as likely as good luck to reverse itself. And when it did, they would all have found it very satisfying to be witnesses to the event. To a man, they wished his luck would change when he opposed Shackleford. It was Marmaduke Shackleford, the most disliked member of the club, who had won from Lady Luck the smile she'd turned away from Denham. And tonight, with Denham's six-hundred stacked up before him, Shackleford was behaving with revolting self-satisfaction in the face of Denham's ill-fortune.

Shackleford was a whiny loser as well as an insufferable winner. The fellow seemed to care nothing for the conventions of gentlemanly gaming. There wasn't a ploy or device he was above using—short of outright cheating—to wrest victory from an opponent. Behind his back, the members all mocked his penchant for scurvy tricks like whistling noisily through his teeth during play, slowing down the pace to an irritating crawl, or finding a flimsy excuse to break up the game when the cards were running against him. Yet none of his strategems was dishonest or heinous enough to permit the management to strip him of his membership.

Every onlooker would have been happy to see Shackleford get a long-deserved drubbing—and at Philip Denham's hands. While they could not, in good conscience, urge Denham to go further into debt by signing vowels again, they couldn't help hoping he would indulge himself one more time. Perhaps *this* would be the time when the unpredictable Dame Fortune would decide to smile on him again.

But Philip's friend, Ned Glendenning, standing directly behind Philip's chair, leaned down and whispered into his friend's ear, "Don't be an idiot, Philip! You're down more than six hundred!"

Philip absently patted the hand Ned had placed on his shoulder. He was indeed too badly dipped to continue to play. An advance of four or five hundred pounds would permit him to continue the game for a couple of hours even if his run of ill-luck should continue, but to throw another five hundred after what he'd already lost seemed a foolhardy act. Ned had his best interests at heart. He ought, he told himself, to listen to Ned's advice.

"Well, Denham, what do you say?" Marmaduke Shackleford urged.

"Don't do it, boy," Lord Lytton advised. "Much as we'd all enjoy seeing you get another chance at Shackleford here, pleasing us ain't worth the danger of getting yourself into Dun territory."

"Thank you, Lord Lytton," Philip responded calmly, waving for a waiter, "but perhaps it *is* worth the danger." He took a pen and pad from the tray the waiter carried, tore off a sheet and scribbled upon it. The onlookers murmured excitedly, but Ned leaned forward and whispered worriedly, "Have you lost your mind? Another five hundred will make your total over—"

"It's for a thousand," Philip murmured in return, signing the sheet with a devil-may-care flourish. He tossed it across the table, nodded to Shackleford and got to his feet. "There you are. My vowels. Now, if you'll excuse me for a few minutes, I'd like a bite of supper before we resume play. Come, Ned, let's go downstairs and sample the buffet."

With a nod to Lord Lytton, a smile for several of his well-wishers and a handshake for a few others, Philip made his way through the crowd, Ned following closely at his heels. But as the crowd dispersed, Philip stopped in his tracks. There at the outer fringe of the circle, frowning at him in disapproval, stood his brother, Roger.

Philip felt his color rise. Roger Denham, the fourth Earl of Arneau, was ten years Philip's senior, had been more like a father than a brother to him, and was the one person in the world whose good opinion Philip craved. Only two months before, Roger had paid all Philip's debts, but with the admonition that he bring his gambling tendencies under control. "Roger," he greeted gaily, valiantly hiding his consternation at having been observed at the card table under these circumstances, "what brings you to Watier's? I was under the impression that the atmosphere at *White's* was more your style."

"It is," Roger Denham replied, taking his brother's arm and maneuvering his way through the dispersing crowd. "The wagering in this establishment is far too unrestrained for my taste—as I'd hoped it would be for yours."

Philip cast a quick, guilty look at his brother's impassive face but then managed a carefree laugh. He could think of no defense against his brother's mild admonition, so he quickly chose to go on the attack. "Don't try to evade my question, Roger, old man. If you so dislike these premises, what brings you here?"

"You do."

"I?" Philip raised an eyebrow in cool innocence. "What do you mean?"

Ned, who had been following discreetly behind, cleared his throat bravely. "*I* told him to come, Philip. Felt you needed some . . . er . . . family guidance."

Philip wheeled on his friend in irritation. "Oh, you *did*, did you? May I ask why?"

Ned chewed at his moustache nervously. Unlike his friend, he did not have the talent to hide his feelings behind a mask of impassivity. "Because I'm your *friend*, you nodcock. *And* your brother-in-law."

"What has *that* to say to anything? Is that a proper excuse for saying God-knows-what about me to my brother . . . and behind my back?"

"Cut line, Philip," Roger broke in, leading them into the almost-deserted lounge. "He only said he feared you might be getting in too deep."

"And what right had he to say that? Just because you married his sister—"

"Letty has nothing to do with this," Ned said in self-defense. "I took the liberty of speaking to Roger because I think you're becoming addicted to gaming...like Lord Alvaney, and...and..." His eyes fell. "And my father, before he died."

"What gammon," Philip scoffed. "Are you seriously trying to compare me to *them*? Lord Alvaney squanders his entire income at the tables—a matter, they say, of sixty or seventy thousand per annum. And, if you'll forgive blunt speaking, your father gambled away his entire estate. In comparision, *my* gambling is child's play. I'm down only a mere..." His voice faltered.

"A mere *what*, Philip?" Roger inquired softly, seating himself on a wing chair near the window and motioning the two younger men to the sofa at his right.

Philip bit his lip. Carefully spreading his coattails, he took the indicated seat, grateful that the action gave him an opportunity to drop his eyes from his brother's piercing gaze. "Only a...a couple of thousand."

"I see."

There was a strained pause. Philip, his eyes on his hands which he'd placed on his knees, could feel Ned staring at him in shock. His friend was well aware that the extent of his indebtedness was far beyond a couple of thousand, but Philip knew that Ned, in spite of having run to Roger with his alarms, would not contradict him now.

"You know, Philip," Roger said thoughtfully, "Ned is not so far off in comparing you to Alvaney and Glendenning. When determining the grip that gaming has made on a man, it isn't the amount lost which is significant but the ability to pay. Alvaney may do as he likes and not be called a gamester, for his income supports his excesses. But Glendenning..." He paused.

Ned sighed. "You may speak your mind, Roger. Everyone knows my father left his family in dire straits. Why, if you hadn't married Letty, I don't know what we should have done. Gaming had so taken hold of my father that even his family's future was wagered away." He sat down beside Philip and laid a hand on his arm. "I don't want to see you take that road."

"Oh, come now, Ned. You don't really believe that I'm as bad as that!"

Ned's hand fell away, and his eyes wavered. "I don't know. Perhaps you are."

Philip snorted disdainfully. "What rubbish!"

"Don't sneer, Philip," Roger admonished, studying his brother's face, a worried frown creasing his brow. "There may be some substance to Ned's fears."

"Why? Just because I'm down a couple of thousand?"

"You have only a modest competence. With an income like yours, even a couple of thousand of debt can be considered excessive."

"Well," Philip said with a sudden grin, hoping to lighten the atmosphere with a bit of levity, "you have only yourself to blame, having been first born."

Roger smiled reluctantly. "Yes, I know. If I hadn't been born, you would have been the Earl and had all the blunt you could wish for to squander away."

"Right!" Philip laughed. It was an old bit of raillery between them, meant to reassure each other that the accident of birth and the laws of primogeniture (which gave wealth to the elder and only a limited competence to the younger) had not caused any bitterness to poison their mutual affection. Roger was as generous a brother as Philip could wish, and there was not a twinge of resentment in his heart against Roger just because he, Philip, had been born a second son.

Ned looked from one brother to the other. "It's all very well to laugh, but the fact remains that Philip has been showing worrisome signs—"

"What signs?" Philip asked, his smile fading.

"Look at the ready way you signed those vowels just now."

Philip glared at Ned in disgust. "You know I only did that to win back enough to get clear. Not because gaming's in my blood, you gudgeon."

"That's what every gamester says," Roger put in quietly.

Philip shot his brother an injured look. Jumping to his feet, he turned his back on them and walked to a nearby window. "So. That's what my brother and my best friend think of me. A wild, uncontrolled, devil-take-the-hindmost gamester."

Roger came up behind him and put an arm on his shoulder. "You know quite well that's not true. We only want to warn you that it can *become* true. Did you realize that Marmaduke Shackleford himself used to be quite good company a few years ago? I've spent many an enjoyable evening with him in my bachelor days. Now I can barely recognize him. Not only has his constant gaming changed his *physical* aspect, but his entire character is altered."

Philip lowered his head. "You needn't worry. I shall not turn into another Shackleford," he said coldly.

"I know that." Roger turned quickly away, afraid he'd said too much. "Well, I'd better take myself off before Letty begins to wonder what's become of me. I'll send round a draft for three thousand to your room tomorrow."

"Why *three*?" Philip asked, looking quickly over his shoulder. "I only said a *couple*—"

"Yes, but you just signed vowels for another thousand, didn't you? I wasn't certain you'd included it. Well, good night. Don't forget that Letty's expecting you both at her little dinner party Friday evening." And he was gone.

"How did he know I signed that note for a thousand?" Philip asked Ned in amazement. "Did you tell him?"

"No, of course not. When could I have done so?"

"Then how the devil did he guess?"

"He knows you better than you know yourself," Ned remarked, rising and joining him at the window. He lowered his voice. "Why did you let him think you only owe a couple of thousand pounds? By my calculations, your outstanding vowels come to almost eight—"

Philip stared out into the darkened street. "The truth is I owe more than ten."

"*Ten thousand*?" Ned's voice rose an octave. "Good God! Have you taken leave of your senses? Why didn't you *tell* him?"

Just then, Philip could faintly discern, in the street below, his brother jumping briskly into his carriage. He remained silent for a moment, watching the equipage move off down the street and out of sight. "I *couldn't* tell him. He'd get that *look* in his eyes, you know."

"No, I *don't* know. What look?"

"I can't really describe it. A sort of *hurt* look . . . as if it were *his* fault that his brother was turning out to be a wastrel or worse. I couldn't have borne it. I'm not going to tell him. I'll work this out myself."

"But *ten thousand*? How on earth—?"

"I haven't the foggiest idea," Philip said, squaring his shoulders, turning about and striding briskly toward the door. "Let's get back to the table, shall we?"

Ned made a gesture of alarm, ran after his friend and grasped his arm. "Wait a minute, Philip! You're not going to *continue* this ill-fated game with Shackleford, are you?"

"Why not? Perhaps my luck will change."

Ned winced. "But, Philip, *listen* to me!" he urged desperately. "Don't chance it. If you withdraw now, you'll save the thousand. And that saving, added to the three thousand your brother is sending you, will reduce your debts by almost half . . . and without any risk!"

"What good is *half*? If I win, I have a chance to make it *all*!"

Ned wanted to shake him. "But . . . what if you don't win?"

Philip grinned. "Don't take on so, Neddie, old man. Everything will come about. It always does."

"No, it doesn't! Good heavens, man, have you *considered*? What will you *do* if you don't win?"

Philip shrugged with admirable nonchalance. "Then I'll think of something else." And with Ned's eyes fixed on his back in consternation, Philip sauntered off down the corridor as if he hadn't a care in the world.

Chapter One

THE TWO CARRIAGES, approaching the modest Glendenning house in Argyle Street from opposite directions, attempted to turn into the drive at the same moment, but (since one was a small and rather shabby curricle and the other an elegant black traveling coach with polished brass fittings and a crest at the side) the driver of the curricle gave way to nobility. Thus, when the curricle drew up to the doorway of the neat residence (with its tall windows, symmetrical facade and its three stone steps leading up to the front door) the red-haired Prudence Peake jumped down eagerly (in alarming unconcern for the life evidently growing in her swollen midsection), Letty, Countess Denham, was already waiting on the lowest step.

"Letty!" Prue chortled eagerly.

"Prue!" The Countess smiled, enveloping her sister in a warm but careful hug.

"Mama sent for you, too!" they exclaimed together.

Grinning at each other in amusement, and keeping up a stream of witty speculation about the nature of this latest disaster which their mother claimed had fallen upon her head, they entered the house and greeted the butler familiarly. "What is it *now*, Hinson?" Prue demanded, handing her bonnet over to his care.

"It's not Clara again, is it?" Letty added, removing her gloves.

"If you mean Miss *Claryce*," the butler corrected tactfully, "I believe there *has* been an altercation involving her."

Letty and Prue looked at each other knowingly. "Is she still using that ridiculous name?" Prue asked bluntly.

"Yes, indeed, Mrs. Peake. She quite insists on it."

Prue looked up at the butler with mock irritation. "Mrs. Peake, is it? Just because Clara—I beg your pardon, *Claryce*—wishes to elevate herself in her own esteem by taking on a romantical name is no reason, Hinson, for you to call *me* Mrs. Peake in that haughty style."

Hinson colored. "But I can't very well call you Mrs. Prue, you know, madam. It would be quite lacking in dignity, especially—" His color deepened.

"—Especially now that I'm breeding, is that it? Oh, very well, Hinson, call me whatever you like. I suppose you call Miss Letty *Countess Denham* now, as well."

"Oh, yes, indeed. Four years now I've been so addressing her, isn't that right, your ladyship?"

Letty, looking in the wall mirror as she removed the wide-brimmed, ostrich-feathered bonnet from her swept-up curls, smiled at his reflection in the glass. "Yes, four years this Friday. Although it took two years for me to become used to it. Tell us, Hinson, is Mama up in the—?"

Hinson nodded. "In the upstairs sitting room, yes, your ladyship."

"Then we may as well go up without ado," Letty sighed, and she made for the stairs. Prue, after placing a manuscript tied with string on the hall table, followed her.

Lady Glendenning was, as her two eldest daughters expected, stretched out on the sofa, her head elevated by the sofa cushions, her feet propped up on three thickly-stuffed pillows, and a wet cloth covering her eyes. One arm was thrown across her forehead in an attitude of despair while the other hung down over the side of the sofa in woebegone listlessness. Hovering over her, handkerchief at the ready, was Miss Dorrimore, once governess to the girls but now acting as live-in companion to Lady Glendenning. And sitting at the window, stitching away at a piece of needlework, was the third sister, Augusta Glendenning. At the sound of the door, Augusta looked up. "Letty! Prue!" She threw her mother a look of mild disgust.

"I might have known! Mama, I *told* you not to send for them again."

"Don't scold, Gussie," Prue said, crossing to the window and planting an affectionate kiss on her sister's cheek. "We really don't mind. How do you do, Miss Dorrimore?"

"Well, Mama, what is it this time?" Letty asked, kneeling down beside the sofa and kissing her mother's brow gently.

"Letty, my love!" Lady Glendenning murmured in a trembling voice, throwing the cloth from her eyes and pulling herself to a sitting position. "How are your babies? How dreadful that I was forced to drag you away from them."

"They are both well. You must come to the house very soon and see them for yourself."

"And Prue!" Lady Glendenning sighed. "You are positively blooming. If I were in a less agitated state of mind, I would be quite overjoyed to see how fit you are looking." She sighed again, lifted a trembling hand to her forehead and fell back against the cushions again. "But that child completely oversets my spirits."

"Claryce is not a child, Mama," Prue remarked. "Now, stop all this sighing and tell us what she's done."

"It's nothing at all," Gussie said firmly. "I've told Mama repeatedly that I don't care a *jot* about Mr. Wivilscombe."

Lady Glendenning sat bolt upright in indignation. "Nonsense! He's a very presentable gentleman."

"*Most* presentable," Miss Dorrimore agreed. "Quite eagerly sought after, they say."

"Yes, and I'm told he has a generous nature, an excellent background and *fifteen thousand* a year," Lady Glendenning added. "How *can* you say, Gussie, that you don't care for him?"

"He is also notoriously indiscriminate, a prattle-box, and thirty-five years old," Gussie muttered, returning to her stitchery.

"I'll have you know, Gussie," Letty said in amused reproof, "that my *Roger* is thirty-five years old."

Gussie threw her eldest sister a quick, affectionate grin. "But your Roger, as we all know, is a *paragon*."

But Prue's mind was on the *real* problem. She frowned down at her mother thoughtfully. "Do you mean that Claryce has walked off with *another* of Gussie's beaux?"

"He was *not* my beau!" Gussie declared.

"Yes, he *was*!" Lady Glendenning insisted, close to tears. "He had come calling on Gussie at least three times! I truly began to believe that he would soon declare himself. But as soon as Claryce suspected that his intentions were serious, she started to flirt with him! She's out riding with him at this very moment!" Shaking her head in dismay, Lady Glendenning dabbed at her eyes with a very damp handkerchief. "I've had five children! *Five*! And every one of them, even Neddie, has been a source of joy to me . . . except Claryce!" She looked up at the ceiling as the tears spilled over. "What did I ever do, I ask myself . . . what error in nuturing . . . what act of neglect . . . to deserve such—?"

"Oh, your ladyship, *don't*!" moaned Miss Dorrimore, applying her handkerchief to Lady Glendenning's left cheek.

"Do stop crying, Mama," Letty said quietly, sitting down beside her mother and wiping Lady Glendenning's *right* cheek with a dry handkerchief of her own. "You can't blame yourself. Being the youngest of five children might have been difficult for Clara—Claryce. We used to tease her and taunt her shamefully. Perhaps it's *our* fault—"

"Don't be a couple of goosecaps," Prue said bluntly, lowering herself carefully into a chair beside Gussie. "She's turned into a beauty and has let it go to her head, that's all. None of us is in the least to blame that she's become a spoiled brat."

No one saw fit to chastise Prue for her plain speaking. Claryce *was* spoiled, and she had been so since childhood. Her selfishness and tendency to whine had been attributed, in her earlier years, to immaturity and lack of special attention from a large and very active family. But now, at eighteen, Claryce had come into her own. Ever since her sister Letty had brought her out six months ago, Claryce had been completely self-centered. Strikingly lovely, with a *retroussé* nose, reddish-gold curls, lively brown-speckled grey eyes and a milky-smooth skin, she charmed every man she met. Nothing gave her more pleasure than to attach a gentleman to her, although she was very careful to keep her own heart untouched. She reveled in the fact that among the gentlemen she was known as Glassheart Glendenning. Her impregnability was a challenge to them and kept them vying with each other for a chance to make a mark on her. She had a larger circle of admirers than any other Marriageable Miss in London, and it was her aim to keep the circle growing for as long as the game pleased her.

There might have been some mothers who would have been *pleased* to see their daughters make so spectacular a success, but Lady Glendenning took no pleasure in it at all. She was painfully aware that, among the young ladies of the *ton*, Claryce Glendenning was universally disliked. The young ladies knew her to be a notorious beau-snatcher. She had not one friend, nor did she seem to care. But what caused Lady Glendenning the most severe suffering was Claryce's callousness toward her own sister. Every young man who called on Augusta was, in Claryce's judgment, fair game. Lady Glendenning had never told a soul, but she secretly suspected that Claryce had even tried to lure Roger Denham, her own *brother-in-law*, into her net. Claryce had always been jealous of her eldest sister, who'd married the most sought-after bachelor in London. Fortunately, Roger was so completely besotted over his Letty that he paid not the slightest attention to the wiles and lures of other women. And as for Prue's husband, Brandon Peake, *he* made so few appearances in society and was so absorbed by his scholarly pursuits that Claryce must have realized there was little point in even *attempting* to attach him.

Prue's gruff honesty caused a bleak silence to fall on the room, for no one present could find it in her heart to deny the truth. Nor did anyone know quite how to deal with the problem. Claryce was a selfish, vain creature, and, as far as her family knew, there was no easy cure for such a condition.

It was Augusta who broke the silence. "If you are all worrying about *me*," she said, her voice mild, cheerful and utterly sincere, "you are unnecessarily troubling yourselves. I am quite happy that Claryce has taken Mr. Wivilscombe for herself. Mama, I *wish* you will believe me and not shed any more tears over this."

"You're quite right," Prue said in hearty agreement, heaving herself up from her chair and patting her stomach as if to tell the little life within that there was nothing out here worth concerning himself about. "If Gussie assures us that she is not distressed, I think we should take her word and not waste another moment discussing the matter. So, Mama, please make haste and dry your eyes, for I would like us to take tea together before I leave for home."

"Oh, *tea*! It quite slipped my mind!" Miss Dorrimore exclaimed in a flurry of dismay and hurried to the door. "Please excuse me . . . I shall see to the arrangements at once."

"While we're waiting, Gussie," Prue said, taking her sister's hand, "I'd like you to come downstairs with me so that I can show you what Brandon has sent you. I left it on the hall table. It's a copy of his translation of the *Agememnon*. He would very much like your opinion of it."

She urged Augusta from her chair and pushed her before her out the door, giving Letty a significant look over her shoulder just before leaving the room. Letty completely understood her sister's glance. Prue was indicating that she thought the matter could better be discussed without Gussie's presence.

"You shouldn't talk about Claryce in front of Gussie in that way, Mama," Letty suggested quietly when she and her mother were alone. "If Gussie *did* care for Mr. Wivilscombe, our conversation might have given her a great deal of pain."

"Oh, dear," Lady Glendenning murmured miserably, twisting her soggy handkerchief in nervous fingers, "do you think she *did* care for him?"

"No, I don't. But in future I think we should be more discreet."

"In future? Good heavens, Letty, do you think we shall have *more* of this wretched business? Oh, I don't know why I ask when I quite know the answer. Of *course* we shall. Claryce will *never* let her sister become a bride!" Her eyes filled again, and she leaned toward Letty and clutched at her hand. "Letty, what *am* I to do?"

Letty bit her underlip thoughtfully. "I wish I knew, Mama. Really, I'd like to give our Claryce a good thrashing!"

"So would I! I should have spanked her years ago, when her selfishness first became noticeable. Now, of course, it's much too late. Why, oh why, is life so unfair? Why is Claryce so pretty and Gussie so . . . pallid?"

"*Pallid*, Mama? What an odd word. I've never thought of her in that way."

"Haven't you? Oh, dear . . . it *is* a dreadful thing for a mother to say, I suppose, but don't you think . . . in company, at least . . . that our dearest Augusta tends to pale out of sight?"

Letty's brows drew together in thoughtful concern. "I don't know. To me, she has always been Gussie—my dear, sensitive, thoughtful sister. I hadn't thought about how she might appear in a ballroom. I've always found her to be quite pretty . . . certainly pretty enough to attract admirers."

"Do you really think so?" Lady Glendenning asked, searching her daughter's face eagerly. "I have always felt that, too. Her hair is so shimmery and silky, and her eyes are quite large and speaking, even if their color is so light . . . but to a mother's eyes, you know . . ." She blinked and sniffed into her handkerchief again. "But then, even to *me* our Gussie appears positively mouse-like beside Claryce. It is dreadfully unmotherly to say so, but I am convinced that Claryce takes perverse *delight* in taking the shine out of her sister!"

"Don't fall into a taking, Mama," Letty said, patting her mother's arm comfortingly. "It's only a squabble between two sisters, after all."

"Only a *squabble*?" Lady Glendenning tottered to her feet and stared down at her daughter in horror. "*Only* a squabble? How can you *say* so? Why, Augusta's entire *future* is at stake! Do you want her to dwindle into an *old maid*?" She sank back down upon the sofa, her eyes filling up again. "I thought that you would understand the *enormity*—"

"I do, Mama, I do. Please don't start to cry again. Prue and I will give the matter some thought. Between us, we shall think of *something*." She stood up and helped her mother to her feet. "But now, put on a brighter face and come down to tea."

She wiped her mother's cheeks again and put an arm around her. Lady Glendenning gave her a brave if tremulous smile. "Yes, you and Prue will find a solution, I'm sure of it. Thank you for coming, dearest. You are always as good as a tonic to my spirits."

* * *

Later, after Lady Glendenning had bravely swallowed a sip of tea (but declared herself incapable of eating a morsel of the delectable biscuits, cakes and sweetmeats which had been spread out on the tea-table in the downstairs sitting room), she permitted Prue and Miss Dorrimore to help her up to her bedroom so that she could rest her nerves. Even this provoked a tearful argument, Lady Glendenning objecting to Prue's assistance when the young woman was in "so delicate a condition." But Prue, who'd made up her mind not to permit her pregnancy to sap her customary vitality, merely teased away her mother's remonstrances and, with Miss Dorrimore's assistance, led her lachrymose mother from the room.

This left Letty and Augusta alone. Letty sat sipping her second cup of tea and gazing rather abstractedly out of the tall double windows, while Augusta looked over the first few pages of her brother-in-law's manuscript. The October sun was rapidly dropping behind the roof of the neighboring house, lighting their faces with a rich, amber glow. Letty, stealing a look at her sister's face, was struck by the beauty in it which the afternoon sun revealed. Who would call Augusta Glendenning mouse-like if he could see her like this, with the golden light etching shadows below her high cheekbones and setting her pale gold hair aflame? If only the unfaithful Mr. Wivilscombe could see her now!

She stirred her tea thoughtfully. "Did you *truly* not care for Mr. Wivilscombe, Gussie, love?" she asked gently.

Gussie turned and smiled at her sister fondly. "Truly, Letty. He is not at all the sort for me. Did you know that he's known as The Seal?"

Letty laughed. "The *Seal*? But why?"

"Well, his appearance does *suggest* a seal, you know—he is big and jovial and has a walrusy moustache. But I believe the epithet comes from his being so slippery and hard to catch. They say that he's pursued any number of females over the last ten years, but whenever they've thought that the situation had arrived at the point of betrothal, he's managed to slip away. It may be fortunate that Claryce took him away before he was able to make a fool of me. You may ask Roger, if you don't believe me. Mr. Wivilscombe told me that he and Roger are quite well acquainted. They used to spend time together before Roger became such a devoted family man, he said. Roger will undoubtedly confirm my statement that I'm well rid of him."

"I'll take your word, you wet-goose," Letty assured her affectionately.

Gussie sighed. "I wish Mama would. It's quite humiliating to have her weeping over me like this."

"I know. Mama does tend to make a to-do over trifles. Nevertheless, Gussie, you should not permit Claryce to take such advantage of you."

"But I don't feel taken advantage of in the least. If Claryce enjoys collecting swains, I don't see what that has to do with me."

"But . . . you mustn't let her collect *your* swains, my dear."

"Why not? *I* certainly don't want them."

"Gussie!" Letty looked at her sister in surprise. "You can't mean that you're uninterested in beaux altogether!"

"Yes, I do mean it," Gussie explained in her mild way.

"I'm not very comfortable with fashionable gentlemen. I find it such a strain to say the proper things and keep the conversation moving."

"Do you, love? Why is that? You find it perfectly easy to speak to all of *us*."

"I know. I don't quite understand it myself. Perhaps I just don't care enough about them to exert myself."

"But you *must* exert yourself!" Letty declared fervently. "You don't want to wake up one morning and find that you've been left on the shelf, do you?"

"Yes, I think I do, as a matter of fact." Gussie gave a small, apologetic smile in response to her sister's appalled expression. "Don't look so horrified, Letty. I find it quite pleasant spending my days quietly here with Mama . . . at least when Claryce isn't raising a dust."

Letty frowned at her in annoyance. "Nonsense!" she said sharply, realizing suddenly that the problem that had set her mother in tears might be more complex and difficult to solve than she had at first supposed. "You sound like someone's *maiden aunt* instead of a pretty girl of twenty. How dare you ask so little of your life! You are entitled to your share of excitement, adventure and *love*, and I think you should exert yourself a bit to find them."

Gussie turned her wide, hazel eyes on her sister with a look that was both serene and amused. "Some people are not cut out for excitement, adventure and love, Letty, and I'm afraid I'm one of them. I'm the sort who dislikes turmoil, you know. If you don't mind, I'll take my excitement, adventure and love from my books."

"*Books*! That's just what she said!" Letty related to Prue a short time later as the two sisters stood outside the door of their mother's house reviewing the afternoon's events before taking leave of each other. "Did you ever hear such nonsense?"

"It's sheer cowardice," Prue said knowingly. "She's afraid of love, afraid of competition and afraid of life."

"Well, what are we going to do about it? We can't permit her to hide away in the house for the rest of her life."

"No, we can't," Prue agreed, "but we shan't solve anything standing about here in the wind. Let's go home and give the matter some thought. No need for haste, you know. Brandon says, '*hasty climbers have sudden falls.*'"

Letty burst into a peal of laughter. "You sound more like Brandon every day. I think your baby will be born spouting quotations instead of crying for his milk."

Prue giggled and looked down at her stomach. "I think so too. He'll be positively brilliant, I'm sure of it." She embraced her sister and started toward her waiting curricle.

But Letty stood rooted to the spot, her smile fading as her thoughts returned to Augusta's plight. "If only we could find a man with sense enough to know that Claryce is a peacock and Gussie a gem."

Prue, climbing aboard her curricle, snorted. "A man like that," she called back over her shoulder, "doesn't exist."

"I don't know about that," Letty muttered to herself thoughtfully as she gave her hand to her footman and permitted herself to be assisted aboard her coach. "There must be someone, *somewhere . . .*"

Chapter Two

AUGUSTA, WITH BRANDON PEAKE'S manuscript under her arm, walked pensively up the stairs to her bedroom. She had intended to remain down in the sitting room in order to finish reading the manuscript (for she did not like to keep her brother-in-law waiting endlessly for her comments), but she'd discovered that she'd been unable to concentrate on it. She was too depressed. Her mother's hysterics and her sisters' visit had disturbed her more than she'd been willing to admit. It was difficult enough trying to keep her outward composure in the best of circumstances; a day like this only made things worse. Why couldn't her family leave her alone?

It wasn't their fault, of course. They meant well. How could they know that she harbored a secret pain like an ulcer in her breast? How could they suspect that she'd been so foolish as to give her heart to a man who, although he'd had four years in which to notice her, seemed barely aware of her existence? It was truly most unfortunate that she'd fallen in love with Letty's brother-in-law. If Philip Denham were a stranger to the family, she might never have met him, and she might have been spared this dreadful pain. As it was, however, she had to pretend to an indifference to a man whose company she was forced to endure every time the family gathered together. It was certainly a discouraging siuation, and one that promised to grow no easier in the future.

She rounded the turn of the stairway so absently that she almost bumped into the wall. It really was too bad about Mr. Wivilscombe, she supposed. He *was* a man of cheerful disposition and substantial character . . . and she'd quite liked him. Perhaps, if he *had* come up to scratch, she would have considered matrimony. With a husband at her side, her situation might be less painful. It would be easier to hide her feelings for Philip if she were safely wed, she supposed.

But no, she told herself as she entered the bedroom and shut the door, *it would not be right to marry a man when my heart is given elsewhere*. That would be dishonest in the extreme. Even though one heard many accounts of women who married for the basest of reasons, she was not the sort to do so. She would not be able to forgive herself. That was why she had to make everyone believe that marriage was not for her.

She tossed the manuscript upon the dressing table and began to pace about her room. Her mother and her older sisters seemed determined to push her into wedlock. She'd not heard the last of the matter, she knew. Letty and Prue both had those *we-must-do-something-about-this* expressions on their faces. Gussie had not the slightest inkling of what sort of action they would take, but she was certain of one thing—whatever they decided to do would be something to cut up her peace.

It had happened before. Her mother and her two elder sisters had decided that she'd needed to see more of the world (and thus expand her opportunities to "meet the proper sort of gentlemen"), so they'd packed her off to spend a fortnight in Bath in the company of Prue and Brandon. To the dismay of the entire family (except, of course, Claryce, who took no interest at all in Gussie's affairs), she'd made friends with only one person during her entire stay—that person being an eccentric old lady of seventy-four years whose claim to fame rested on having met the poet Thomas Gray in her youth. She had committed to memory Gray's complete poetical works and would declaim them at the slightest provocation.

Gussie grinned as she recalled the day she'd introduced Mrs. Dolphiner to her sister and Brandon, and the old lady had launched into her favorite of Gray's works, *An Ode on the Death of Favorite Cat, Drowned in a Tub of Goldfishes*. There they all had stood, right in the center of the Pump Room, drawing the attention of all the crowd as the old lady's voice had grown louder and louder. By the time Mrs. Dolphiner had reached the fourth stanza, (the part where the cat puts her head and paw into the fishbowl), her hands were waving in the air, her voice was high and dramatic, and her face was screwed up in perfect imitation of the cat's in the water:

> *"The hapless nymph with wonder saw*
> *A whisker first and then a claw,*
> *With many an ardent wish*
> *She stretched in vain to reach the prize.*
> *What female heart can gold despise?*
> *What cat's averse to fish?"*

she recited excitedly, while Brandon and Prue had grown red with embarrassment. Gussie, however, had been enormously entertained. She'd grown quite fond of old Mrs. Dolphiner and corresponded with her to this day.

But her affection for Mrs. Dolphiner had not been enough to make her stay in Bath a pleasant experience, for Prue had been overzealous in attempting to push her to take an active social role. She and Brandon had brought every eligible bachelor in the neighborhood to Gussie's attention; they'd introduced her to every man they'd met and dragged her to every concert, ball or fete to which they could wangle an invitation. Gussie had found the experience awkward and painful in the extreme, and she'd felt nothing but enormous relief when the fortnight had come to an end.

She dropped down upon the window seat and stared out on the darkening sky. Was it so very dreadful to wish to remain unmarried? Why did marriage have to be the be-all and end-all of a girl's life? She could readily understand that Letty and Prue desired to see her as happy as they were, but their marriages were quite exceptional. Letty's marriage to Roger was almost like a fairy-tale alliance—a true love-match quite in the tradition of Cinderella. And because of Roger's wealth and station—and the maturity and generosity of both their natures—the pair *did* seem to be living in the happily-ever-after style which fairy tales require. But Letty surely did not believe that *other* marriages were likely to turn out that way!

Prue, too, seemed to be quite happy in her wedded life, even though her circumstances were not nearly so certain to lead to the rhapsodical state in which Letty existed. Prue's husband, Brandon, was a delightful, scholarly fellow of whom Gussie was very fond, but his relatively modest income would keep Prue's ability to indulge in luxuries quite at a minimum. And Brandon was much more likely to fall into moodiness and behave childishly than Roger was. Prue's nature, however, was so effervescent and affectionate that she could probably make their household a happy one under any circumstances. But what made them think that she, Augusta Glendenning, would be equally fortunate?

Gussie was not at all convinced that she was as ideally suited for wedded life as her sisters, even if she had *not* so foolishly bestowed her heart on a man who was not interested in her. She was essentially a shy and private person, quite content to spend time alone with her thoughts. And whereas she did not object to attending large parties, where she could sit unobtrusively in the background and watch and listen to the doings around her, she was very uncomfortable when she was required to participate in intimate conversations with relative strangers. Cosy little chats with gentlemen she hardly knew (which is what courtship seemed to her to consist of) made her completely miserable. She could neither bring herself to giggle at their foolish sallies (as she'd heard so many girls do) nor enter into long and serious discussions of any of their favorite topics (which in her experience seemed to be three: the weather, their horses or the excellence of the buffet which their hostess had set). And it was completely beyond her to make the baldly-flattering remarks about their reputations as sportsmen, the quality of their dancing, or the cut of their waistcoats which the other girls seemed to utter with appalling regularity whenever they conversed with gentlemen.

Her brother Neddie had scoffed when she'd confided these feelings to him. "Don't be such a dashed ninnyhammer," he'd exclaimed. "Why can't you talk to *them* as you talk to *me*?"

But how could she talk to a man—one she hardly knew and barely liked—in the same fashion as she would to her own brother? No . . . not one member of the family seemed to understand . . . not Mama, not her sisters, not even Neddie. Only Katie, their self-sufficient, strong-minded abigail, was capable of understanding that a woman could learn to rely on her own resources—

There was a light knock at the door, and it was promptly

pushed open to reveal the very person she'd just been thinking of. Katie-from-the-Kitchen herself stood in the doorway, peering into the dimness of the room with a puzzled expression on her face. "You 'ere, Miss Augusta?" she asked.

Gussie shook herself from her reverie and got to her feet. "Yes. Come in, Katie."

"'Ow do ye come to be sittin' there in the dark?" the abigail queried, busily lighting the candles in the sconces near the door.

"I didn't realize how dark it's become," Gussie said with a guilty shrug.

Katie gave her a quick, piercing glance. "If it wuz anyone but me," she scolded, "they'd a thought you wuz sittin' there broodin'."

Katie's London-streets accent and attitude of familiarity—both qualities of singular inappropriateness in so important a member of the domestic staff—would have caused an uninitiated visitor to frown in disapproval, but the Glendennings were not in the least perturbed by the young woman's eccentricities. They were all fond of Katie, and all agreed that she was worth her weight in gold. She'd served as abigail to the Glendenning sisters ever since Claryce had discovered her in the kitchen almost five years before. Claryce had been only thirteen then, and she used to enjoy stealing down to the kitchen whenever she felt put-upon by her sisters to console herself with a sweet wormed from Cook. It was there, in the nether regions of the house, that she'd discovered the scullery maid called Katie who, although only a few years older than she, seemed to know all manner of interesting tidbits of information. Claryce had quoted Katie so often at the dinner table that Neddie had finally suggested they send for her. The result was that they were all charmed, and Katie was raised at once from scullery maid to abigail. This post she'd maintained ever since, despite lucrative offers from any number of admiring ladies who, learning of her skill with herbs and medicinal potions, had been eager to tempt the girl away from the Glendennings. But Katie had been content to remain where she was. A young woman of rare good sense, Katie-from-the-Kitchen (the name Neddie had given her and which she herself took a perverse delight in keeping) had been dresser, confidante and advisor to all four sisters in the following years—caring for Letty and Prue until they wed and now shared by the two sisters still remaining under the Glendenning roof.

With the candles lit, Katie scrutinized Gussie's face with shrewd yet kindly eyes. "You ain't been frettin' over Mr. Wivilscombe, 'ave you, Miss Augusta?"

"You know better than that," Gussie said. "It's only that—"

"I know," Katie said sympathetically. "'Er ladyship's been at ye again."

"Yes, and Letty and Prue as well." She sighed and dropped down on the window seat again. "I suppose I shall have to endure this sort of thing forever . . . unless I surrender and permit them to make a match for me."

"There ain't no need for 'em to do that," Katie said matter-of-factly. "You'll find a proper sprag fer *yourself*." She marched energetically to the heavy oak wardrobe and pulled open its double doors. "An' it won't be too long afore that 'appens."

Gussie frowned at her. "I don't want a 'proper sprag.' I thought that *you*, at least, understood how I feel. Don't tell me you're on *their* side!"

"There ain't no sides 'ere, y'know, Missy. Everyone wants the best fer you."

"But they don't *know* what's best for me."

Katie threw a sympathetic smile over her shoulder. "I *do* un'erstand you, Miss Augusta, truly. I know y've no wish to wed right now. I even tole 'er ladyship not to go naggin' at you. 'No need fer ridin' grub,' I said, ''til the girl finds a suitor to suit 'er.'" She chortled at her own pun as she pulled a dress from the recesses of the wardrobe.

"*Really*, Katie!" Gussie declared, dismayed at the defection of her last ally. "I'm not *looking* for a suitor, and you know it. I don't want to be wed at all."

Katie shook out the dress briskly. "That's what you may think now, but I'd go bail ye'll change yer tune one day. Meantimes, you might recall that there's always talk o' *wedded* bliss, but I ain't never heard no one blabbin' about *un*wedded bliss."

"Well, you can hear *me* blabbing about it! It would be bliss to me if everyone would *stop* trying to marry me off!"

"That may be," Katie said, throwing the dinner gown across the bed, "but if we don't stop gabbin' an' get you dressed, Miss Claryce'll be back and shoutin' fer me to—"

The sound of the door being flung open with an unceremonious abruptness caused them both to look up. Claryce, draped in a fashionable blue-velvet riding dress and with a cocky little hat perched on her reddish curls at a decidedly rakish angle, stood poised in the doorway. "I might have know I'd find you here, Katie," she said in disgust. "Don't you realize how late it is?"

"Evenin', Miss Claryce," Katie answered cheerfully, calmly undoing the buttons at the back of Gussie's afternoon dress.

"It must be after *six*!" Claryce fumed. "I wasted the entire afternoon trying to find out if Mr. Wivilscombe intends to attend the Cranshaws' ball. He is the most non-committal, *guarded* sort—I couldn't get a definite answer from him. And now I shall be late for dinner. Come along, will you? I need you to help me out of these blasted riding things."

"You can go with Claryce, Katie," Gussie offered. "I can manage—"

"No need for that," Katie said placidly. "'Er ladyship's set dinner back a bit."

"Set dinner back?" Claryce asked. "Why? Are we having guests?"

"No, not guests. It's on account of 'er ladyship 'avin' lost 'er appetite this afternoon...an' you know very well why," Katie muttered, giving Claryce a look of disapproval. "So there ain't no call t' kick up a dust."

"In that case," Claryce said, sauntering in and seating herself at her sister's dressing table, "I may as well stay and chat a while. Though it was very thoughtless of Mama to delay dinner. Doesn't she know that I've agreed to make an appearance at the opera with Lord Garvey tonight?"

"Oh?" Gussie asked, her eyes lighting with interest. "You *are* in luck, Claryce. I think it's *Don Giovanni* tonight. Do go and help her dress, Katie. I shall run and hurry Mama, for we mustn't permit them to be late for *that*."

"Don't bother, Gussie," Claryce murmured, smiling at herself in the mirror as she removed her riding hat. "I don't mind arriving late, really. Sitting through an entire opera can be a great bore, you know."

"Now, really, Claryce," Gussie said disapprovingly, "*Mozart* a bore?"

Claryce shrugged. "Besides, don't you want to ask me how I enjoyed the ride with Wivilscombe?"

"I'm sure you found it a great bore," Gussie muttered with

a touch of asperity, although the effect of her annoyance was muted by the dress which Katie had seen fit to pull over her head at that moment. "You always say your rides with your various swains are great bores," she added when the dress had been removed.

"Yes, they are, although today's was more enjoyable than most. Denny has such a great number of friends that we had constantly to stop and greet people along the way."

"Is it *Denny* already?" Gussie couldn't help remarking. "How very quickly you can come on terms of intimacy with gentlemen, Claryce. It quite fills me with awe. But why did the constant stopping make the ride so enjoyable? I should have supposed that such interruptions would interfere with your conversation with your escort."

"Who cares for that? It's much more entertaining to stop and talk to interesting people along the way and have the gentlemen tell Denny what a lucky fellow he is to have such a charming companion. That's what they all said . . . and *that*, my dear sister, is what makes a ride enjoyable."

"Is it?" Gussie asked dubiously. "Did *Mr. Wivilscombe* enjoy the interruptions as well? I suspect that he must have found them tiresome."

"Oh, pooh! What difference does *that* make?"

"But . . . you went riding to become better acquainted with him, isn't that so?"

"That was part of it, I suppose," Claryce replied, eyeing her sister with scornful amusement. "But primarily, I went to see and be seen. And even if Denny had become annoyed at having to stand about and watch while I flirted with his friends, his annoyance wouldn't lessen his interest in me. In fact," she grinned as she looked back at herself in the glass, "quite the reverse."

Gussie shook her head. "How very puzzling. Gentlemen can be very strange, can't they?"

"They're not at all strange. Really, Gussie, you're painfully naive about men." She got up, picked up her hat and strolled to the door. "I sometimes think that it's *I* who's the older of the two of us. You can be so infantile at times." She paused in the doorway and looked back over her shoulder. "Don't take forever, Katie. We'll have to re-comb my hair, you know."

Claryce swept out, leaving Katie and Gussie staring after her. "I'll be bum-squabbled," Katie murmured, putting her hands on her hips and staring at the door, "if I don't think yer sister ought to 'ave a paddle to 'er rump!"

Gussie broke into a grin. "And *I'll* be bum-squabbled if I don't agree . . . especially if I were the one to wield the paddle!"

But even as she and Katie gave way to giggles, Gussie couldn't help feeling a nip of envy in her chest. Claryce was selfish, spoiled and irritating. But if Gussie had only a small portion of her verve and charm, perhaps a certain oblivious gentleman by the name of Philip Denham would by this time have taken note that she was alive.

Chapter Three

LETTY RETURNED TO her home on the very fashionable Curzon Street with her mind completely preoccupied. Her sister Gussie was the dearest girl, and she couldn't forgive herself for not having noticed that, during the four years since she'd married, her sister had been pushed into the background of the social scene. Something had to be done to remedy the situation—and at once!

Her abstracted air remained with her as the evening progressed, but it was not at first noticed by her usually observant husband, for he himself was busily occupied in playing with his son. Letty and Roger always spent the two hours before dinner in the upstairs sitting room, playing with their offspring before the nurse took them off to bed. During so lively and cheerful a time, Roger found himself too much entertained to think of anything else. This evening, he was seated on the floor before the fire, helping his three-year-old son Roddy to build a bridge with his blocks, while Letty sat in an armchair nearby bouncing their baby daughter on her knee. But her movements were merely instinctive; her mind was elsewhere. "Are you acquainted with a gentleman named Dennis Wivilscombe, Roger?" she asked at last.

Roger looked up from the rickety structure his son was

busily assembling, his eyebrows raised. "Yes, quite well, although I can't say I've seen much of him lately."

"Why not? Don't you like him?"

"Yes, he's a very good fellow. But he's a bachelor, you know. I don't much frequent my old bachelor haunts these days. Why do you ask about him?"

"It seems that he's been calling at Argyle Street. I only wondered what he's like."

"He's a quite decent chap. Very good natured, open-handed, always ready to help a friend in distress, and—"

A crash of blocks interrupted him. "Oh, Papa! It c'lapthed!" wailed the little boy.

Roger turned his attention back to the blocks. "Collapsed, has it? That *is* too bad," he sympathized, looking over the wreckage. "One weight too many for the supports, I'm afraid. But don't look so downhearted, Roddy, my lad. We can build it up again."

Letty waited for her husband to resume his comments, but his absorption in bridge-erection seemed to have driven the matter from his mind. "Well, go on," she prompted.

"What?" he asked, not looking up from the precarious structure that was again rising to dangerous heights.

"About Dennis Wivilscombe. You were saying—?"

"Oh, yes. I was saying that he's an entertaining, generous fellow, that's all."

"Is he a philanderer?" Letty persisted.

Roger glanced up, amused. "Is that what Claryce says of him?"

"*Claryce?*" Letty stiffened in offense. "What made you assume it was Claryce he called to see?"

Something in her tone—a touch of asperity—caught his attention. His eyebrows rose again, and this time he studied his wife more closely. "Was it *Augusta* he came calling on? I didn't know Wivilscombe had so much sense."

"He doesn't," Letty snapped irritably. "He *dropped* Gussie and took off after Claryce the moment she crooked her finger at him."

"I'm not a bit surprised. No, Roddy, not such a big one. It'll collapse again."

Letty was staring at her husband in disgust. "Not *surprised*? Why *not*, pray? Why is it that you—and all your sex—ignore the charms of a girl like Gussie?"

"I?" Roger asked, looking up at his wife shrewdly, a grin on his lips. "I ignore her charms, my dear, because any other course would be decidedly improper."

"Jackanapes!" Letty, permitting only a trace of a smile to peep through, made a face at him.

Roddy, who had lost his father's attention, eyed his parents interestedly. "What'th a jackanapeth?" he asked.

"Someone naughty, like a little boy who listens to conversations not meant for him," his father told him promptly. "A good engineer concentrates on the task at hand."

"I'm a good engineer," the boy asserted, turning back to his blocks.

"And as for you, ma'am," Roger said, now fully aware that his wife had something on her mind, "what's troubling you?"

"It's Gussie," Letty confessed. "I hadn't realized what's been happening to her."

"Is something wrong with her? Is she ill?"

"No, nothing like that. But, Roger, what you just said is symptomatic of the problem."

"Really? What did I say?"

"You jumped to the conclusion that your friend had gone calling on *Claryce.* Why wasn't it just as likely he'd called to see *Gussie?"*

Roger rubbed his chin embarrassedly. "I'm sorry, love. I hadn't meant to cast aspersion on her. But in my defense, I didn't believe that Wivilscombe would take notice of Augusta."

"But why *not?"*

"I know you're completely devoted to your Augusta, my dear, but don't let your affection blind you. Only a man possessed of subtle discrimination in his judgment of women would choose Augusta over Claryce. And Dennis, while I don't mean to disparage him, was always rather superficial about the fair sex—dashing after this girl one day and that one the next."

"Yes, so I understand. Did you know they call him The Seal?"

"No, I didn't. Why?"

"Because he slips so easily out of the grasp of any female who tries to hold him."

Roger laughed. "So Dennis is hard to catch, is he?"

"Then I suppose he *is* a philanderer," Letty said with a regretful sigh.

"No, that's not what the epithet means, you goosecap. It

only means the fellow is marriage-shy. However, it does add support to my theory that he's the sort who's more likely to succumb to Claryce's more obvious attractions than to Augusta's more quiet ones, since he tends to be rather indiscriminate. However, once some clever female nets him, he'll settle down all right and tight. He's basically a good sort."

"Ah, I see." She paused for a moment and stared thoughtfully into the fire, while Roger turned back to the pile of blocks to admire his son's handiwork. "But what if he *were* to become interested in Gussie ...?" she asked after a while. "Do you think the match would be suitable?"

"There! *Finished*!" announced Roddy proudly.

"That's very good, Roddy." His father stood up and lifted his son in the air proudly. "You've the makings of a fine engineer, if I'm any judge."

"I *told* you tho," the boy chortled proudly.

Letty glared at them in mock offense. "It quite takes the shine from a lady to find herself playing second fiddle to a toy bridge," she declared. "Did you hear me, Roger? I asked if you think a match between Gussie and Mr. Wivilscombe would be suitable."

Roger, who was not nearly so interested in a match for his sister-in-law as he was in tossing his son in the air and hearing him gurgle, put the boy down and blinked at his wife bewilderedly. "But I thought you said it was *Claryce*—"

Letty shifted the baby to her shoulder and jumped up impatiently. "I'm only asking you to *suppose* ..."

Roger realized that his wife's preoccupation would not be easily turned aside, so, with a laugh, he turned to face her. "Heaven defend me from the determined matchmakers of the world!" he exclaimed, softening his words by planting an affectionate kiss on her brow. "But the answer is yes, my dear. Yes, Wivilscombe is probably a *very* good catch—for *either one* of your sisters ... if one of them can manage to nab him. But then, I'm only a man, and in these matters, the opinion of a mere man are not worth very much."

"About *that*, my lord," his wife said disdainfully, "I am in complete agreement."

"What'th a matchmaker?" Roddy wanted to know.

"A kind of busybody," his father said, throwing a glinting look of amusement at his wife before he bent and lifted his son up to his shoulder. "And before you ask me what a busybody is, I'd better take you off to bed."

"And about time, too," his wife agreed, following her husband out the door.

By the time the children had been turned over to their nurse, Roger began to hope that his wife had forgotten her earlier ruminations about her sister. But as the pair walked down the corridor toward their rooms to dress for dinner, Letty brought up a subject which he knew must be in some way related to the matter. "Roger, my love," she said sweetly, slipping an arm about his waist, "do you think I might arrange to hire a few musicians for our anniversary dinner?"

"Of course, if you wish it. But I thought you'd said you wanted only a small, simple celebration."

"I think I've changed my mind. I may increase the guest list somewhat . . . just so that there will be a large-enough group to engage in a bit of dancing. Are you certain you won't mind?"

"I'm quite certain." He leaned down and kissed her with reassuring fervor. "Just as I'm certain," he added with a twinkle, "that you've some scheme up your sleeve."

Her lips twitched, but she looked up at him with wide-eyed innocence. "*Scheme*? I don't know *what* you mean."

"Oh, don't you?" Grinning, he walked on, not adding another word. He knew there was more to come, but he didn't intend to make it easier for her to broach her next request.

She said nothing more until they'd entered their bedroom. "By the way," she asked, elaborately casual, "do you think you'd like to invite your friend to the party?"

"Friend?" he echoed, his voice exaggeratedly bewildered. "*What* friend?"

She wheeled on him impatiently, and then caught the amused gleam in his eye. "You . . . *gamecock*!" she exclaimed, snatching a pillow from the bed and pummeling him with it until he retreated, laughing, into his dressing room and shut the door on her.

He waited, grinning, behind the closed door until she spoke again. "You *will* ask Mr. Wivilscombe to come, won't you, Roger?" she pleaded after her laughter had subsided. "Unless . . ."

"Unless . . . ?" he prodded from the other side of the door.

"Unless you think it will be too strange to do so after not having seen him in all this time."

"I shall ask him, my love, just as you wish," Roger said

reassuringly, "even if it *will* seem strange to him. And I'm sure Dennis will be delighted to accept. I only ask two favors of you in return."

"What two favors?" she asked suspiciously.

He opened the door and stuck his head out. "*One* is that you admit here and now that you *do* have a scheme up your sleeve—"

She grinned at him guiltily. "Well, perhaps the *beginnings* of a scheme..."

"Well, then, when you've worked it all out, I hope you will grant me my second favor..."

"Which is—?"

"That you keep it to yourself. Whatever little matchmaker's game you've decided to play, my dearest, I don't want to know a thing about it!"

Chapter Four

PHILIP LOOKED UP from the figures on the paper before him, a feeling of sickening despair creeping up from his stomach to his throat. It was as if his *brain's* awareness of the trouble he was in was not enough—his *body*, too, was warning him that he'd fallen more deeply in the suds than he'd ever done before...and that there was no apparent way to get himself free.

Repeated checking of the numbers had not made a difference. The total of his outstanding vowels came to more than twelve thousand pounds. Wincing, he thrust the paper across the table toward his friend, Ned Glendenning, who had been watching him from behind the bottle of port with silent tension. Then Philip heaved himself up from his chair and crossed the room to the fireplace, where he stared down into the flames in mute depression.

Ned looked across at his friend's lowered head for a moment in wordless sympathy and picked up the paper gingerly. The total at the bottom made him gasp. "Twelve thousand?" he asked in a choked voice. "Good God!"

"Yes," Philip said without turning. "'Good God' is as effective a summation of the situation as any."

"*Twelve* thousand? Are you *sure*?"

"I've only added the figures a dozen times. Do it yourself, if you don't trust my arithmetic."

There followed a long, painful silence, during which Ned studied his friend's back with a worried frown. In the dimness of the room, Philip's tall form was only a dark shadow outlined by the firelight, the only other light (from the branched candlestick on the table) too faint to reach across the room. But even in the darkness, Ned could see the slump of Philip's shoulders. His silhouette revealed far better than words the extent of his anxiety. Ned expelled his breath in a silent sigh. If only he could help.

Ned had never before had a friend of whom he was so fond. He'd met Philip four years before, at his sister's wedding. Ned had been only eighteen at the time, but Philip had been a dashing, sophisticated twenty-one-year-old who'd excited Ned's immediate admiration. Ned had not, at first, quite understood why Philip had befriended so dull and unexceptional a fellow as himself, but later he realized that Philip respected his cautious, sensible, practical outlook. The two had become fast friends almost immediately, each one bringing to the other something that was missing in himself. For Ned, it was Philip's charm, his daring, his dazzling style with horses, cards and ladies; for Philip it was Ned's reliability, his sturdy common sense and his unflappable good nature. But Ned did not see how he could be of help to his friend now; he had not a spare penny in the world.

He reached for the port and downed a glassful in nervous haste. "Have you anything to sell? Your horses?" he suggested.

"I've only the greys left," Philip muttered hopelessly, "and Roger would be bound to notice if I got rid of *them*."

"Your ring, then. That diamond must be worth a good deal."

"I'm not certain. Perhaps two or three thousand." Philip lifted his head and looked at the gem sparkling on the little finger of his left hand. "Mother left it to me. It was my father's, you know, and she always treasured it." He sighed regretfully. "I hate to sell it. It should, by rights, have gone to Roger, but Mama wanted *me* to have it. Said it was because I'm so much like my father." He snorted bitterly. "Ha! So much like him, indeed. My father never gambled in his life."

"No, I shouldn't sell it then, if I were you." Ned took another drink to give himself courage. "Look here, Philip, I think it's time you stopped behaving like a stubborn fool and confessed the whole to Roger," he advised bluntly. "With the three thousand he's already sent, you need only ask for nine—"

"*Only* nine!"

Ned shrugged unhappily. "What else is there for you to do?"

"I don't know," Philip answered, turning slowly to face his friend, "but whatever I do, it won't be that. I *can't* tell Roger! He's helped me twice before, and I promised him—! Damnation, Ned, I can't *face* hurting him again."

"You should have thought of that—"

"If you say *once more*," Philip cut in angrily, "that I should have thought of it before I sat down at the card table with Shackleford, I shall plant a facer on your *chin!*"

Ned lowered his eyes. "Sorry, old man. Stupid of me."

Silence fell again, except for the sound of Philip's boot as he kicked at the fireplace fender absently. Ned eyed his friend warily over the edge of his wineglass. If only he had some money of his own. . . .

Chewing his moustache, as he always did when nervous or upset, Ned let his eyes roam about the room. Philip had chosen this flat when he'd come down to London after taking his degree at Cambridge. It was modest but serviceable, located near Pall Mall in what was considered the most desirable section of London. When he'd first moved in, Philip had furnished the place elegantly with the gifts of silver, paintings and furnishings which his mother had sent from one or the other of the family estates, and he'd engaged a manservant of admirable efficiency to care for it. But his debts had forced Philip to discharge his man and sell off his possessions piece by piece. Now the walls were quite empty and the rooms stripped of decoration. Only the most necessary furniture remained, cared for cursorily by a woman who came in mornings to "do for Mr. Denham."

Fortunately, only Ned knew this. Like most bachelors, Philip did little entertaining in his rooms. Even his brother had not found it necessary to visit here. Since Roger invited Philip to dine at Arneau House quite regularly, there was no reason for him to seek Philip out in his flat. Thus Roger had never discovered the extent of Philip's present impoverishment. Nor had anyone else, since Philip had managed to keep up his wardrobe and, when he left his rooms, looked every inch the prosperous, carefree Corinthian. Although by this time rumors of his gambling debts were rife, no one could have guessed the true extent of his financial predicament.

It was too bad that Philip's mother, the Dowager Lady Denham, had died two years ago. She'd doted on both her sons, but she'd understood the difficulty of being a second-born and had been of enormous support to Philip while she'd lived. Roger was equally sympathetic, of course, but Philip was too proud—and too eager to win Roger's approval—to permit his brother to learn the truth.

Suddenly Ned blinked. "Wait a minute!" he burst out. lifting his head with hopeful enthusiasm. "I *have* it!"

Philip turned from the fire and eyed his friend suspiciously. "*What* have you—a secret cache of gold sovereigns you've just remembered?"

"I have the *solution*! *Marriage*!"

"Marriage?" Philip echoed in disgust. "You're foxed!"

"Not a bit," Ned assured him earnestly. "It's a perfectly splendid idea! Didn't you tell me that Roger has promised you a very generous settlement when you're wed?"

"Yes, that's true . . . but it would take almost a whole year's income from that settlement to pay my debts. How could I manage to keep a wife without money for a year?"

"Easily . . . if you choose the right girl. There are many families, you know, who deal quite generously with gentlemen who take their daughters off their hands. Why, they say that Yarbrough won a dowry of thirty thousand and a yearly income to boot when he married Jane Hapgood."

"Jane Hapgood was an *ape-leader*," Philip said in revulsion. "Surely you're not suggesting that I sell myself to an old prune like—"

"No, of course not. But there are any number of quite presentable girls who would be happy to accept a proposal from Philip Denham."

Philip snorted. "You're touched in your upper works! What young lady of means and looks would wish to settle for a second son?"

"*Many*, I tell you! Haven't you noticed how the ladies look at you?"

"No, I haven't." He stared at his friend dubiously. "*How* do they look at me?"

"Oh, you know . . . in that *measuring* way they have when they're attracted—"

"Balderdash!"

"It's *not* balderdash," Ned insisted. "The other night at the Revingtons' ball, Mary Blanchard's eyes followed you all—"

"You are being nonsensical. Perhaps I *do* make a good impression in a ballroom, but what woman of sense would care for that? They'll all have heard by this time that I'm a gamester and in debt, and they'll shun me like a plague-carrier."

Ned shook his head. "No, Philip, I think you're out in your reckoning. Women are strange creatures. They are often *attracted* to gamesters and rakes. I live in a household of women, and I know."

"Attracted to gamesters and rakes?" Philip asked incredulously. "That's ridiculous. Your sisters would *never*—"

"Yes, they would, under certain circumstances. The sort of qualities women like in a man are not the sensible ones but . . ."

"But what?" Philip asked interestedly, dropping down in his chair. "*What* sort of qualities?"

"The most surprising things, really. Like a good leg . . . or curly hair . . . or sometimes a cleft chin or an easy smile will send them into transports."

"You don't mean it!" Philip gaped at his friend in amazement. Then he reached for the port and poured himself a glassful. After downing it, he shrugged dismissively. "Well, I haven't a cleft in my chin or curly hair . . . so there's an end on it."

"But you *have* a pleasing appearance, you know . . . and considerable address. A veritable Corinthian, I'd say. So you needn't sell yourself short. Why not give it a try?"

"I'm not in the petticoat line, as you know quite well," Philip told him flatly. "I have no intention of getting myself leg-shackled." Then, eyeing his friend thoughtfully, he added, "But if you think this idea is so promising, I don't see why *you* don't try it yourself."

"Me?" Ned gaped at him. "Why should *I* do it?"

"Why not? At least *you* have your *title* to offer. And since *your* income is far from luxurious, it seems to me you might very well benefit from your own advice."

"But I'm not in the petticoat line either. I'm surrounded by females at home as it *is*. I shall wed one day, but I'm not quite ready for it yet."

Philip raised his eyebrows with ironic amusement. "Oh, I *see*! Entrapment in wedlock is fine for *me* but not for *you*, is that it?"

"I'm not the one who's in debt to the tune of twelve thousand," Ned reminded him gently.

"True," Philip agreed, deflated. "Very true. Your point, old fellow."

"Then you'll consider the idea?"

"Perhaps." He rose from his chair again and began to pace about the room like a caged animal. "It's quite lowering to think of oneself as so mercenary—the sort who would marry for no other purpose than to get out of debt."

"You needn't consider the matter in that light," Ned said comfortingly. "After all, if you truly *like* the girl, the fact that she brings some wealth with her can be considered merely incidental. You may very possibly find a girl who'll suit you quite well."

"Unlikely," Philip responded gloomily. "I haven't *yet* met a woman I couldn't live without."

Nevertheless, Ned reached over for the inkstand, pulled it toward him and picked up the pen. On the back of the paper on which Philip's debts had been listed, he promptly began to list the names of ladies who might be eligible. Every name he suggested, however, elicited from Philip some remark of disparagement—this one was too young, that one too stout, the third was a notorious shrew and the fourth had long ago taken him in dislike. Thus they bandied names back and forth for two hours without apparent success. When the candles finally guttered in their sockets and Ned rose to take his leave, only three names remained uncrossed on the list of scratched-out suggestions. "You *will* call on Mary Blanchard and Cora Ainsley, won't you?"

"Yes, I suppose so," Philip said wearily, looking over the paper without enthusiasm, "but you can put Lady Lucia Greland out of your mind. I don't see why you bothered to circle her name. I told you she quite terrifies me."

"Well, she doesn't terrify *me*," Ned declared, snatching the sheet from Philip's hand. "I shall call on *her* myself and speak in your behalf."

"Don't you dare!" Philip declared in horror.

"But she's the most promising of the lot—"

"I don't see why you insist on that. The girl is a virtual *virago*. Under no circumstances would I consider—"

"Oh, very well," Ned agreed reluctantly, shrugging into his greatcoat, "but promise that you'll call on the others—and soon!"

"You have my word," Philip said glumly, ushering him out — the door. "I'll do it tomorrow."

"Tomorrow?" Ned, quite pleased, smiled over his shoulder as he went out the door. "That *is* a good chap!"

Philip shut the door after him and sighed. "Only because, if I wait another day, I shall completely lose my courage," he muttered.

*   *   *

The morning dawned grey and overcast, and a chill October wind rattled the windows. It was enough to make Philip regret his rash promise to Ned the night before. This was not the sort of morning to pay calls. Besides, the dark hours of the night had brought second thoughts. He didn't *want* to be wed. He'd much rather engage in shallow flirtations with *many* ladies than to tie himself down with one. Ladies could be very irritating, demanding creatures even when one was *not* married to them; once wed (he had no doubt), their demands would be increased and their little irritating qualities would become much more vexatious. He wished he had not been so hasty in giving his word.

But he had. And he was not a man to break his word, no matter *what* misgivings that pledge might arouse in him. With a sigh, he rose from his bed and dressed himself with care. He chose a dark-green superfine coat, a swanskin waistcoat with horizontal stripes in shades of green and silver, and a pair of buff-colored pantaloons which fit as closely to the leg as skin. By the time he emerged from his rooms less than two hours later, no one would have guessed from his appearance that he'd suffered any inner turmoil. He'd added to his costume a pair of gleaming French top-boots, a neckcloth tied expertly in the popular *Waterfall* style, and a high crowned beaver with a flat top and rounded brim. He looked in the very first style of elegance. And the expression on his face was calm and assured, his step was lively as he walked to the stables to get his curricle, and his swing of his cane was decidedly cheerful.

His arrival at the residence of Cora Ainsley caused an immediate flurry. The butler ushered him into the drawing room with great ceremony and, shortly thereafter, he could hear cries of excitement and running footsteps above his head. In a few moments, the door of the drawing room slid open a few inches, and a little girl peeped in at him. When she saw that he was looking at her, she emitted a loud giggle and hastily withdrew, pulling the doors together with a bang. Her footsteps clattered up the stairs, and he could hear quite distinctly her cry of "He's a reg'lar top-of-the-trees!"

"Cissy, you little beast, shut *up*!" a young lady's voice warned. "D' you want him to *hear* you?"

Those too-obvious signs of the intense interest his arrival had generated made him extremely uncomfortable, and he was casting about in his mind for a graceful way to take his leave when the doors slid open again and Cora Ainsley's mother, Lady Alice Ainsley, entered with a broad smile and an out-stretched hand. "My *dear* boy," she cooed breathlessly as he bent over her hand, "how delightful that you have come to call. Cora will be down directly. She is the greatest slugabed, you know, and didn't expect any callers . . . that is, not before noon, of course—"

"If I'm too early—" Philip put in quickly, moving to pick up his hat and cane.

"No, no, not at all!" Lady Alice assured him, stepping between him and the table where he'd placed his things and taking his arm. "You are not early at *all*. We are positively *overjoyed* that you've stopped in, for I have said to Cora any *number* of times that Philip Denham is as *well-bred* and *delightful* a gentleman as any in *London* and asked her to be *sure* to invite you. *Do* sit down here next to me and tell me how you do."

"I'm quite well, your ladyship," Philip said, taking a seat beside her obediently but feeling as if he were an animal who'd stepped with eyes wide open right into a snare.

"Yes, I can *see* that you are," she remarked, beaming at him approvingly. "My friend, Lady Revington, and I were remarking only the other evening, at her ball, you know, that you've never been in better looks. There *was* a time, after your dear mother passed away, that you seemed to be quite thin and pale, which was of course *completely* understandable, but I'm *so* happy to see that you've recovered your robust health. It does not do to neglect one's health, I always say."

"Yes, very true," Philip murmured with a polite smile. "I—"

"And one should *not* hide away from one's friends, either, and I'm *quite* pleased to see that you've come to call at last!

Many's the time I've said to Cora, 'you *mustn't* neglect Philip Denham, my dear,' I've said. 'I hope you've made it *clear* to him,' I've said, 'that he is *most* welcome at our home at any time . . . any time at all . . .'"

"Thank you, ma'am. It is most kind—"

"And now you're *here*!" She clapped her hands together on her broad breast and beamed at him again. "To take Cora for a drive, I expect. I *told* her when we looked out and saw your curricle and those *beautiful* greys of yours, 'Cora,' I said, 'put on the lavendar jaconet and a warm pelisse, for sure as check he means to take you driving.'"

"Yes," Philip nodded, his calm posture and slight smile in no way revealing his growing distaste, "I *had* intended—"

She clapped her hands again and guffawed with pleasure. "There! You see? Mothers are always right in these matters. 'Cora,' I said, 'Guineas to a groat he's brought round his curricle *particularly* to take you driving. Mothers *know* about these things,' I told her. And so it has turned out, much to my satisfaction. How *delightful*, my dear boy, that you have decided to call at last."

She kept up in this vein for the next quarter-hour, giving Philip no opportunity to speak, much less to make excuses to take his leave. But Lady Alice showed herself quite capable of ceasing her monologue when her daughter finally made her entrance. Cora Ainsley stepped into the room, a tremulous smile on her lips and high color in her cheeks. She was a pretty little thing, with large blue eyes, shiny auburn hair which fell in bouncy curls over each ear, and a form which billowed here and there with enticing curves. It was the allure of those curves (as much as the fact that her father had left an estate that was rumored to exceed thirty thousand per annum) that had caused Ned to put her name at the top of the list. "Mr. Denham," she breathed excitedly, "how delightful that you've come to call!"

"Yes, *isn't* it?" her mother gurgled, rising and grinning as Philip, who was already on his feet, bent to kiss the girl's proffered hand. "He's come to take you *driving*, just as I predicted! But you needn't rush off at once, you know. I'm sure I shan't feel the *least* qualm about leaving you alone to discuss your plans for a few minutes. I've *always* said—haven't I, my love?—that Philip Denham is a young man of *impeccable* character. If I've said that once, I've said it a *thousand times!* *Impeccable* character—those were my very words . . ."

After she left, her daughter took her place on the sofa and

smiled up at Philip invitingly. "Won't you sit down, Mr. Denham? I'm sure we needn't rush off right away. It will be *so* pleasant to be able to spend a few moments in re-acquainting ourselves, you know. As I've always said to Mama, 'Philip Denham may be a famous sportsman and a Corinthian of note, but one doesn't always know what he's thinking.' Although I must admit I *do* admire someone who doesn't reveal *everything* he's thinking, don't you?"

"Well, I—"

"Exactly! I truly cannot *abide* those babbling-brook sorts who prose on and on without a stop. As I said to Mama just *yesterday*, after a certain gentleman had paid a call, 'Mama,' I said, 'I truly *cannot* encourage him to call again, for he prosed on and on quite like a babbling brook, without a *stop!* Truly, one can *not* enjoy such companionship when one has scarcely an opportunity to get a word in, can one?"

"No, I don't suppose—" Philip mumbled dejectedly, realizing that the daughter, despite her curves, made as oppressive a companion as her mother.

"Certainly. A bit of *moderation* in speech is always desirable. I have always said, as the Romans used to do—or was it the French?—that there should be moderation in all things. I told my little sister only this morning, 'Cissy,' I said, 'you should learn to moderate your voice, for when you grow up to be a Young Lady, you will learn that moderation in all things will be your best course.' That's what I told her only this morning. And *I* am not the sort, you know, to give advice which I don't follow myself. I'm quite scrupulous about that. Aren't you?"

"Yes, I am," Philip said firmly, getting to his feet. "I quite agree with you, Miss Ainsley. Moderation in all things. Therefore, so that you shall not think me immoderate in my stay, I shall take my leave."

She blinked up at him in dismay. "Your . . . *leave?* But you've barely stayed half-an-hour!"

"Yes, but I cannot fail to take the hint you so graciously and kindly concealed in your words. Moderation, because you so admire the quality, has now become my *law*." With a smile and a bow, he turned and crossed the room to fetch his hat and cane.

"But I didn't mean . . . you mustn't think . . . I mean, weren't we to go for a drive . . . ?"

Philip paused, cast about in his mind for an excuse and

turned to her with his assured smile. "Yes, I had hoped so. But the weather is certainly inclement . . . not in any sense moderate, you know . . . so I shall have to curb my impatience and leave the drive for a milder day. Thank you, Miss Ainsley, for a most *instructive* morning." With another bow, he hastily quitted the room.

His encounter with Miss Ainsley had been depressing enough to drive from his mind whatever faint glimmers of hope he'd entertained that he might make a match that would be both financially beneficial and emotionally satisfying. He was now ready to dismiss the entire scheme as impossible. But he'd given his word to visit Mary Blanchard, too. With a shudder of distaste, he jumped into his curricle and headed for the Blanchard residence. He might just as well conclude the matter at once.

Mary Blanchard was tall and somewhat angular, but her face, with its high cheekbones and well-modeled chin, was the sort that men often described as 'haunting.' When she arrived in the sitting room after keeping him waiting only five minutes, looking pleasantly disconcerted and only a trifle abstracted (and without a mother in tow), he permitted himself to hope that this visit would turn out better than the last. It took only another five minutes, however, to make him realize that, in its own way, this call would be equally disastrous.

In the first place, the room was smotheringly warm, for although it was small, it boasted a huge fireplace in which a roaring fire was burning. In the second place, Miss Blanchard, who had taken a place close beside him on a small loveseat (the room's only comfortable-looking piece of furniture), had doused herself with a musk-like perfume which threatened to overpower him. And in the third place, he discovered to his intense discomfort that Miss Blanchard was *soulful*.

Mary Blanchard had little faith in words. She didn't speak much but let her eyes do the speaking for her. "Really?" she would murmur after every remark he made, accompanying the word with a deep stare into his eyes, as if she were searching for corroboration in his very psyche. She reacted to every one of his statements with the same concentrated stare . . . as if his remark about the bite of the wind was as fraught with significance as his prediction that a Regency would be established by the year's end because of the King's very serious indisposition.

What with the heat, the perfume and the eyes which she so determinedly fastened on his face, Philip felt a growing anguish. What was she trying to find, or to express, by peering so fixedly into his eyes? Was she trying to declare that she was a woman of unimpeachable sincerity? Was she trying to indicate an all-consuming interest in his thoughts? Or was she trying to read, in the depths of his irises, the true motive for his call on her? Whatever the answer, the steadiness of her intense gaze convinced him that he could *not* spend a lifetime subjected to that unwavering scrutiny. As soon as he could politely take his leave, he did so.

Once on the street, he took a deep breath of cool, fresh air in almost inexpressible relief. His future had been decided: *he would not permit himself to marry.* The two ladies he'd called on today had seemed, the night before, to be the most desirable of all the eligible girls he and Ned had been able to think of, and it was now clear that a life with either of them would have been insupportable. If they were the *best*, what might the *rest* of them have been like? He shuddered at the thought. Anything, even the burden of his enormous debt, would be preferable to marriage. Ned's plan was out of the question. And he would tell the fellow so, when he saw him this evening, in no uncertain terms!

Chapter Five

THE NEWS THAT Letty meant to have dancing at her anniversary dinner sent a ripple of excitement through the Glendenning household, for, as Claryce pointed out, that fact indicated that the affair was to be much more important than they'd originally supposed. "Yès, Claryce is right," Lady Glendenning agreed. "It will be more like a *ball* than a simple family dinner."

Under those altered circumstances, therefore, the members of the Glendenning household had to make more elaborate preparations than they'd planned. Ball gowns, rather than ordinary dinner dresses, were required. Hair styles had to be more ornate. Velvet cloaks were called for instead of the pelisses the ladies would have worn with their dinner dresses, and those had to be removed from their places at the backs of the wardrobes and aired and steamed so that all the creases would be removed. And, since long white gloves were *de rigueur* for balls, every pair had to be inspected for smudges or missing buttons.

The entire household bustled on the appointed day. Katie ran hither and yon collecting sashes to be ironed, dancing slippers to be polished and laces to be stitched onto necklines. Miss Dorrimore hurried from bedroom to bedroom in an endeavor to help each of the ladies with her hair. Even Hinson

46

undertook the role of valet to young Lord Glendenning, wishing
to ensure that the young man's evening clothes would be "bang
up to the mark." By the middle of the afternoon, everyone in
the household except the cook was in some way involved in
the preparations for the night's festivities.

Ned, however, had not been able to throw himself into the
spirit of the occasion. Philip's problem had completely depressed him. Ever since he'd learned that his brilliantly-con-
ceived plan to get Philip leg-shackled had failed, he'd felt
deflated. The debt of twelve thousand pounds weighed almost
as heavily on *his* mind as it did on his friend's, and he could
think of no stratagem—other than matrimony—to solve the
problem.

He paced about his bedroom disconsolately. With his sisters
and his mother busily preparing themselves for Letty's party,
there was no one lingering about the house to offer him companionship. He had absolutely nothing to do but to dwell on
Philip's plight. Why the females of the household should find
it necessary to begin their *toilettes* so early in the afternoon
was a mystery to him. He could wash, shave and dress in less
than two hours—why should it take women almost all day?

He'd whiled away the earlier part of the day by reading the
Times from first page to last. What was there for him to do
with himself now? Searching about the room for something
with which to occupy himself, his eye fell upon a crumpled
paper on his dressing-room table. It was the sheet on which
he and Philip had listed the names of the various young ladies
who might be likely candidates for Philip to wed. He sighed
and picked it up listlessly. How unfortunate that none of them
had turned out to be suitable. Wedlock would have been a most
propitious solution to Philip's dilemma. Not only would it have
enabled him to discharge his debts, but it might very well have
given him the impetus to mature, to become less profligate,
to bring his gaming tendencies under control and to live in a
less devil-may-care way.

He noticed, as he ran his eyes down the list of rejected
females, the name which he'd circled. Lucia Greland. Lady
Lucia was the girl whom Philip had said terrified him. How
strange! While it was true that she had a somewhat booming
voice and a tomboyish manner, Ned had felt, during the two
or three times he'd been in her company, a decided warmth
in her personality and a straightforwardness in her address

which were quite likeable. In addition, when her father had died three years ago and left her orphaned, she'd come into a considerable estate.

Of course, it was said that Lady Lucia Greland was wild—given to riding a horse much too powerful for a girl, to driving a high-perch phaeton with reckless abandon, to keeping a number of huge dogs in her house and, in general, to behaving in so eccentric a way that she set tongues wagging all over town. But Ned was not one to set store by gossip. He very much doubted if even *half* of what they said of her was true. Philip had been too hasty in his judgment of her. Perhaps he, *Ned*, should investigate the lady in Philip's stead. If he took the matter in his own hands—as he'd threatened to do—he himself might be able to arrange a match between the lady and Philip. Of course, Philip might become furious with him, but Ned wouldn't tell him a word about it until the groundwork had been well laid. *Dash it*, he muttered to himself, *why not*?

And what better time than right now—during this otherwise dull and empty afternoon? He would do a service for a friend and give himself an interesting occupation with which to while away the time. With a burst of eager energy, he threw on his coat and took himself off without further ado.

* * *

An elderly butler, bent with age and dressed in decidedly shabby livery, opened the door of the large, haphazardly-designed house which Lord Greland had built in Upper Berkeley Street some thirty years before. The neighborhood was too far from St. James to be fashionable, but neither Lord Greland nor his daughter had seemed to let that fact annoy them. "I hate living in town in any case," Lucia had been said to have remarked, "so I may as well live in Upper Berkeley Street when I'm in town as anywhere else."

As the butler made his slow, tortuous ascent of the stairway to inform his mistress that she had a caller, Ned, who had been left standing in the hallway, looked about him in considerable surprise. He could see into the open door of an oversized drawing-room, and he was at once struck by its deplorable condition. He had had it on very good authority that Lady Lucia Greland was as rich as a nabob. Why, then, was the house so run-down and poorly kept? The carpets, which might have been costly orientals to begin with, were faded and torn, and they seemed not to have been swept in weeks. The window-draperies were thick with dust and were rent in so many places that they seemed on the point of falling apart. And the furniture, too, showed signs of wear, age and neglect, being chipped, scratched and even chewed on the legs. Yes, of *course*! She was said to keep a number of dogs...

A sudden, loud barking—as if the dogs had read his thoughts—sounded from the staircase above his head. With a start, he looked up. Two enormous Irish wolfhounds were bounding down the stairs, restrained only by the leashes being held tightly by the lady of the house. "Éasy, Benvolio!" she shouted. "Quiet, Mercutio! Do you want to frighten our guest to death?"

Ned, who had indeed been frightened to the extent of turning quite pale and feeling his heartbeat increase considerably, tried to appear calm. "G–good day, your ladyship," he stammered awkwardly.

By this time, Lucia Greland had reached the bottom of the stairway and was studying his face. "My man tells me you are Lord Glendenning," she said in her mannish, powerful voice. "Do I know you?"

Since the dogs were equally curious and sought to discover the answer by jumping upon him and sniffing his face, Ned was hard-pressed to manage an answer. He backed away from their attack, unable to keep from putting up an arm to protect his face from their claws.

"Down, down, you great beasts!" their mistress ordered firmly, and the two hounds obediently, if reluctantly, heeled at her sides.

"Y–yes, my lady," Ned offered hesitantly, his confidence in himself and his mission quite shaken, not only by his fright at the attack of the dogs but by the lady's failure to recognize him, "we've met a number of times. In fact, you s–stood up with me for a country dance at the Revingtons' the other evening."

She came up close to him, turned him so that his face was angled toward the light of a tall window at the top of the staircase, and examined him again. "Ah, *yes*! Ned, isn't it?"

Ned blushed. "Yes, that's right. The nickname suits me better than the title, I'm afraid. Nothing very lordly about me."

She cocked her head and looked at him with a judicial shrewdness. "Oh, I don't know," she said after her scrutiny had been completed. "You're more lordly than some I've known." Then, with a sudden, flashing smile, she thrust out her free hand. Almost held spellbound by her steady stare, he grasped her hand and was about to stoop and kiss it when she squeezed *his* firmly and shook it as heartily as a man. "How do you do?" she asked warmly. "How kind of you to call. Come into the library where it's warm. I don't bother keeping fires in most of these rooms, you know, since I never use 'em."

With the dogs jumping and frisking about them, they made their way down the hall to the library. That room was in much better condition than the others he'd glimpsed. The floors and carpets were clean and the furniture polished. Though the hangings were shabby and the furniture scratched, the glow of the fire gave a warm patina to the wood paneling, and the leather bindings of the many books added a touch of richness to the atmosphere. "Sit down, sit down," she urged cheerfully. "Don't wait for me. I've got to settle the dogs."

While she ordered the dogs to lie down near the fire, Ned took the opportunity to catch his breath and study his hostess. She was certainly not in the common way. Her hair was loose and hung about her face in wild disarray, a light-brown mass of crinkly waves. Her skin was darkened and somewhat weathered from many hours out-of-doors, making her look slightly older than her twenty-four years. But her eyes were bright and shrewd, her upturned nose gave her face a look of pert amusement, and her lips were red and full. As she knelt beside her dogs, untying their leashes, he could see that her body was muscular and that she moved with an athlete's purposeful grace. Eccentric though she was, Ned felt that anyone with a grain of sense would have to like her.

"I'm not at all sure I care for that calculating stare," she remarked, looking up at him quizzically. "You are giving me the most uncomfortable premonition that you've come here for a purpose I shall not like at all."

Ned blushed again. "I beg your pardon, my lady. I didn't realize that I was staring."

"My title doesn't suit me any more than yours does you." She stood erect in one fluid movement and walked with a mannish stride to a chair facing his. "I shall not object to your calling me Lucy." She sat down, leaned back in the chair, stretched out her legs before her and put her hands behind her head, fingers linked, in comfortable informality. "Now, then, Ned, my lad, let's have it. What is it that brings you so far from Mayfair?"

Suddenly and quite belatedly, it struck Ned that he'd been much too hasty and thoughtless in making this call. What was he to say to her—*My friend is in need of money and is interested in arranging a match with an heiress?* Certainly it wouldn't do to tell her so bluntly the reason for his visit. What *was* he to say? "Well, I . . . er . . ." he began uncomfortably, "I've come on . . . er . . . behalf of a . . . friend—"

"A friend?" she asked, cocking her head and looking at him curiously.

"Yes. A friend who is interested in . . . er . . ."

"Yes?" she asked encouragingly, her eyes brightening in amusement.

"In . . . er . . . furthering an acquaintance with you."

One of her eyebrows lifted in surprise as she watched his face with interest. "A *friend*, you say?"

"Yes. A friend."

"A very *good* friend, I imagine," she remarked with a decided touch of sarcasm.

"Oh, yes. The very best. We are very close, you see."

"Yes, I had assumed as much. And why, may I ask, does this *friend* wish to further an acquaintance with *me*?"

"Well . . . er . . . because he . . . er . . . very much admires you."

"*Does* he, indeed?" She drew in her legs, dropped her arms and, with lithe deliberation, got up from her chair. "Why?"

"Why?" Ned echoed in an agony of embarrassment, getting up too. "Because . . . because . . ."

She put a hand on his shoulder and pushed him down into the chair. "Don't get up, Ned. I like to prowl about. You needn't jump to your feet every time I do." She circled his chair, studying him from all angles with such cool dispassion that he felt his ears redden in confusion. "Well, why?" she demanded again. "Why does he admire me? Because of my excessive beauty, perhaps?"

"Y—yes," Ned stammered gamely, "he finds you very striking—"

"Ah, *striking*! Hardly a reason for beginning an acquaintance, however." After one more circumnavigation of his chair, she returned to her own. "Perhaps he was drawn to my ladylike charms? The gentle softness of my voice? The exquisite feminity of my manner?"

The unmistakable irony in her voice made him miserably awkward, but he saw no reason for her apparent self-disparagement. "I–I don't know why you should sound so satirical, ma'am. My friend sees you as possessing any number of charms . . ."

"Oh?" Her eyes twinkled mischievously as she resumed her position of shocking informality, her hands behind her head again and her legs stretched out before her. "What charms?"

"He thinks of you as a woman of . . . er . . . considerable spirit and . . ."

"And?" she encouraged, a slight smile turning up the corners of her mouth.

"And he admires the fact that you are . . . are . . ."

"Yes?"

". . . that you are not just in the common way, you know."

She smiled. "How very nice of your . . . er . . . *friend.*" She got up, walked round her own chair, leaned her elbows on its back and put her chin on her hands. "I don't suppose your friend is *also* aware that I'm an heiress of a quite respectable fortune, is he?"

Ned reddened to the roots of his hair. How had he blundered into such a coil? Instead of *helping* Philip, he was probably ruining his chances *completely.* "I'm sorry," he muttered feebly. "I'm afraid I'm making a mull of this."

She responded with a surprising gurgle of laughter. "Not at all. I find myself quite fascinated. But I like direct speaking. *Does* your interest . . . or, rather, your *friend's* interest . . . have something to do with my wealth?"

Ned, fixing his eyes on her face, forced himself to make a quick decision. If the girl did indeed like direct speaking, perhaps it would be best to make a clean breast of the entire matter. She was the most direct-speaking young woman he'd ever met—so why not speak to her with complete honesty? "May I be frank?" he asked, leaning forward earnestly.

"Yes, I wish you would."

"My friend, you see, finds himself in considerable financial difficulty. An advantageous marriage might very well help in that regard. But his character is such that he would abhor making an alliance for that purpose alone. That is why I . . . we . . . thought of you."

"Because he . . . or you . . . so admired me, eh?"

"Yes."

"And you say that you . . . or your *friend* . . . is of the belief that an alliance between us might hold the promise of *more* than mere convenience, is that what you're trying to say?"

"Yes, my lady, I am."

"How very optimistic of you." She came round her chair. "Especially since you know me so little."

"That is quite true, but I'd hope that—"

"For instance, did you know that I am very much accustomed to having my own way?"

"That is something to be expected in one who has had to be alone so long and is forced to rely on herself to make all her decisions in life."

"How *very* understanding you are, Ned," she said, the ironical tone in her voice deepening.

He didn't understand her mood and, instinctively, kept silent.

"And does your *friend* know that I can't abide to live in London for more than three months at a time?"

"I don't see what difference *that* can—"

"Does he know," she went on, approaching his chair, "that I breed Irish wolfhounds for a hobby, that I ride in the park in most unladylike abandon—?"

"I'm sure that—"

She came around behind him and leaned over, speaking portentously into his ear. "And that I'm known among the members of the *ton* as a virago?"

"I'm convinced, ma'am," he said, trying unsuccessfully to turn and catch the expression on her face, "that such an epithet is a gross exaggeration."

"No, it is not," she said, still behind him. "It is one that I quite deserve. And what's worse, I am clutchfisted and penny-pinching to a high degree, reluctant even to spend a groat to improve the condition of this house—"

"Please, your ladyship, stop this!" He jumped up from his chair and turned to face her. "Perhaps I deserve that you should taunt me like this . . . I realize that I've been completely tactless in presenting the case to you in this thoughtless way. If your father—or *any* parent or guardian—had been available, you could have been spared a conversation of this sort—I could have made the suggestion to *him*. But even if I've offended you, I cannot bear to hear you disparage yourself in this fashion!"

She smiled at him complacently and, with a hand on his shoulder, urged him down into his chair again. "I have said nothing about myself which is not completely true, my dear sir. Nothing." She strolled back to her chair. "But my claim of absolute veracity is one which I fear *you* cannot make."

Ned, completely taken aback, blinked at her. "What do you mean, ma'am? Do you think I've *lied* to you?"

"Haven't you?" She grinned at him in amused rebuke, as if he were a little boy who'd claimed not to have eaten the missing piece of cake all the while his face was smeared with chocolate. "This talk of a *friend*! Why not come right out and admit that you've been speaking of *yourself*?"

Ned's brain felt sluggish. What was she talking about? "Myself?" he asked stupidly.

"You needn't be afraid," she assured him, smiling. "You've made a very appealing presentation of your case. Very appealing. Preposterous as it is, I may almost be inclined to give the matter serious consideration... when you've shown the courage to admit that it is you, yourself, who—"

M—me?" Ned felt the blood drain from his face. "But... whatever gave you the idea that...?" He rose clumsily to his feet. "What have I *said* to give you the impression that...?"

She gazed at him a moment in obvious perplexity as her smile slowly died away. "Are you saying that you *aren't* speaking for yourself?"

He put a shaking hand to his forehead. "Good God, what have I *done*?"

"Do you mean... there really *is* a friend...?" Her voice was so low it gave him a strangely ominous feeling.

"Yes, your ladyship, there is. Truly!"

Her body seemed to stiffen and her lips grew rigid. "You... you had the *temerity*," she hissed, rising slowly from her chair, "to come here and speak to me on a matter of such... such *intimacy*... in behalf of someone *else*?"

The words seemed to quiver in the air, held aloft by the power of her suppressed fury. He felt sickened in shame and fear. "But I... didn't think..." he muttered lamely.

"How *dared* you come here and offend me so! *Get out at once*!" she shouted like an enraged Juno, gesturing imperiously toward the door.

He backed away, stumbling. "But ma'am, please... let me explain—"

"*Out*, do you hear? And don't ever bother to come back!

I never wish to see your face again!"

Ned's thoughts and senstaions were in chaos. What had he done to upset her so? He didn't see why the misunderstanding should have caused her to take such offense. "Please," he begged desparingly, "tell me what I've *done*! I never meant to—"

"If you don't take yourself off at *once*," she muttered through clenched teeth, "I shall call the dogs!"

"But if you'd only give me a *moment* . . . one moment to—"

"*Mercutio! Benvolio! Up!*"

The dogs' ears shot up, and, with low growls, they sprang. Ned waited for no more. He ran out, barely shutting the library door behind him before the dogs flung themselves upon it, barking loudly enough to wake the dead. Without another moment's pause, he stumbled from the house, his heart beating in his throat and his head pounding in humiliation and misery. It was not until later, when he was back in his bedroom, his breath returned to normal and his pulse somewhat calmer, that he realized that, above the mass of conflicting emotions— above the fear of the dogs, his shame at somehow having betrayed his friend, his confusion at having offended the lady unknowingly—above all that was the mortification of having been, in some completely bewildering way which he still couldn't understand, a complete, utter, indisputable and unmitigated fool.

Chapter Six

OF THE THIRTY-ODD guests whom Letty welcomed to her party, there was not one she surveyed with greater interest than Mr. Dennis Wivilscombe. His appearance did not fall short of her expectations. He was a pleasant-looking gentleman, several inches over average height, bulky in girth, with a thick neck and large hands. His dark, curly hair was cut short, but his sideburns grew down almost to his chin. The sideburns and the wide, walrus-like moustache gave him a look of cheerful masculinity, an impression confirmed by his hearty handshake and deep voice. "I can't tell you, ma'am, how delighted I am to make your acquaintance at last," he boomed when Letty greeted him in the entrance hall. "You are every bit as charming as they say."

Although Letty was very eager to observe Mr. Wivilscombe's behavior toward her sisters, she was too much the hostess to neglect her duties during dinner. She had to see that each course was served at just the right moment, that the wines were kept flowing, that the pearled-barley soup was adequately hot, the hazel-hen sufficiently doused with sauce and the Apricot Ice properly chilled. Nevertheless, her busy eyes took note of the fact that Mr. Wivilscombe kept Claryce laughing during the meal (even though Letty had placed her on the opposite side of the table from him), while Augusta (who had been seated to his right) seemed to get very little of his attention. Luckily, Philip had been placed at Augusta's left, and the dear boy politely exerted himself to keep the shy girl entertained.

Letty was disturbed to see that, despite Philip's efforts to converse with her, Gussie never looked up to meet his eye or favor him with a smile. Every time Letty looked across at her, Gussie's eyes seemed to be fixed on her plate. *When*, Letty wondered, *did my sister become so withdrawn?*

To give her further cause for anxiety, Letty couldn't help noticing that Ned, too, was unusually quiet during the meal. She'd placed him near her own place at the table, so it was not difficult to observe that her brother was abstracted—his eyes glazed over as if he were engaged in some inner debate. Fortunately for the success of her party, the room rang with so much lively chatter and such frequent bursts of laughter that Ned's distraction and Augusta's shyness were not particularly noted by the others.

Letty tried not to let her concern for Augusta and for Ned interfere with her joyous celebration of her anniversary. Roger had been so generous in helping to make this party a memorable occasion—even going so far as to present her with a pear-shaped emerald pendant so large and lustrous it took her breath away—that she wanted no cloud to shadow his enjoyment of the evening. She fingered the emerald, suspended on a heavy, wrought-gold chain (which Roger had, with the most satisfying of endearments, hung about her neck earlier that evening), and she looked down the long table at him. He met her eyes, smiled and surreptitiously winked at her. His eyes held a look of such suggestive intimacy that she blushed, and a wave of happiness swept over her. If only her family could each find the kind of contentment in their lives that she enjoyed!

When the ladies left the table, the musicians in the drawing room immediately struck up a lively gavotte. The sounds were so attractive that the gentlemen did not long linger over their ports. Within half an hour, two sets had been formed for a country dance, and the gaiety had begun.

After Letty had danced with her husband, her brother-in-law and Mr. Wivilscombe, she begged to be allowed to take a respite on the sidelines. Prue had already given up her exertions on the dance floor (performed despite the fact that the time of her lying-in was not far off) and had taken a seat on one of the sofas, her hands resting lightly on her amply-curved midsection as she attempted to catch her breath. Brandon hovered solicitously over her, repeatedly asking if she were quite sure she felt well. Letty took a place beside them. "Prue looks very well to me, Brandon," she assured the worried husband. "You must not be so excessively fearful."

"Am I excessively fearful?" Brandon asked, considering the matter with his usual seriousness. "You are probably right. Sophocles does say, *'To him who lives in fear, everything rustles.'*"

"Good for Sophocles," Prue declared. "Now let us have no more talk about my health." She threw Letty a look which clearly said that men can be such fools. "A little dancing can do the baby no harm."

"No, but you mustn't overdo such exertion, you know, Prue," Letty cautioned.

Prue laughed. "You, too? Really, Letty, I hope *you* won't start to fuss over me. It's quite annoying enough to have Brandon do it. Brandon, my love, why don't you ask Gussie to stand up with you for a dance? She's sitting over there with Mama for all the world like an aging spinster. I haven't seen her dance *once*."

"I'd be quite happy to stand up with Augusta," Brandon said, rising and looking down at his wife reprovingly, "but you don't have to pretend that you're asking me to do it for *her* sake. You and Letty wish to gossip, and you want me out of the way, isn't that it?"

Prue giggled. "Perhaps. But *do* go along, my dear. The set is beginning to form."

"Very well, I'll go. Not another word will you have from me. *'Words are for women, actions for men,'* as someone— I can't remember who it was—once said." Brandon obligingly took himself off, confident that Letty would make a satisfactory substitute for him as caretaker of his headstrong wife.

Prue leaned close to her sister. "What do you think of the notorious Wivilscombe, Letty? Attractive, is he not?"

"Very. Although the clunch has stood up with Claryce for three of the last four dances. Doesn't he think of Gussie at *all*?"

Prue shrugged. "Men! They are all of them quite buffle-headed when it comes to judging women."

"With the exception of Roger and Brandon, of course," Letty said with a grin.

"I can add another name to that list," Prue remarked, looking across the room to where, in front of the tall windows which faced upon a walled garden at the back of the house, Philip Denham was now standing. "Your brother-in-law."

"Philip? What makes you say that?"

"He *spurned* Claryce!" Prue said in a gleeful whisper. "I *saw* it."

Letty's eyes widened with interest. "Did he *really*? When?"

"Just a little while ago. The vixen walked right up to him and, from what I could judge from this distance, actually invited him to take a turn on the floor with her."

"Prue! She *didn't*! You must be mistaken."

"What else could she have been asking? He shook his head, bowed politely, made some excuse and *left* her! I could see that she was excessively chagrined."

"You don't say!" Letty murmured as she fixed her eyes on Philip with thoughtful speculation. *Prue might very well be right*, she said to herself. If Philip had indeed rejected Claryce's advances, it would not be very surprising, for Philip was no easy prey. Letty had watched him, in the four years of her married life, resist the wiles of any number of calculating females. She'd often teased him about it. "I'm just not in the petticoat line," he'd respond. "I prefer the unshackled bachelor life."

She studied him now with renewed interest. Tall and slim as he was, his well-developed shoulders and legs revealed the sportsman in his form as clearly as the enigmatic gaze of his blue eyes hid the gambler in his nature. Philip was what the ladies liked to call a nonpareil—an attractive, charming, town-bred Corinthian who took for granted the respect of his fellow men and the admiration of the ladies. But he was probably unaware of the waves of excitement he could generate among the young ladies merely by brushing back his straight, light-brown hair from his forehead or flashing his sudden, heart-warming grin at them. In addition, his obvious lack of interest in pursuing them was as stimulating to the ladies as catnip is to cats. And Claryce was as susceptible to that sort of catnip as any feline creature. But if Letty were any judge, it would take a female of extraordinary finesse—much more than Claryce possessed—to ensnare Philip.

While she sat observing him, she saw Ned approach him. The two young men exchanged words, their faces suddenly serious and worried. *What on earth is wrong with them?* Letty wondered. *Has one or the other of them fallen into some sort of trouble?*

"Have you noticed anything strange about Neddie this evening?" Letty asked Prue. But before Prue was able to respond, a burst of laughter caused them both to look round. Just to their left, Claryce (looking quite ravishing in a mulberry-colored Mantua silk, her hair pulled back *à la Greque* and threaded enticingly with silver cord) stood surrounded by three gentlemen importuning her for the next dance. One was Lord Garvey (whom Claryce had specifically asked Letty to invite), the second was young Neville Trevithen (one of a half-dozen young men whom Letty had invited to ensure a lively crowd on the dance floor), and the third was Mr. Wivilscombe. "Come now, Miss Glendenning," Wivilscombe was saying to her, "you must make a decision. The next set will be forming in a moment. Surely one of us—if you'll forgive a pun—is worth your *wiles*."

Another burst of laughter greeted this sally, but Wivilscombe's wit did not win him her hand. Claryce merely directed a look of amused disdain in his direction, took Mr. Trevithen's arm and walked off to the dance floor with him, the swing of her hips giving ample evidence that she was aware that her two rejected swains were watching her as she moved away. But both Mr. Wivilscombe and Lord Garvey were experienced campaigners, and neither one looked as crestfallen as Claryce would have supposed. They exchanged smiling shrugs, and each went off quite philosophically to find other partners.

Mr. Wivilscombe, noticing his hostess near by, turned immediately in her direction and asked her to stand up with him again. Letty gently refused, pleading weariness. "But perhaps you would care to pull up a chair and join my sister and me for a while. We are both approaching the age, I fear, when it is more enjoyable to sit and gossip than to exert ourselves in dancing."

"I don't believe that for a *moment*, Lady Denham," he responded, obligingly pulling up a chair, "for I have watched you *both* on the dance floor this evening, and there was not a young girl there who was livelier or more energetic."

"Yes, but we haven't the staying power, you know," Prue sighed. "It's the staying power that makes the difference. Look at Claryce there. I don't believe she's missed more than one dance all evening."

Mr. Wivilscombe turned to look in Claryce's direction. "I

must agree with you *there*, Mrs. Peake. Your sister always seems quite boundlessly animated."

"That is a very charming compliment to my sister," Letty said with the slightest, almost unnoticeable, touch of irritation in her voice, "but I find that animation is not necessarily the most admirable of virtues."

"No, of course not," Mr. Wivilscombe said agreeably.

"But you like animation in a lady, do you, sir?" Prue inquired, looking at him with interest.

"It is *one* of the things I like, I admit."

"What other qualities do you like in a lady's character, Mr. Wivilscombe?" Letty asked curiously.

He smiled at her affably. "Oh, all sorts of qualities please me, your ladyship. I am not one to set up requirements and strictures. I like this lady for her dimples, that one for her laugh, and a third for her musical voice. I'm not at all hard to please."

"How very nice for the ladies," Prue murmured, amused. Mr. Wivilscombe was certainly a good-natured fellow. It was hard to feel annoyed with him, even though it had been this very quality—his lack of discrimination—that had moved him so easily from Gussie to Claryce.

"But certainly you must have *some* requirements in mind for the lady you will eventually make your wife," Letty persisted.

Wivilscombe stroked his heavy chin thoughtfully. "I suppose I've thought, from time to time, about what sort of lady I'd like to wed, but . . ." He broke into a rather sheepish grin. "But my vision seems to keep changing. Do you think that means I'm likely to remain a bachelor?"

"I don't know what it means, I'm afraid," Letty responded. "I suppose *that's* why you're known as The Seal."

He chuckled. "So you've heard that, have you? It's an appellation I find quite embarrassing. I know I look a bit like a walrus, but I'm not nearly as hard to hold on to as the epithet seems to suggest. Why, if your sister there would give me the slightest sign that she's not just toying with me . . ." His voice died down, and all their eyes turned to watch as Claryce, executing a graceful turn, passed by on the floor in front of them.

Letty could barely keep herself from uttering a sharp rejoinder. If this large, good-natured fellow (who must have *some* sense in his head, having been, at the age of thirty-five, successfully side-stepping matrimony for years and *years*) truly intended to permit himself to be caught by a frivolous charmer like Claryce, Letty had little sympathy for him. But, fortunately, before she was tempted to let her thoughts find utterance, Brandon returned. Feeling that she'd heard enough of Mr. Dennis Wivilscombe's jovial imbecilities, she stood up and politely excused herself. "It's time," she said as she took her leave of them, "that I found my brother. The cawker hasn't come near me all evening."

After much searching, she discovered Neddie huddled with Philip in the library, the two of them staring into the fire in the hearth and looking as dismal as she'd ever seen them. Philip jumped to his feet the moment he caught sight of her, his grim expression immediately replaced with one of cheerful welcome. So smooth was the transition that she almost doubted that she'd correctly interpreted his earlier look. "Whatever are you both doing?" she said with overblown vivacity. "Why are you hiding away here? This is a *party*, you know. Philip, my dear, you are to go out at once and dance with my mother. And Ned, you've not asked me to stand up with you *once* this evening— and on my anniversary, too!"

With this combination of bullying and badinage, she marched them out of the library and back into the drawing room. When she'd maneuvered her brother onto the dance floor, she wasted no time in asking him what was wrong. But the movements of the dance made intimate conversation difficult, and, in addition, Ned's answers were terse and evasive. "Don't know what maggot's got into your head," he muttered uncommunicatively.

"See here, Neddie, there's no need to run sly with *me*," she said bluntly. "I know you well enough to be able to detect when something's on your mind."

"Don't be a silly widgeon," he insisted with vehemence. "Nothing is at all amiss."

But by the time the dance had ended, Letty had managed to learn enough to guess that, although Ned was troubled with something personal, it was *Philip* who was in the greater difficulty. She was then able, quite easily, to deduce the nature of her brother-in-law's problem: Philip, she reasoned, had accumulated some sizeable gambling debts.

Letty had been aware for some time that Philip, because of a tendency to indulge in too-deep play, had been causing Roger

serious concern. And she realized, too, how much Philip valued
Roger's good opinion. If her surmise was correct—if Philip
had fallen into debt again—she would not be surprised that
the young man wished to keep that information from his
brother. Roger was the last person in the world in whom Philip
would wish to confide such a matter. Letty could quite sympathize. Roger was wont to get a *look* in his eyes—a hurt,
startled, disappointed look—when someone he loved fell from
grace. That look was always devastating to the guilty party.
She herself had inspired a mild version of that look once or
twice, when she'd done or said something foolish. It was not
a look she'd like to see again. Poor Philip. Perhaps she could
offer some help to him.

Precisely at that moment, she was struck with an inspiration.
Of *course* she could help him . . . and *he could help her as well*!
Why had she not thought of it before? She almost wanted to
laugh out loud with delight. The idea was truly ingenious—so
inspired that it almost made her gasp at her temerity in con-
cocting it. Not since the tempestuous days of her courtship had
she invented so cunning, so Machiavellian, so *precarious* a
scheme. Her heart began to beat in youthful excitement. Why,
she felt as quivery as a green girl! She could hardly wait to set
things in motion.

But now was not the time. She needed, first, to think the
scheme through. Then she needed an hour alone with Philip.
Her little plot could not be initiated now, in the midst of a
dinner party being held in her own home. Her brilliant scheme
would have to wait. Now was the time to act the role of hostess,
to enjoy the festivities she'd so carefully planned, and to bask
in the glow of the celebration of her four years of marital bliss.
So, with a forceful effort of will, she pushed her scheme to the
back of her mind, looked round the room for her favorite partner
and went off to dance—with her husband.

Chapter Seven

PHILIP WAS QUITE surprised, the next morning, to receive a note from his sister-in-law. What could Letty possibly want with him, he wondered, when she'd seen him just a few hours ago? The wording of her missive was irritatingly mysterious: *I must talk to you on a matter of some urgency. Can you come to Curzon Street at about two? Roger will be visiting his solicitor at that time, and I shall be quite alone.* Why on earth did Letty want him to come when Roger was out? If a stranger had chanced upon this note, he might well have assumed there was something havey-cavey going on between Lady Denham and her brother-in-law. Of course, anyone knowing Letty even a *little* would realize how ridiculous such an evil interpretation would be—Letty's devotion to Roger was indisputable. Still, a bit of discretion when one wrote letters was advisable. He'd have to give her a scold.

Feeling more curious than concerned, Philip presented himself at the doorstep of Arneau House on the stroke of two and was immediately ushered into the downstairs sitting room. "Good Lord, Letty," he said at once, putting his hat and cane on a table near the door, "what's the blasted *mystery*? You've had me playing guessing games all morning. And why did you make a point of saying we'd be alone? Anyone would think this was an *assignation*!"

"I'm sorry, Philip," Letty said with a little laugh. "I was *afraid* that the wording of my note might be somewhat theatrical. But never mind that. Do sit down, my dear. Shall I pour you a glass of madeira?"

"Not for me, thanks. I don't wish to prolong the suspense." He sat down opposite her and looked at her curiously. "What is this urgent matter?"

She leaned forward, her eyes searching his face. "It concerns my sister. I need your advice, my dear."

"*My* advice? About your *sister*?" Philip was completely dumbfounded. Whatever inchoate thoughts had suggested themselves to his mind while he'd waited for this interview, he'd never imagined a subject of this sort. "Which sister?"

"Augusta. What do you think of her, Philip?"

"What do *I* think of her? Why? What difference can it make what I—?"

"I'll explain in a moment. Just tell me quite frankly your impression of her."

"Well, she . . ." Philip was quite at a loss for words. He'd known Augusta ever since they'd met at Roger's wedding, but at this moment, caught unawares, he couldn't even bring her *face* to mind. "She seems to be a . . . a very fine young lady."

"Fine?" Letty watched him with interest. "What do you mean by that?"

Philip rubbed his chin. His impressions of the girl were so vague that he scarcely knew how to reply. "Oh, you know . . . well-bred . . . sensitive . . . restrained . . ."

"I see. But not very *interesting*, is that what you mean?"

"I didn't mean that at all," he said defensively. "Of *course* she's interesting—"

Letty looked at him earnestly. "You mustn't feel you have to be polite, you know. I need to have the absolute truth."

He shrugged. If she wanted the truth she could have it. "Well, then, to be quite honest, I haven't noticed if she's interesting or not. She's a bit shy and retiring, you see, so I haven't got to know her very well."

"I'm not surprised," Letty sighed. "Claryce completely overshadows her, doesn't she?"

"Does she? Well, I *suppose* that may be the case," Philip murmured, wondering somewhat uncomfortably where all this was leading.

"It *is* the case. Don't *you* think Claryce overshadows her?"

Letty asked with intent curiosity.

"I can see where *some* might think so," he said dubiously.

"But not you?"

"Do you want *more* blunt speaking? If you do, I'll admit to you that your sister, Claryce, is not . . . er . . . to my taste."

"Oh, Philip, my dear," Letty sighed, giving him a warm pathetic smile, "if only the other London gentlemen agreed with you. But they don't, you know. Claryce has managed to snatch away every suitor Gussie's ever had."

Philip squirmed in discomposure. This was not the sort of revelation he felt comfortable in discovering. "I don't understand, Letty," he said, bemused. "What have your sisters to do with me?"

"I hoped you could advise me. I'm quite in despair about Gussie's future." She turned her lovely, lustrous eyes meltingly up to his. "I cannot let the girl dwindle away into an old maid, can I?"

Philip had been too often the target of just such melting glances to be taken in. "See here, Letty, what are you up to? If there's something you want of me, just ask. There's no need to use your feminine tricks to turn me up sweet."

She burst into a peal of laughter. "There, you *see*? That's *just* why I sent for you. You're the only unmarried man I know who can't be taken in by what you call 'feminine tricks.' That's why I have such need of you."

He eyed her suspiciously. "To do what?"

"What I wish to ask you," she said, rising and coming to stand before him in urgent appeal, "is to *transform* my sister Augusta. I want you to make her the toast of the *ton* . . . a reigning belle . . . a diamond of the first water, capable of competing successfully against her sister in the ballroom, at the dinner table and on the Marriage Mart."

Philip gaped at her, scarcely able to believe his ears. "You . . . you want *me* to do this? *Me?*"

She nodded briskly. "You."

"Letty, you must have rattled your *think-box*! Why me?"

She grinned at the appalled expression on his face. "You're the perfect choice, Philip. Your reaction to my female wiles just now *proved* that, didn't it?"

He shook his head. "Not to me."

"Don't you *see* how perfect you'd be? You're at home to a peg in matters of dress, deportment and social courtesies.

You're familiar with the likes and dislikes of men of the world. And best of all, you've been evading designing females for so long that you must by this time be completely familiar with their machinations. All you need do is teach Gussie what you've learned."

"Oh, is *that all*?" His tone was heavy with sarcasm. Completely disinclined to grant her request, he got quickly to his feet and frowned down at her. "I tell you, Letty, you're out in your reckoning if you think I'm your man."

"Then who *is*?" she countered promptly. "Can you suggest a substitute?"

He paused for a moment in thought. What fellow of his acquaintance would make a suitable instructor to train a girl in matters of coquetry? Even if he could think of one—and he had no doubt there were many—would Letty want a *stranger* to be privy to such an intimate matter? He could see, suddenly, why she had fixed on *him* to fill the post. He, at least, was *family*. But this was not the sort of task he had any desire to undertake. He felt a rising wave of irritation that she had thrust this request upon him. "Perhaps your entire plan is best forgotten," he suggested. "Why don't you go upstairs, take a long nap and forget this wild scheme."

"No, Philip . . . you don't understand how much this means to me." She looked up at him, her face a study in dashed hopes. "I *can't* forget it."

Her obvious distress couldn't fail to touch him. Gently, he took her chin in his hand and tilted up her face. "Don't look so dejected, my dear," he said kindly. "What you desire to accomplish is probably akin to making a silk purse from a sow's ear, and that, my mother used to tell me, can never be done. It's no use to yearn after the impossible."

"Oh, dear," Letty sighed, "I wish Brandon were here."

He dropped his hand in surprise. "Brandon? Brandon *Peake*? Why?"

"Because *he* would have an appropriate epigram to contradict yours."

Philip laughed. "Yes, I see what you mean. He'd say something like: '*Nothing is impossible to a willing mind.*'"

"Yes, exactly." Letty smiled wanly. "What brilliant mind conceived that saying?"

"I have no idea." Philip crossed to the table and picked up his hat and cane. "I haven't Brandon's talent when it comes to epigrams, you know. Just as I haven't the talent to do as you ask."

Letty, deflated, dropped into a chair. "Do you think poor Gussie is as hopeless a case as all that?" she asked in low-voiced despondency.

Philip felt a twinge of guilt. "No, that's not what I meant at all." He put down his hat again and came back across the room. "I only meant that the task is beyond my capabilities. I'm sure that Augusta, if she could overcome her shyness, would be as sought-after as any—"

"But you . . . you called her a sow's ear," Letty reminded him.

Philip colored in embarrassment. He wanted to bite his tongue! "I didn't mean to . . . ! Dash it, Letty, it was only a figure of speech. Please believe that I never meant to imply—"

She waved her hand as if to wipe out her previous remark. "It's all right, Philip. I know you didn't mean it. It's only that I'm so utterly *disappointed* . . ."

Philip knelt beside her chair and took her hand. "Don't look like that, my dear. You'll find a way to make your sister shine. You've overestimated *my* abilities in these matters, that's all. Why, I would scarcely know how to *begin*—!"

Letty lifted her despairing eyes to his. "I ask you only to *try*, Philip. Only to try."

The pleading, soft voice, the appeal in those melting eyes—these were almost too much even for Philip to withstand. He hated to refuse his sister-in-law anything. But what she asked was truly impossible. Firmly, he got to his feet and went back to pick up his hat. "I wish I could oblige you, Letty," he said earnestly, "but I'm quite out of my depth in these matters." He put on his stylish beaver, picked up his cane and made for the door.

Letty looked after him in some desperation, but she had not yet played her trump card. "Wouldn't you even oblige me if I offered to pay your gambling debts?" she called after him.

He stood stock still for a moment. "Gambling debts?" he asked, turning about and studying her with a look of cool appraisal.

"You *are* in debt, are you not?"

His steady blue eyes didn't blink. Not a muscle in his cheek quivered. Not a finger twitched. "No, of course not. Whatever gave you such an idea?"

So this is how gamblers hide their feelings, Letty thought, watching him with reluctant admiration. She even began to doubt if her supposition about his problem was correct. If he was so skilled in masking his emotions, it might take more skill than she possessed to shake him into making a confession. And without it, how could she ever set her plan in motion? "I wish you would treat me with candor, my dear," she urged, attempting to hold him with the compelling sympathy in her eyes. "I want to help *you* as much as I want you to help *me*. And . . . I promise to say nothing to Roger of what you reveal to me."

For a moment, Philip maintained his attitude of aloof innocence. But then his eyes fell. With a shrug, he took off his hat again and tossed it upon the table. "Did Neddie give me away?" he asked quietly.

"No, of course not. The two of you seemed to me to be depressed last night . . . and I added two and two."

Philip nodded and threw her a respectful glance. "Clever of you. I was convinced that my manner last night was decidedly jovial. I must be losing my touch."

"Not at all. You were the perfect ballroom beau."

"If I was so perfect, how did you find me out? That moment in the library surely was not enough—?"

"I spent a *good deal* of time observing you, you see."

He looked at her closely. "Did you? Merely to discover if you could find a way to entice me into agreeing to your plan for your sister?"

"No, of course not. How unkind of you, Philip! Do you think I care nothing for *you*? It was not until *after* I realized that you were troubled that it occurred to me that we could help *each other*."

He turned away, ashamed. "But we *can't* help each other, my dear," he told her, his voice low and discouraged. "I owe a great deal more blunt than I would care to admit even to you."

She jumped from her chair and ran up behind him. "Don't say that, Philip," she urged, placing a hand on his arm. "All you need do is tell me the extent of your indebtedness, and I'll send the money round to your rooms *tomorrow*."

Unable to face her, he put a hand on hers and shook his head. "No . . . it's quite impossible . . ."

Letty had never seen him so depressed. In alarm, she took hold of both his arms and turned him round. "Philip, if things are as bad as that, you *must* let me help you," she cried. "Forget Gussie's problem, if you feel it beyond you, but you *must* let me help you out of this fix you're in!"

He met her eye bravely. "You *can't* help me, love," he explained miserably. "You'd have to go to Roger for a large sum of money, wouldn't you? If I'd have wanted Roger's help, I'd have gone to him myself." His expression suddenly darkened. "I say, you haven't said anything of this to *him*, have you?"

"No, of course not!"

He sighed in relief. "Thank you, my dear. And thank you for *wishing* to help. It was a very kind gesture."

She turned away from him with an impatient stamp of her foot. "I want to do more than make a gesture. And I *can* help you without going to Roger." Turning back to him, she smiled gently. "He's been the most generous of husbands, you know. I have a quite sizeable account of my own. And he never questions me about how I use it. How much do you need? Three thousand? Four?"

Philip gave a bitter laugh. "I'm afraid it's more than twice that," he said in self-disgust.

Her breath caught in her throat. "Philip! More than *twice*—? Good heavens!"

Shamed, he turned back to the table and picked up his hat again. "I did try to warn you—"

"Oh, dear!" She threw him a worried look. "I hope this doesn't mean that you've gaming in your blood, my dear. Roger would be quite broken-hearted if he thought that—"

"That's why he mustn't know! *Ever*!" He turned a white, agonized face in her direction. "You must *promise* me, Letty!"

"You have my word, my dear. But this gaming of yours . . . *is* it in your blood?"

He shrugged. "I don't know. Perhaps. How can one judge one's own nature? Sometimes, when I'm challenged to a card game, or I hear of an interesting wager, the urge to participate is . . . almost irresistible . . ." He had never admitted those thoughts aloud. He met her eyes, a look of horror at his situation deep in his own. Then, with a groan, he dropped into a chair and put his head in his hands. "Oh, God, Letty, what *am* I to do?"

Letty, touched to the core by his plight, placed a soft hand on his shoulder. The poor boy was sunk in despair. *Could gaming be in his blood?* She studied his bent head intently while her mind searched for an answer. *No*, she decided, *I don't believe it for a moment*. She felt sure he was not addicted beyond the attraction for gambling felt by many young men who are forced by their situations into idleness and dissipation. She was certain that if Philip could be encouraged to find a *purpose* in life . . . an occupation of worth, an interest in the study of government, of finance, of history . . . a *wife* . . . *any* of these would be the making of him. This situation of his cried out for the remedy which she, with her ingenious plan, had already foreseen. All she had to do was put it into motion, and both Gussie *and* Philip might be saved . . .

"Dash it, Philip," she said with renewed cheerfulness, "let's not look on the black side. If you must wager, then at least you can wager with *me* instead of some dastardly, card-playing Captain Sharp."

He looked up, baffled. "Wager—?"

"Yes. My money against your skill and proficiency in social situations. I'll wager the entire amount of your debt that you can't make Gussie win back Mr. Dennis Wivilscombe from the clutches of her very ravishing, spectacular and predatory sister."

Her spirited good humor, coming so soon after his tortured admission of the fear that had been preying on his mind, seemed to diminish the import of his dire situation. A laugh was forced out of him. "What a persistent little chit you are, Lady Denham," he declared with admiration, pulling himself up on his feet. "If your plan for your sister is so important to you, I'll do as you ask . . . and never mind the wager."

"Oh, Philip, *will* you?" She threw her arms around his neck and kissed his cheek with delighted enthusiasm. "But you *must* agree to the wager. I *insist* upon it."

"Don't be a goosecap," he said, turning away from her and going once more to pick up his hat. "What sort of creature do you take me for? Do you think I could possibly let you give me nine thousand pounds?"

The sum almost made her pale, but she managed to keep her inner tremors from showing. "It *is* a shocking amount, my dear. But I'll send it round to you as soon as I've managed to collect it."

"No, no, my little innocent," he corrected, grinning down at her. "Don't you know *anything* about wagering? You don't have to pay until—and unless—you've lost."

"But I'd rather do it *my* way," she insisted. "You want to pay your debts as soon as possible, don't you?"

"Yes, it would be a delightful relief to do so. But what if I fail to accomplish my task with your sister?"

"You won't fail."

"But if I do—?"

"Then you'll be in debt to *me*. Won't that be better than to owe the money to strangers?"

He stared at her, feeling a disconcerting surge of humiliation and hope warring in his breast. The glimmering of hope was the first bright ray to gleam through the darkness of those long days of desperation, and it flickered in his breast too brightly to be easily quenched. "Oh, God, Letty, if *only*...!" But he couldn't permit himself to thrust such a burden upon her. "No... you *can't*! You could hardly explain to Roger that you needed nine thousand pounds because you wanted a new *gown*, you know... no matter *how* generous he is," he pointed out sensibly.

"I know." She smiled up at him confidently, but her eyes were thoughtful as her fingers curled around the emerald pendant hanging from her neck on its gold chain. "I shall find another way. Don't trouble your head over it. Well, Philip, my dear... *have* we a wager?"

He searched her face but could read nothing in her eyes except a pleased serenity. The flickering ray of hope ignited into a blaze. If Letty felt so confident that she could raise so enormous a sum without Roger's knowledge, he would let her do it! He would pay her back some day... somehow. And meanwhile, he'd show her the extent of his gratitude by making her sister into the most dazzling female in London!

Suddenly he felt his spirit lift in relief, like a bird gliding aloft on an upward gust of air. "Yes, my dear," he said, his voice choked, "a wager it is!" He bent down and tenderly kissed her cheek. "But I very much fear that you'll have the worst of it."

"No such thing," she assured him happily, taking his arm and walking with him to the door. "If you can accomplish what I've asked of you, Philip, I shall consider that this, my first and only wager, is the very best bargain I've ever made."

Chapter Eight

LATE THE FOLLOWING morning, a day of grey sky and threatening wind, two letters of very different but equally astounding import were delivered to the Glendenning household in Argyle Street. The first to arrive was addressed to Miss Augusta Glendenning and was passed into her hands by the butler at the moment when she emerged from the morning room after she'd finished her breakfast. "It's from your sister, Lady Denham, Miss Augusta," Hinson informed her as he handed her the envelope. "The footman didn't wait for an answer."

Gussie took the letter and nodded placidly, completely unaware that the news carried in the missive would shock her to the marrow of her bones. She strolled down the hall to the sitting room, took a chair near the window—for the dark sky permitted very little light to filter into the room—and broke the letter's seal. It was indeed from Letty, and she leaned back in her chair to savor its contents. Letty was probably writing to ask her to come to Arneau House for luncheon or to join her sister on a shopping expedition. Letty always sent notes to her for such purposes. She unfolded the crested paper and was mildly surprised to see that the note was too lengthy to be a mere invitation. Perhaps one of the babies had done something extraordinary, and Letty wanted to tell her about it.

With an anticipatory smile, she began to read. *Dearest Gussie*, the note began, *I hope you will not think me an incorrigible meddler when I tell you that I have taken a Certain Step in regard to your future.* ("Oh, dear," Gussie sighed aloud, shaking her head in amused irritation. She'd *known* that her sisters were in their we-must-do-something-about-Gussie moods. What was it to be this time? She read on.) *Although my plan may not meet with your complete approval at first, I am convinced that when you think it over you will agree with me that it is a wise course. Mama, Prue and I are all convinced that you cannot go on as you have, hiding your light under a bushel and permitting Claryce to take advantage of you.* (Gussie winced. It was dreadfully discomfiting to have to endure this sort of thing. Must her sisters and her mother forever pluck away on the same harpstring? Why couldn't they be content to let her remain as she was?) *Dearest, don't be angry at me for saying this, but it seems to me that the only practical solution to this problem is to find a way to draw you out of yourself . . . to teach you how to show to the world your very considerable charm and attractiveness.* ("Ha!" Gussie sneered. Did her sister think she would be taken in by such blatant flattery? Letty should know better.) *In order to do this, I have taken the liberty of arranging a course of private tutoring for you . . .* (Gussie read those words with some sense of relief. Private tutoring, foolish and bewildering as it seemed to her, was not so bad as *some* of the schemes her sisters might have concocted. Although what sort of tutoring Letty had in mind Gussie couldn't even imagine.) *. . . a course of private tutoring for you with a person whose qualifications are impeccable and with whom you can feel completely comfortable, for he is one of the family. It is Philip Denham—* (The name seemed to leap off the page, and it struck Gussie's consciousness with the force of a dropped bombshell. She felt herself stiffen and her breath catch in her throat. Her mind seemed to freeze; for a moment she was incapable of any thought or feeling. Her eyes simply went on reading, her brain barely registering the meaning of the words.) *—Philip Denham who has agreed to help you to 'come out of your shell.' He will call on you early this afternoon to begin the tutoring. I hope, when you've thought this matter over, my love, you will see this, not as an interference in your life, but as the start of an exciting new adventure. I shall stop by later this week to see how you are progressing. In the meantime,* *dearest one, please remember that I am, as always, your very loving sister, Letty.*

For a long time Gussie sat, unmoving, in her chair, staring out ahead of her at nothing. How could her sister, the most beloved friend she had in the world, have done this dreadful thing to her? How could Letty have *humiliated* her before the one person in the world whose opinion of her mattered—Philip Denham? She wondered what Letty had said of her to Philip— what description of her lack of social grace, what explanation of her failures in the Marriage Mart, what analysis of her lack of vibrancy or color—to convince him to run to her aid? What a pathetic dowd he must think her! Good *God*, how could she ever *face* him again?

She noticed that the sheet of notepaper was trembling in her hand. Some instinct warned her that there was a phrase in the letter that she'd better read again. Fearfully, she scanned the sheet. Yes, there it was: *He will call on you early this afternoon to begin the tutoring.* She had not been mistaken about that detail. Letty had arranged matters so that Gussie would not have time to circumvent this little scheme. Why . . . Philip Denham might present himself on the doorstep *at any moment*!

Gussie felt sick. What was she to do? The fellow would soon be on his way (it was already close to noon) and here she sat like a lump, transfixed. Her hair was not properly dressed, her gown was an old, faded morning dress not at all appropriate for receiving guests, and her spirits were so agitated that she would undoubtedly stammer if she tried to speak. She could no more face Philip Denham in this condition than she could dance *naked* on the stage of the Covent Garden Theater! She must hide herself away, and quickly, before he loomed up in the doorway and confronted her!

"Hinson!" she cried, jumping up from her chair and racing to the hallway. "*Hinson*, where *are* you?"

The surprised butler came running up from the back stairs, pulling on his coat. "Miss Augusta," he asked breathlessly, "is anything amiss?"

"*Yes! No!* That is, I am *not at home*, do you understand? If anyone calls this afternoon . . . *anyone at all* . . . you are to *insist* that I am not at home. I will *not* come down under any circumstances, and you are not to let anyone in. Is that *clear*, Hinson?"

His mouth dropped open. Miss Augusta was not the sort to

become agitated. If anyone in the household could keep her head in emergencies, it was Miss Augusta. What had *happened* to the poor girl? he wondered. "Yes, of course, Miss. I quite understand. You may rely on me," he assured her. But even before he'd concluded his reassurances, the girl had turned, sped up the stairs and had disappeared from sight.

The second letter arrived a short while later and was addressed to Edward, Lord Glendenning. Hinson observed that it was delivered by a footman in shabby livery who'd emerged from an antiquated and decidedly dilapidated coach which nevertheless bore a crest on its side. Since the earlier letter—which had come from Lady Denham and had given him no hint that it contained bad news—had apparently caused a considerable disturbance despite its innocent appearance, *this* letter, delivered in such an eccentric fashion, filled him with misgivings. It seemed to presage all sorts of trouble, and he was in no haste to deliver it into Mr. Ned's hands. Besides, the young man was still asleep.

Carrying the missive gingerly between his right thumb and forefinger—as if it contained a covering of deadly poison—he went down to the kitchen to report this latest event to Cook and Katie, who were taking their luncheon. "Do you think this means *more* trouble?" he asked when he'd related the strange manner of the letter's delivery.

"Ain't our business, Mr. Hinson, whether it does or no," Katie said flatly. "Ye'd better take it up t' the lad."

Cook clucked her tongue. "I felt it in me bones this mornin' that this wuz t' be a donsie day. The wind's 'owlin' in the chimney and the sky's so dark it give me th' shakes. Did ye ask Miss Augusta what the matter wuz, Katie?"

"I tried. But she's locked 'er door. She's layin' in there, weepin' a flood and not wishin' to talk to a soul." She shook her head worriedly. "Ain't like my little poppet t' carry on so. She's put me plumb in the dismals."

Hinson nodded in agreement. "Never *have* seen the girl in such agitation. Well, p'haps I'll hold *this* letter 'til later. Don't want to give it to his lordship now and put *him* in the dismals, too."

"Y' cain't do that, Mr. Hinson," Katie pointed out. "What if it's somethin' o' momentous importance? *I'll* bring it up to 'im, if you'd prefer it."

"*Would* you, Katie? I'd be much obliged, I can tell you. I've no stomach for excitement, you know."

Ned had just come down to the morning room and was reaching for the coffee-pot when Katie came in, letter in hand. "A note for you, m'lord," she said, eyeing him nervously. "Delivered by a footman, it was, 'oo comed in a b'zarre ol' carriage wi' a crest."

Ned looked up at her and grinned. "Well, Katie, you're supposed to know everything that's worth knowing. Who's crest was it?"

"I didn't get a peep at it meself, so I cain't say," she answered, not the least discomposed by his flattery. She studied the seal of the letter carefully, as if it would offer her a clue.

"Let me have it, girl. The seal isn't likely to tell us anything." He reached for the letter and looked at it curiously. "Is the coffee still hot, Katie? If it is, you may pour me a cup."

"I'll fetch ye a fresh pot," she offered. But instead of leaving, she pretended to be occupied with clearing away the cups. "Ain't you goin' t' open it?" she urged impatiently.

"The crest has made you curious, has it?" Ned teased, throwing her a grin. "Well, if you think I'm going to tell you who—" His smile disappeared as he broke the seal and caught a glimpse of the signature. "Good *Lord*!" he gasped, astounded.

"Well, m' lord?" Katie prodded impatiently. "'Oo's crest *is* it?"

"Never you mind," he muttered, his eyes fixed on the note. "Go on about your business."

"Bad news, then?" she persisted, not at all bothered by having overstepped the bounds of proper behavior for a household servant. If there was trouble in this house, she wanted to know what it was. Ignorance of the facts would not help her to help the family.

But Ned waved her away. "No, no. Leave me alone, will you?"

Something in his tone made her peer at him closely. The intensity of his manner of reading the letter, as well as a bit of redness she detected on his ears, suddenly made her chuckle. It was a *love* letter! "I might a knowed," she muttered to herself as she left the room, relieved that she could report downstairs that "it was on'y a letter from a *lady*."

But it was not a love letter. It was from Lucy Greland, and Ned, completely amazed at what he was reading, scarcely noticed Katie's withdrawal. *My dear Lord Glendenning*, the letter began, *I fear that my behavior toward you during our recent interview was somewhat lacking in propriety. Please accept my sincere apology for what can only be called my shocking rudeness. I have reviewed our entire conversation in my mind, and I find—to my own surprise—that the subject you embarked upon continues to pique my interest. If you can permit yourself to accept my apology and return to pay another visit to Greland House, I would be happy to receive you and to pursue the subject further. If you can call today, after one o'clock this afternoon, you will find me at home. You have my assurance that I will refrain, this time, from setting the dogs on you again. Yours, etc., Lucy Greland.*

The note left Ned in a whirl of confusing emotions. His first reaction of surprise soon gave way to a kind of self-satisfaction. So . . . Lucy Greland was sorry she'd thrown him out! That knowledge gave him more pleasure than he'd felt in a long time. It made him want to laugh out loud to realize that she was attempting to make it up to him. The little fool had set the dogs on him for no good reason; it pleased him that she now felt ashamed.

But his sense of satisfaction soon changed to a feeling of anger. She had asked him to call on her *again*. This very day! What *cheek* the woman had! If she imagined that he would subject himself to further humiliation, she was fair and far off. *Set the dogs on Ned Glendenning, will you, ma'am?* He'd be *dashed* if he'd give her a second chance!

Forgetting completely that he hadn't yet eaten a bite of breakfast, he got up and went directly to the writing desk in the sitting room. He pulled a sheet of paper from its pigeonhole, trimmed a pen and began to write. *My dear Lady Lucia, I thank you for your note and invitation to call, but I find myself unavailable at the hour you suggested. . . .* No, that wouldn't do. It was too ingratiating, too forgiving. Besides, she might very well suggest another appointment. He tore up the sheet and took another. *Your ladyship*, he wrote, *I find myself unwilling to subject my nerves to another experience such as that which occurred . . .*

No, that was much too rude to be gentlemanly. He had to find a way to reject her invitation which would be both cutting and polite. He took a third sheet. *My dear madam, I thank you for your kind invitation, but I believe there would be little purpose in my calling on you again . . .*

He threw down the pen in disgust. None of his attempts had managed to achieve the proper tone. Perhaps he should just be straightforward and tell her frankly that he no longer believed that his friend and she would suit. Under those circumstances, she would understand that there was no point in pursuing their conversation any further.

On the other hand, of course, he could not really be *certain* that his judgment was sound. Philip might very well *enjoy* dealing with a woman of such spirit. If one looked at the matter dispassionately, one would have to admit that Ned had achieved the first step of his plan—he'd interested the lady in making a marriage of convenience. And Philip still had *need* of such an arrangement, hadn't he? Perhaps Ned should not be hasty in deciding to call the matter off.

I ought to think of Philip's needs, not mine, Ned told himself. The lady had written that she found herself *piqued* by the subject of an arranged marriage. If he, Ned, had managed to arouse her interest, he'd taken a giant step forward. If he was to call himself a friend to Philip, it was his duty to follow through on this promising beginning. He *should* pay the call on Lucy Greland after all, just as she'd suggested.

Without further debate, he tore up the scribbled sheets, checked the time on the mantel clock and went to change his clothes. An hour later, without a word to anyone, he left the house and ran quickly down the front steps. The wind's bite made him wish he'd worn a greatcoat. He turned up the collar of his coat, and in so doing, he failed to see his friend, Philip, about to mount the stairs and almost bumped into him.

"Ho, there, Neddie," Philip greeted, "don't you look where you're going?"

Ned gaped in surprise. "I say, old fellow, did we have an engagement? I'm dreadfully sorry, but I've an urgent appointment elsewhere."

"No need to concern yourself," Philip said with a smile. "I haven't come to visit *you*!"

"You *haven't*? Then, who—?"

"I've come to call on Augusta, you coxcomb. You're not the *only* person in the family worth talking to."

Ned raised his eyebrows, startled. "Gussie? You've come to call on *Gussie*? Whatever for?"

"I'll tell you about it later. In fact, I have a *great deal* to tell you later. But for the nonce it will have to wait. I promised Letty I would not be late."

"What has Letty to do with it? Well, never mind. I mustn't be late either. Shall we have dinner together this evening? I may have a great deal to tell *you*, too."

"Then let's say my rooms at seven." Philip nodded his adieu and started up the steps. "I take it that Augusta is at home?" he asked over his shoulder.

"Oh, yes," Ned declared, setting off briskly down the street. "I haven't seen her myself today, but at this hour you'll *surely* find her in."

Chapter Nine

"I'M SORRY, MR. DENHAM," Hinson said firmly, "but Miss Augusta is *not* at home."

Philip frowned at the butler in annoyance. "Lord Glendenning has just told me that she *is* at home. Will you please take my card up to her? I believe she's expecting me."

"It will be of no earthly use, sir. I have very strict instructions on this matter. The lady herself has ordered me to tell any callers that she is *not* at home."

"Perhaps she left those orders so that she and I will not be disturbed. I'm certain she did not mean the message for me."

"There were no exceptions, Mr. Denham, I assure you."

"Look here, Hinson, I don't like standing about on the doorstep sparring with you. Are you going to take my card up to the lady, or do I have to do it myself?"

"I'll take your card, sir, if you insist, but I must ask you to remain outside the door while—"

"Hinson!" came Miss Augusta's voice from the stairway behind him. "Why do you keep Mr. Denham standing on the threshold in this wind? Admit him at once!"

Hinson jumped as if he'd been shocked by a lightning bolt and wheeled about. There on the stairs was Miss Augusta, smilingly holding out her hand in welcome and looking as calm

and composed as if her earlier display of nerves had not occurred at all. Despite his years of experience in maintaining
a proper, butlerish impassivity, Hinson gaped at her open-
mouthed. Was the girl demented? Hadn't she specifically *told*
him, not more than two hours since, to refuse admittance to
anyone who called? "B-but, Miss *Augusta*—!" he stammered
in bewilderment.

"Good day, Mr. Denham," Augusta said in cheerful greeting, ignoring Hinson's pop-eyed stare. "Please come in. Hinson, you needn't stand there like a statue. Take Mr. Denham's
hat."

Gussie's change of heart was not quite as shocking as it
seemed to the stupified butler. Her bout of tears in her bedroom
had eased her feeling of near-hysteria, and as soon as she'd
been able to think rationally, she'd begun to realize that something might be salvaged from the humiliating situation in which
her sister had embroiled her—something which might turn out
to be to her benefit.

Her sister's discussion with Philip had probably convinced
him that she was a hopeless dowd, completely inept in dealing
with men, but Gussie had decided that she needn't *add* to
Philip's disdain by hiding away in her room like a frightened
puppy. She would go down, she'd decided, and face him like
a woman of sense and dignity . . . and tell him quite calmly that
she didn't require his services. By her demeanor and her words,
she would manage to show him that even a *dowd* could be
possessed of valuable attributes—qualities like Good Sense,
a Calm Disposition and a Lack of Vanity. And, in addition,
she would have the satisfaction of having gained, just this once,
a few moments of his undivided attention.

So she'd washed her face, combed her hair and slipped into
a more presentable dress. (It was only a plum-colored kersey-
mere—a dress that Claryce would have scorned to wear—but
it was neat and comfortable and didn't have the sort of low
neckline or short sleeves which would make her feel self-con-
scious.) Thus arrayed, she'd gone out to the stairs and had
heard the altercation in the hallway.

Now that the moment of greeting was over, she was quite
pleased with herself for having changed her mind about hiding
away. She had never before had the opportunity to speak to
Philip Denham privately, and she suddenly felt very eager for
the experience. It was true that she'd always had the greatest

difficulty in making conversation with strange gentlemen, but *this* time there would be no such problem, for she had something of definite substance to say. She would tell Mr. Denham—in quite the most polite terms, of course—to take his *Impeccable Qualifications* and jump in the lake with them!

"Come into the sitting room, Mr. Denham, where we can be private," she said pleasantly, leading the way. "It was certainly very kind in you to permit Letty to impose my problem on you in this way."

"Not kind at all, Miss Glendenning," Philip responded as they entered the sitting room. He looked the girl over carefully while she turned away to close the door, adding, "I have more to gain by this...er...experiment than either you or your sister."

She threw him a quick, surprised look over her shoulder. Then, her calm, pleasant expression returning, she came away from the door and crossed the room to a chair near the fire. Motioning him to the loveseat near by, she sat down and said, "I cannot pretend to understand what *you* have to gain, sir. Nor do I understand what the nature of this experiment *is* which you and my sister have concocted between you, but—"

"I'd be happy to explain—"

"Excuse me, but perhaps I can save you the time and trouble of making explanations, for I've invited you in only to inform you that I haven't the slightest desire to be tutored in the social graces."

If her blunt announcement startled him, Philip's long experience as a gambler kept him from showing his astonishment in his face. "I hadn't thought of the plan as *tutoring*, exactly," he ventured, trying to understand why she was showing this unexpected resistance.

"Hadn't you? I'm certain that *tutoring* is the word Letty used when she wrote to me about the matter this morning." She pulled out a sheet of note-paper which she'd tucked into her sleeve. "'*I have taken the liberty*,' it says here, '*of arranging a course of private tutoring for you.*'"

Philip's astonishment was now quite apparent. "She wrote you about the matter this *morning*? Let me be certain I understand you. Are you saying that this is the first you've *heard* of it?"

"But of *course*." It was now Gussie's turn to be surprised. "Did you think otherwise?"

Philip ran a hand through his hair, disconcerted. "Well, I'd assumed . . . that is, it never *occurred* to me that you hadn't been involved in formulating the plan!"

"Today, Mr. Denham, was the first time I'd heard of it."

He jumped up from his seat in embarrassment and began to pace about the room. "But surely you and Letty discussed the idea in some *general* way—?" he asked, pausing.

"No, we did not. Belive me, sir, when I tell you that my sister's letter dropped into my lap this morning as unexpectedly and shatteringly as a bombshell."

He stared at her, confounded. "Dash it all! I ought to wring Letty's *neck*!"

Gussie lowered her eyes to her hands. "I suppose she meant well," she said without conviction, not yet able in her heart to forgive her sister for causing her this humiliation before Philip Denham's very eyes. "But now that you realize that this—what is it you called it? *Experiment*?—was not of my arranging, you can understand why I haven't the slightest intention of proceeding with it."

He didn't answer for a moment but studied her face speculatively. "Yes, I can certainly understand your reluctance," he said softly after a while, taking his seat again. "In your place, I should probably have resorted to outright *violence*! But your sister, in spite of having gone about arranging things in an awkward way, has concocted a very promising scheme. It would be too bad to scotch the plan merely in angry retaliation against her. That would be akin to throwing out the baby with the bathwater, you know."

"Would it?" Lifting her eyes, she looked across at him. "I think you overrate the scheme, Mr. Denham . . . unless I have failed fully to grasp its import." She looked again at the letter in her hand. "As I understand it, my sister desires you to help 'draw me out' of myself . . . for the purpose—if I understand this rather cryptic message—of my making more of a mark on society. Isn't that the substance of the plan?"

He flashed a sudden, wide grin at her. "Oh, much more than that, Miss Glendenning, *much* more than that! We are to be content with nothing less than making you the toast of London!"

His smile had caught her unaware, and, to her chagrin, she felt a tug of response right in the pit of her stomach. *He can probably charm the birds from the trees*, she thought irritably, and to depress any pretensions he may have felt by recognizing that she'd reacted so readily to his grin, she frowned at him coldly. "Make *me* the toast of London?" she inquired with eyebrows raised haughtily. "Letty must think you a *magician*."

"Not at all, ma'am. Now that I've had this chance to study you, I'm convinced that the task will be quite easy."

"You needn't try to flummery me, Mr. Denham. I own a mirror."

"I *assure* you, Miss Glendenning—" he began, leaning forward earnestly.

But she would not permit herself to be taken in. "It's foolish to continue this conversation, sir. I'm quite determined against the scheme. You see, even if it were a possibility, I do not *care* to be the toast of London."

"Don't you?" His lip curled in a skeptical smile. "Then you must be a rare creature indeed."

"I don't believe that the desire for a quiet life is so rare," she said, looking down at her hands again. "There must be many like me who do not wish to draw attention to themselves . . . who prefer to stay in the background rather than the forefront . . . and who wish only that . . . that . . ." But realizing that she'd said more than she'd intended, she fell silent.

"Wish only that *what*, Miss Glendenning?" Philip pursued, leaning forward and watching her face intently.

She cast him a quick glance. "That they could be . . . cherished . . . just as they are," she admitted, her voice hesitant and low.

Philip felt a stab of shame. He had been treating her with condescension, as if she were a pathetic, lonely little creature yearning for his help, when all the while she had more character and sense than he. He stared at her, sitting so quietly across from him, her head lowered and her hands folded in her lap like a governess who'd been scolded. Even her plain, purplish dress and the way her light hair was pulled back tightly into a knot at the nape of her neck suggested a governess. But behind the modest exterior, he perceived, was a person of considerable depth and feeling, someone too sensitive and individual for him to tamper with.

He had no right to be here, despite Letty's urgings. Letty was a loving sister and wanted her Gussie to be happy, but this was not the way to achieve that goal. Miss Augusta Glendenning seemed to him, now that he'd gotten this intimate glimpse of her, to be quite capable of finding her own way to happiness, and he intended to inform his sister-in-law of that observation at the first opportunity. In the meantime, there was nothing left for him to do here but take his leave. "You are quite right, Miss Glendenning," he said abruptly, pulling himself to his feet. "The entire scheme was shallow and superficial. I was presumptuous and thoughtless to have entered into it. I can only ask that you forgive me." He made a quick bow and started toward the door.

She looked after him with a sinking heart. The first really significant conversation with the man she'd adored for four years had just taken place, and it was ending without having changed anything. Of course, she hadn't really *expected* anything to change, but she hadn't expected, either, to feel so devastated by its conclusion. Everything had happened so quickly. Perhaps she'd been too hasty in refusing to take part in Letty's scheme. If she'd had more time to think, perhaps she might have been able to prolong the encounter. Had she let her pride push her to take a wrong turn?

He was leaving . . . and unless she said or did something *immediately*, this provocative encounter would pass, leaving her emptier of hope than ever. Her mind, racing about wildly to find some hook with which to catch his attention again, leaped—in the remarkable way minds have of remembering forgotten but needed bits of information in times of desperation—upon a remark Philip had uttered when he'd first arrived. *I have more to gain by this . . . er . . . experiment*, he'd said, *than either you or your sister*. "Mr. Denham," she said quickly, turning in her chair, "before you go . . . there is something I'd like to ask you."

"Yes, ma'am?" His hand was already on the knob as he paused.

"I couldn't help wondering . . ." She got up and crossed the room toward him. "What was it that *you* were to gain from your participation in Letty's little scheme?"

"I?" He smiled a rather rueful smile. "Nothing worth speaking of. The matter isn't worthy of your attention."

"But I would like to know. Please."

He shrugged and dropped his eyes from her level gaze. "If the plan had . . . had been successful . . . Letty would have paid my gambling debts."

"Oh! I see." So *that's* how Letty had inveigled him into her scheme. He had done it for *money*! She suddenly felt sick. Her mouth was dry, and her fingers began to tremble. Her throat burned with a sudden, tearful sting, and, to keep the tears from spilling over, she put both hands behind her and clenched the fingers together tightly. She'd been a fool not to have let him go when she'd had the chance. She could have spared herself this additional pain.

He was looking at her closely. There was no question that she was in some way disappointed in him. "Did you think I'd offered my services out of brotherly affection for Letty?" he asked, feeling another wave of shame sweep over him. This girl had a definite talent for making him feel crass. His voice took on the rasp of self-mockery. "I haven't the generosity of character for that, ma'am."

"Th–There was no reason in the world f–for you to have undertaken such a task out of generosity, sir," she said bravely. "Letty is only a sister-in-law . . . and you and I are . . . b–barely acquainted."

"You make me all the more ashamed of myself," he muttered, and with another bow he turned to the door again.

"Was it . . . a great deal of m–money?" she asked timidly.

"A *very* great deal," he admitted, not turning round.

"And . . . my refusal, I suppose . . . puts you back into a position of . . . difficulty?"

He looked over his shoulder at her, a brow upraised. "Don't trouble your head about that, ma'am. I shall contrive."

"But I can't *help* feeling troubled." She twisted her hands, which she still kept clenched behind her, in nervous indecision. "I didn't realize that, in spurning Letty's little plot, I would be in any way hurting . . . anyone else."

Philip turned and walked toward her, smiling down at her wryly. "But my dear Miss Glendenning," he pointed out with a touch of irony, "why should you let *my* situation affect you at *all*? If, as you pointed out a moment ago, you and I are barely acquainted, there is no more need for generosity on *your* part than there was on mine."

She shook her head as if his arguments were drops of rain which needed but a gesture to be brushed aside. Her mind had flown ahead to other matters. "But even if I had *agreed* . . . it's too ridiculous to suppose that you could have succeeded. The toast of London, indeed! Did you and Letty really convince yourselves that there was any possibility of my . . . of your . . . your . . . ?"

"Of my *winning* the wager?" he supplied. "I hadn't any doubt at all."

"You must be mad!" she declared, throwing up her arms helplessly. "Utterly mad." Disconcerted, she turned and wandered over to the fireplace where she stood staring absently into the flames. "What, exactly, did you and Letty expect me to . . . er . . . accomplish to win you your 'very great deal' of money?" she asked after a while.

"I believe that Letty had chosen a symbolic moment when she would have considered that we'd achieved our goal—and that would be the instant that Mr. Dennis Wivilscombe made you an offer."

"Mr. *Wivilscombe*?" She looked at him with sheer astonishment. "But *why*?"

Philip shrugged. "Mr. Wivilscombe is notorious for slipping out of the clutches of many a designing female, even when the most canny sharpers were betting at White's that he would be landed at last. So if you'd succeeded in catching The Seal where so many beauties have failed, Letty would have found that to be a significant achievement."

Gussie shook her head in disbelief. "I trust that I would not have had to *accept* him, too, would I?" she asked drily.

"Wouldn't you have wished to? I had assumed . . . but then, I'm beginning to realize that I should never make assumptions about *you*, Miss Glendenning. In any case, neither Letty nor I would presume to tell you what answer to make to Mr. Wivilscombe's offer."

"*Letty* would so presume," Gussie muttered a bit resentfully.

"But we are speaking to no purpose, aren't we? The scheme, we've agreed, is quite beneath your notice—"

"I've changed my mind, Mr. Denham," she replied, lifting her head and giving him a firm, decisive smile. "I shall try my best to help you win your wager."

"But . . . *my dear girl*," Philip objected, "I can't permit you to do this for *my* sake!"

"It's not entirely for your sake. I see certain advantages for *me* as well. So if you're still of a mind to proceed, I shall be happy to do my part to try to land The Seal."

Philip, after a moment of hesitation during which he studied her from beneath tightly-knit brows, gave her another of his brilliant smiles. "Very well, then, ma'am, it's settled."

She nodded. "I hope I shall be a good pupil, sir."

"You needn't worry on that score. And I wish you will not

think of me as a tutor. I shall be like a fond parent, Miss Glendenning—or a brother, rather— who is helping his sister come out into the world."

She smiled and crossed the room to open the door for him. "Well, then, if you are to be brotherly, you must stop calling me Miss Glendenning. I'm Gussie to the family."

He stopped and regarded her with a measuring objectivity. "No, not Gussie. Gussie is not an appropriate name for a toast of the *ton*. You are to be *Augusta*. Nothing but Augusta from now on."

Gussie giggled. "How silly I shall feel. It's quite like my sister Clara calling herself Claryce."

"Not at all, my dear. Your name *is* Augusta, isn't it? You must begin to think of yourself in an Augusta sort of way—graceful and important—and not like a *Gussie* who hides herself away in corners. But enough of that for now. Tomorrow will be soon enough to start our game."

"Yes," Augusta murmured, a spot of color coming into her cheeks as Philip bowed over her hand and went briskly down the hallway, "*tomorrow*."

Chapter Ten

THE DOGS SEEMED much less threatening to Ned this time. His scent was now familiar to them, and when they jumped up on him, they licked his face instead of snarling. "*Down*, Mercutio," he ordered with a smart show of bravery. "*Stop* that, Benvolio!" And to his surprise, the dogs obediently heeled.

Lady Lucia, watching from the stairway, beamed. "I think they like you, Lord Glendenning," she said as she resumed her descent. "That is very much in your favor, you know. The opinions of my dogs are very important to me."

He studied his hostess with some surprise as she led the way down the hall. Her appearance was considerably different from what it had been during his last visit. If Ned did not believe the thought to be ridiculous, he would almost have imagined that she'd made an effort to primp for him. Her hair had been plaited and twisted into an intricate knot at the back of her head, her gown was of a shiny, luxurious material which he felt certain was not intended to be used for an everyday dress, and she'd even put on a long strand of pearls. She appeared, today, less of the wild, free-spirited creature she'd seemed on his last visit. While he was more at ease with the lady in her present, more conventional aspect, he rather missed the excitement of her previous guise.

"I thought we might continue our conversation over a small luncheon," she said, moving past the library to the dining room, the dogs leaping and bounding at her sides and Ned following closely behind. Once in the dining room, he was again struck with a vague, instinctual feeling that she'd taken pains to impress him. The room was spotlessly clean, the windows and the faceted prisms of the crystal chandelier sparkling, and the floor and furniture gleaming from the effects of vigorous polishing. He could even smell the wax.

The table had been set lavishly with fine crystal goblets and gold plate which twinkled and shone in the light of the many candles of the chandelier and the grey afternoon light filtering through the windows. And when they'd taken seats, and the butler—this time dressed in impeccable livery and followed by two neat housemaids bearing platters of cold roast chicken, ham and pickled salmon—began to serve them with silent but stately deliberation, Ned felt almost certain that the lady had set out to make a favorable mark on him. But why? Was she as eager to make a *mariage de convenance* as all that?

Through the first course, under the eyes of the servants, conversation was desultory at best, but after the second course had been served (a mere insignificancy consisting of steamed river trout, piping hot poultry filets *à la maréchale*, assorted garden vegetables, escalloped potatoes, poached eggs, gooseberry tarts and three cream desserts which included a confection known as the Antioch Ruin), and the servants had been dismissed, her ladyship settled down to converse in earnest. "I hope, Lord Glendenning, that you've found it possible to forgive my rudeness of the other afternoon."

Ned, surveying the awesome viands spread out before him, smiled at her diffidently. "I could scarcely maintain a feeling of resentment, my lady, while basking in the warmth of such lavish hospitality. But I can't help wondering what . . . that is, why—?"

"Why I've asked you here again? I shall tell you in a moment. But first, please try some of the trout. My cook is very talented in the preparation of fish, you know."

"I don't think I can eat another bite—"

"Nonsense! You've barely done justice to the poultry, and you have *yet* to sample the Ruin. But to get to the matter at hand, I must admit to you, my lord—"

"We had agreed, if you remember, to forget about our titles."

"Ned, then. I must admit, Ned, that I found myself curious, after you'd left, about many things you'd omitted to explain."

"What sort of things, ma'am?"

"You must call me Lucy, remember?" She played with the fish on her plate for a moment, and then glanced across the table at him. "Well, for one thing, did your suggestion for this . . . er . . . marital arrangement originate with your friend? Or was it your own idea?"

His eyes flickered from hers to his plate. Would she take it amiss if he told her the truth? "I . . . I believe it was *my* idea . . . at first . . ."

She seemed to be pleased. "Yes, I . . . suspected so. But it is not very clear to me why you singled *me* out. I know you said a number of very polite but quite nonsensical things to me in answer to that question the last time we spoke, but I'm still puzzled."

"It's not so very puzzling, ma'am. I . . . we . . . noticed you at the Revingtons' . . . and on other occasions as well . . . and we *liked* you."

Her shrewd eyes were watching him mockingly. "How convenient it must be to have a friend whose tastes are so close to yours," she murmured drily. "And was it your *friend* who suggested that you come here to . . . sound me out?"

"Well . . . not exactly. My friend was not very sanguine about his chances, you see."

She laughed. "*Afraid* to come himself, was he?"

"No, it was not that. He doesn't know . . . that is, I decided that perhaps it would be less awkward if I came to see you *first* . . ."

"Ah, I see. Your friend doesn't yet *know* that you've made this . . . effort on his behalf?"

"No . . . not yet."

The amusement at the back of her eyes was very disconcerting. *What on earth*, Ned wondered, *is she laughing at?* While she rang for the butler and waited for the servants to clear the table and serve the tea, they sat observing each other interestedly. Ned found her enigmatic stare completely puzzling. He would have given much more than a penny to know what she was thinking.

"Now, *do* take a bite of that Ruin, Ned," she urged, the laughing light still dancing at the back of her eyes, "and see if I'm not right that my cook is a genius. To be able to choose a good cook is one of the best talents a wife can have, you know. If you like the luncheon, you can go back and report to your friend that, despite my short temper, my wild disposition, my clutchfistedness and my general contrariness, I am quite proficient at choosing a cook."

The Ruin was indeed a memorable confection, and Ned dispatched a large portion with considerable enjoyment. When at last he sat back and sighed with satisfaction, he found that her eyes were still on him with that teasing glint. "You were right, ma'am," he murmured, smiling back at her. "Your cook is a treasure. And I will be happy to report that fact to my friend."

"Will you tell him about all the *rest* that you've learned about me as well?"

"That you're short-tempered, wild, clutchfisted and contrary? No, I don't think I will."

"But why not? Don't you want your friend to know the truth?"

"Those epithets do not at all conform to my impression of you, ma'am. You mustn't object to my reporting the truth as I *see* it rather than as I'm *told* to see it."

"And how *do* you see it, Ned?"

"Frankly," he admitted courageously, "I'm still too puzzled to say."

She eyed him with approval. "That's better than the foolishness you uttered about me the last time. But tell me about your friend. What sort of man is he? Studious? Shy? Retiring?"

"Oh, no, not at all. I'm sorry if I've given that impression. On the contrary, he's quite dashing. He's a noted sportsman, very well thought of by everyone. You will undoubtedly know his name: it's—"

"No, don't tell me," she cut in quickly, holding up a restraining hand. "Not yet. I'm not yet sure I wish to proceed with this matter. And until I am, it would be less awkward if I didn't know . . . in case I should ever come face-to-face with him." She picked up an apple from the epergne in the center of the table and played with it thoughtfully. "So he's a sportsman, is he? I shouldn't have thought it. You've led me to believe, from the similarity of your tastes, that he was quite like you. Yet I have the feeling that you are not the sporting sort."

"You're right, I'm not. In fact, my friend and I are not alike at all. He is very outgoing, jovial and attractive, while I'm . . . well, I'm much duller and more commonplace."

"I don't find you commonplace, Ned," she said, her eyes on the apple in her hand. "Not at all." She looked across the table at him with a shrewd, appraising stare. "Which leads me to believe that you are not a very accurate judge of character."

"But I am, ma'am. If you'd permit me to arrange a meeting between you, you'd see for yourself—!"

"First tell me some more about him. I must make certain that I shan't find myself in an unpleasant situation. Have you known the gentleman long?"

Ned began to relate the story of how he met Philip, omitting the details of the wedding so that Lucy would not guess the identity of the man he was discussing. Her occasional questions and her interested stare made him feel quite expansive, and he found himself relating little incidents and adventures which he and Philip had shared. Amusing reminiscences or revealing vignettes popped into his head—things he hadn't thought of for years or only half remembered—and he talked easily and comfortably for a long time. It was only when the sound of rain spattering on the windows caught his attention (and he looked up to see that it had become quite dark outside), that he realized he'd talked the afternoon away. With a shamefaced apology, he jumped to his feet to take his leave.

Reassuring him that she'd found his tales delightful, his hostess took his arm and led him back down the hallway, the dogs (who had slumbered peacefully under the windows while they'd talked) again bounding alongside. "Shall I arrange a meeting between you, then, ma'am?" he asked, taking his hat from the butler.

"No, Ned, not yet. I think we should talk about this a bit more. Would it be possible for you to call again . . . say . . . *tomorrow*?"

*   *   *

Letty, too, was spending the dark, overcast afternoon in an out-of-the-ordinary way. As soon as she'd learned that Roger intended to spend the afternoon in the City in conference with his man of business, she decided to take advantage of his absence by using the time to raise the money she'd promised to Philip. She sent a hurried message to Katie that she desired the maid's company on an errand and requested that the girl be ready to be taken up in an hour's time. *Please don't mention this to anyone*, she instructed. *Make some excuse and walk to the corner of the street just before two o'clock, and I shall take you up there.*

As soon as the message was sent, she ordered a footman to tell the groom to have the small phaeton brought round. (The small phaeton would not be very warm on a day like this, but it had the advantage of bearing no crest on its side.) Then, dismissing her abigail, she locked herself in her bedroom and began to search through her wardrobe for a bonnet with a veil. This found, she put it on, making sure the veil shadowed her face sufficiently so that she would not be readily recognized. Then she removed from her jewel-case the large, lovely emerald pendant which Roger had given her and, with fingers that trembled ever so slightly, placed it gently into the velvet-lined box in which it had come. Trying to ignore the sharp twinge of regret and guilt which threatened to weaken her resolve, she carefully tucked the box into her thick muff. Finally, she put on a warm pelisse, picked up the muff, squared her shoulders and went out to the carriage.

Katie was waiting on the corner but not looking at all pleased. "What sort o' havey-cavey business are you up to, yer ladyship?" she demanded as soon as she'd taken a seat beside Letty. "I 'ardly knowed what t' say t' Mr. Hinson 'bout where I wuz off to."

"I'm sorry, Katie, but you were the only one I could trust. I have some very private business to transact, but I didn't dare to go alone. It shan't take very long."

"Is that *all* yer goin' t' say?" Katie shook her head in decided disapproval. "You must be up t' somethin' smoky if you wouldn't even stop at th' *door!*" She looked at her erstwhile mistress through narrowed eyes. "You ain't gotten yourself into a coil, 'ave you?"

"No, of course not. I'm only doing a favor for...for a friend. I can't tell you anything more. Just trust me, and stay close beside me."

"You c'n count on *that*, m'lady, fer certain. I'll stick t' you like glue. I on'y wish y' moughtn't be gettin' yerself in some sort o' fix, that's all."

Letty patted the girl's arm comfortingly and relapsed into silence. She wished, too, that she might not be getting herself into a fix. This was not the sort of adventure she desired at all. If only she could confide in Roger! But that was not possible—she'd given her word. She might as well not dwell on the fact that, for the first time since her marriage, she would have to deceive her husband. It was best not to think about that. She took a quick glance at Katie's set face. The girl did not approve of these secret intrigues, but she was certainly intrepid. It gave Letty courage just having her along.

When the carriage drew to a stop, Katie peered out of the window curiously. They had drawn up before a beautifully-appointed shop with large, many-paned bow windows on each side of its double doorway. Over the doorway waving noisily in the gusty wind, hung a neatly-lettered sign which read BIRD-WELL AND KERR, JEWELERS ROYAL, CLERKEN-WELL. She gave Letty another puzzled, piercing glance before she hopped down from the carriage and gave her assistance to Letty to alight.

When they entered the showroom, a carefully-dressed, meticulously-barbered salesman leaped immediately to attention. He was the most highly valued employee of the establishment and a man of considerable experience. Although he didn't know the identity of the lady in the veiled hat, he could recognize a member of the nobility when he saw one. "May I be of assistance, my lady?" he asked deferentially.

"I would like to see Mr. Birdwell, please," Letty said, her voice not reflecting the trembling of her fingers clutched round the box inside her muff.

The salesman hesitated. He knew that Mr. Birdwell had no patience for trivial interruptions, but one could hardly ask a lady, especially one who was accompanied by a sharp-eyed, inquisitive maidservant, the nature of her errand—not, that is, without incurring her displeasure. "If your ladyship is interested in the purchase of a pair of earrings, a bracelet, a necklace, a torque, or anything of that sort, I'm sure I can show you—"

"You 'eard 'er ladyship, didn't you?" Katie put in impatiently, aware of Letty's strained tension. "She says she wished t' see Mr. Birdwell. If you ain't Mr. Birdwell, you c'n just take yerself off 'n *find* 'im!"

The salesman gaped at the maid in astonishment, his eyes sliding from her face to the veiled lady's and back again. A little cockney abigail was a very strange sort of servant for a lady of quality, if he knew anything of the ways of nobility. Either the lady was a very grand eccentric or a complete fraud. "May I t-tell Mr. B-Birdwell who is c-calling?" he stammered, completely unsure of his ground.

"No, you may not!" Katie snapped.

"But you may show him this," Letty offered, removing one gloved hand from her muff and handing him the little jewel-box.

The salesman took the box, bowed and backed away. Then, turning, he hurried to the rear of the showroom, entered a little hallway, tapped nervously on the opaque glass window of a heavy door and disappeared inside. A moment later the door opened, and a small, balding man with a *pince-nez* affixed to his nose, its black ribbon streaming out behind him, came hurrying out, the salesman at his heels. "Your ladyship!" he exclaimed, scurrying into the showroom and bowing to Letty in obvious agitation, "you must forgive us . . . we had no *idea* . . . ! I sincerely hope you have not been kept standing this way for long."

"Mr. Birdwell?" Letty asked, extending her hand graciously. "I take it you recognize the . . . er . . . merchandise."

"Oh, yes, of course. I trust your ladyship is pleased with it. I can assure you that the item is perfect . . . without a single flaw—"

"I don't doubt that, Mr. Birdwell."

The jeweler adjusted his *pince-nez* and peered at the lady carefully. She was closely veiled, and he could see through the bow window that the carriage which waited for her outside his shop lacked the familiar Arneau crest. "I beg that your ladyship would do me the honor of accompanying me to my office, where we can be perfectly private," he suggested tactfully.

Letty nodded. "Wait for me here, Katie," she murmured to the little abigail. "I shan't be long." And she followed the jeweler to the office in the rear.

The room was a large, square office, tastefully appointed with Persian carpets, wing chairs of expensive leather, a number of large mahogany chests with brass locks, and an ornate desk on which were spread some ledger books and papers. Mr. Birdwell led Letty to the chair nearest his desk, and he took his seat behind it. "Now, Lady Denham," he said, smiling at her eagerly, "we may be comfortable. How may I assist you? Do you plan a surprise for his lordship? If you do, we shall be hard-pressed to find a gem for *him* comparable to the emerald he bought for *you*."

Letty's eyes flickered to her hands. "I haven't come to make a purchase, Mr. Birdwell. I've come to . . . return the emerald."

"Return the *emerald*?" the jeweler echoed, unable to disguise his surprise. "Can it be that you are not *pleased* with it?"

She shook her head. "It is impossible not to be pleased with it. It is the most beautiful gem I've ever seen. But . . ." She looked up at his face worriedly. "Can I rely on your discretion, sir?"

"Of *course*, your ladyship. The transactions which take place in this room are as privileged as in the confessional of a cathedral, I assure you."

"Then I shall speak bluntly. I have need of a . . . a sum of money . . . a rather large sum of money. And it occurred to me that you might be willing to let me have it in exchange for the jewel."

"Certainly, your ladyship. I have any number of buyers who would be interested in purchasing a gem of such—"

"Oh!" Letty exclaimed, alarmed. "I didn't wish you to *sell* it, you know. Merely to . . . I mean, couldn't you *hold* it for a while? I don't know its value, of course—I don't *want* to know it!—but if you could let me have a . . . a certain sum . . . and hold the gem as—what is the term? Collateral?—I'm certain that I can manage to pay back the amount in six or seven months . . ."

Mr. Birdwell did not alter his expression. This was not the first time a member of the nobility had found himself (or herself) scorched and had tried to climb out of Dun Territory by selling the family jewels. He and his partner had always turned those occasions into handsome profits. "Yes, my lady, I'm certain that something of the sort can be arranged. What was the sum you had in mind?"

She looked across at him in some trepidation. "N–nine thousand pounds," she said in a low voice.

He didn't permit himself to smile. How ignorant these people were in the ways of the world. The gem was worth a great deal more. "Whatever you say, my lady," he said, getting to his feet and opening a drawer in a chest behind him. "Did you wish for the money at once?"

Later, after he'd ushered her and her maidservant to the door, he stood in one of the bow windows watching the phaeton disappear down the street into the mist of rain and wind. He wasted not a moment's thought in wondering how the lady had got herself so badly dipped. His only concern was what action he should now take. He could sell the gem at a handsome profit, of course, but if Lord Denham should ever get wind of it, Birdwell and Kerr could find themselves in deep trouble. No, it would not do at all to antagonize a patron of the wealth and importance of Lord Denham. Mr. Birdwell put his hand in his pocket and removed the little jewel-box. He opened the lid and looked down at the twinkling, pear-shaped stone. *No, he decided, it would not be wise to turn a profit at Lord Denham's expense.* He had a much more practical solution. He would merely inform his lordship of what had transpired. In that way, he would not only get his money back, but he'd earn Lord Denham's everlasting—and undoubtedly profitable—gratitude.

Chapter Eleven

His DEBTS PAID, Philip was in the very best of spirits. He swung his cane cheerfully as he climbed the steps of the Glendenning house to make his fifth call in a week on his new, if not very promising, pupil. Augusta, although expressing a willingness to cooperate in the attempt to make her a social success, seemed underneath the surface to exert an instinctive resistance to his instruction. It was a puzzling problem. He was uncertain of the cause of her feelings of reluctance to play the game to the hilt. And, worse, he had no idea how to *overcome* that reluctance.

But the girl's recalcitrance failed to depress him. In fact, nothing could depress him at this moment! He'd been some-how—miraculously!—delivered from the slough of despond by the remarkable generosity of his sister-in-law, and although he had no idea of how Letty had managed to find the money, he was wholeheartedly grateful to her for it. His debts were paid—and it had been accomplished without his having had to resort to marriage, to exile, or to facing his brother with the truth! He could hardly believe his good fortune. He would find a way, one day when his luck at the tables returned, to repay Letty, but in the meantime he intended to concentrate his attentions on accomplishing the goal she had set for him—the goal of making Augusta a reigning belle.

He whistled merrily to himself as he waited for Hinson to answer his knock, and, when the door opened, he greeted the butler with cheery familiarity. "In the sitting room, is she?" he asked, tossing his beaver and cane onto the marble-topped pier table and strolling across the hallway.

"Yes, sir," Hinson answered, watching Mr. Denham speculatively as the young man sauntered down the hall and knocked at the sitting-room door. From the frequency of Mr. Denham's visits, anyone would have suspected that Miss Augusta had found herself a new suitor, but if this was courtship, it was unlike any that Hinson had ever before observed. There was an air of easy informality about their attitude toward each other that puzzled the butler. It was all much too casual, if he was any judge. "I don't know what young people are coming to these days," he muttered under his breath as he withdrew to the lower regions.

Philip entered the sitting room and found Augusta posing stiffly in the center of the room, modeling one of the new dresses which she had, with Philip's guidance, ordered just a few days before. Katie was kneeling on the floor at her side, pinning up the hem. "Turn a wee bi' t' yer righ'," the abigail was saying, her mouth full of pins.

"Oh, there you are, Philip," Augusta greeted him familiarly. "I'm glad you've come before I'd taken this off. I'm full of misgivings about it."

"Again?" Philip shook his head in mild reproof. "I thought I'd reassured you—"

"I don't think we should have chosen quite such a bright shade of salmon. I shall not feel comfortable wearing it."

"Why not?" Philip circled her, surveying the effect of the gown on her slim form with critical attention. "The color gives a very pleasant glow to your cheeks."

She made a rueful face. "I shall look like a platter of steamed fish," she muttered, looking down at herself in disapproval. "I think we should have taken the figured crape."

Philip fixed a frowning eye on her. "Are you still harping on that puce-colored cloth? Really, Augusta, that's the outside of enough! I've explained again and again that browns and purples are more suited to dowagers than to young ladies. You'll wear nothing but pinks, coppers and reds, if I have anything to say on the matter."

"Then perhaps," Augusta replied with a touch of resentment, "you shouldn't *have* anything to s— *Ouch!*" She gave a little jump as one of Katie's pins pricked her ankle.

Katie removed the pins from her mouth with bland innocence. "Turn a bit more, Miss Augusta, please," she requested.

Augusta glared down at her. For almost a week now—ever since this 'tutoring' had begun—Katie had been behaving like a cat in the cream. She'd convinced herself that, in the person of Philip Denham, Miss Augusta had found her "proper sprag." The girl grinned and winked and looked 'knowing' whenever Philip's name was mentioned. Augusta had protested every grin and had denied vehemently that there was anything even remotely romantic between herself and her tutor. "We are like brother and sister," she'd declared repeatedly, but Katie would not be convinced. Augusta had realized, after a day or two of repeated denials, that she was protesting too much. Somehow she'd given herself away to the perspicacious abigail, and no denials or objections would change Katie's conviction that she'd discovered the truth. Fortunately, Katie was absolutely discreet and would reveal to no one else that her Miss Augusta had lost her heart to the young Mr. Denham. But Gussie couldn't keep her from her little attempts to encourage the match. The pinprick in her ankle was Katie's way of telling her mistress not to be quarrelsome.

Philip, having completed his circumambulation, smiled at Augusta's appearance with satisfaction. "The drapery at the back is very becoming," he said, ignoring his pupil's recalcitrance, "and the embroidery at the neck is even more enticing than I'd expected. I don't know how Madame Challier managed to complete the work so quickly."

Katie sat back on her heels and gazed up at the dress. "All o' them tiny, wee stitches..." she said, shaking her head admiringly. "That dressmaker must 'ave magic in 'er fingers." She stuck the extra pins in a large pincushion on the floor beside her, got to her feet, gathered up her things and went to the door. "I wish I could learn t' make small stitches. All thumbs I be. But 'ave no fear, Mr. Denham, it won't be *me* doin' the sewin' on the 'em. Miss Dorrimore's goin' t' do it." And with a quick courtsey, she scurried out.

Philip smiled after her. "At least your Katie approves of my taste," he remarked.

But Augusta would not be placated. "Nevertheless," she insisted stubbornly, "I'm convinced that the color is too garish. I shall have everyone *staring* at me!"

"*That*, my little shiver-mouse, is *precisely* my goal."

She dropped down on the sofa, carefully lifting the pinned hem so that she would not be punctured again, and turned a pair of doubtful eyes up to his. "But, Philip . . . don't you think people will say I'm dreadfully vulgar?"

"I don't much care *what* they say," he responded callously, seating himself beside her, "so long as they take notice of you."

She shuddered. "I shall die of embarrassment."

"No, you won't, my dear. You'll be very much admired, and you'll enjoy every moment of it, I promise you."

Augusta only shook her head. She'd made a bargain, and she would try to live up to it, but the entire prospect filled her with dread. Merely to have the opportunity to spend some time in Philip's company, she'd compromised her basic nature. She would not in the least enjoy becoming the object of attention, whatever he chose to believe. She had put herself into a situation in which it was imperative that she make herself noticeable. How was she to endure it? The mere *anticipation* of it made her feel decidedly ill.

Philip was beginning to know her well enough to read some of her misgivings in her face. "Don't look so frightened, my dear," he said gently. "I shall not thrust you, unprepared, into the center of the social circle like a fledgling acrobat in a circus. You'll be completely confident of yourself beforehand." He studied her in the new dress as an idea struck him. "What do you say to going for a drive in the park with me tomorrow, if the weather is fine? You can wear this dress—if Miss Dorrimore can manage to finish her hemming in time—and see for yourself that the experience will not be painful."

Her heart gave a little leap. "A drive? W—with you?"

"Yes." His mind warmed to the idea. "Yes, indeed. We can pretend that I'm a new beau, and you can try some of those conversation stratagems I've suggested. It could be a sort of rehearsal."

The appeal of a drive in his company was irresistible to her. It would be a joy to sit beside him in his carriage, to have the pleasure of his escort, even if it was only a pretense . . . even if she had to wear this horrid dress and endure a number of disapproving stares. "Yes, Philip," she said, keeping her eyes meekly lowered, "if you think it will help . . ."

* * *

Five in the afternoon was the hour set for the drive, for that was the time when most of the fashionable set could be seen driving, riding or strolling through Hyde Park. Augusta had objected to that hour, afraid that the park would be terribly crowded, but Philip had overridden her objections by saying that the late-October winds were bound to keep many of the usual company at home. Therefore, at a few minutes before five on the following day, Augusta came down the stairs, fully dressed in her salmon-colored gown, with a fetching black shawl (which her mother, foolishly excited by what she thought were signs that Philip Denham had taken "an interest" in her daughter, had taken from her own wardrobe and insisted that Gussie wear "for warmth") thrown over her shoulders, and a little chip hat perched on the top of her head and tied under the chin with a ribbon whose color matched her gown. Philip had decreed that she tie her hair tightly at the back of her head and permit the long tail to fall in one thick coil over her shoulder. The entire effect had surprised her. She looked quite changed. She was feeling most distractingly ambivalent—one half of her mind beset with consternation over making a public appearance in such dramatic, attention-seeking attire, and the other half exhilarated by the heady anticipation of an afternoon of pleasure at Philip's side.

She was a few steps from the bottom of the stairway when the front door opened to admit Claryce, just returning from a shopping expedition. Her arms were loaded with boxes and packages, and her eyes were shining with excitement. Taking only a quick glance at Augusta, she deposited the parcels on the pier table and clarioned happily, "You'll never believe, Gussie, what I found in a little shop on the Strand. It's a fur tippet, and I paid only— Good *heavens*! What have you *done* to yourself?"

"D–done to myself?" Augusta asked in consternation.

"That *dress*!" Claryce studied her sister with narrowed eyes. "I haven't seen it before, have I?" She walked up a few steps to get a closer look and eyed the gown covetously. Then she began to notice other details. "You've done something to your *hair*, too!"

"I've only let the knot down . . ." Augusta explained hastily. "Isn't it all right?"

Claryce shrugged. "I'm not sure it suits you. The *dress* certainly doesn't."

Augusta blinked worriedly. "*Why*, Claryce? What's *wrong* with it?"

"I don't know. Too . . . too striking, I think, for *you* to carry off. May I borrow it to wear when Denny takes me to see the Elgin Marbles?"

Augusta put up her chin defiantly and marched down the remaining stairs. "No, you may not. Perhaps I *can't* carry it off, but at least I won't have to hear people whisper that I'm wearing your cast-offs when I appear in it again. You have plenty of striking gowns of your *own* to wear to see the Elgin Marbles."

"Very well, if that's how you feel," Claryce said indifferently, picking up the largest of the parcels and starting up the stairs again. "You needn't fall into a taking. I don't know what's come over you lately, Gussie, really I don't."

"*Nothing*'s come over me," Augusta snapped. "And I'll thank you to call me by my proper name—Augusta!"

Claryce, halfway up the stairs, hooted and turned to throw her sister a mocking sneer. "*Augusta*, eh? Now I *know* some maggot has got into your—"

A knock at the door silenced her. Augusta, not waiting for Hinson to make his leisurely march from below stairs to the door, ran to answer it. Philip entered, holding a small nosegay in his hand. Not noticing Claryce on the stairs, he grinned at Augusta, made an exaggeratedly formal bow and held out the flowers. "Miss Glendenning, you are looking so lovely you make my flowers pale."

Claryce gasped audibly. Philip, startled, looked up at her. "Oh, good afternoon, Claryce," he said, feeling a bit foolish to have been caught in his little game of pretense with Augusta. "I didn't see you standing there." He threw Augusta a surreptitious wink. "I couldn't tear my eyes away from Augusta, I'm afraid. Your sister Augusta is in quite her best looks today, isn't she?"

Augusta looked up from her delighted contemplation of her flowers and muttered to him in an undertone, "Claryce says the dress doesn't suit me. She says I can't carry it off."

Philip took her hand and twirled her around. "*I* think you are *something like*!" The enthusiasm in his voice was unmistakable. "Don't you think so, Claryce?"

Claryce was so shocked that she had difficulty finding her voice. "Y—yes. Qu—quite . . ." she managed. But before she had time to recover her wits, Augusta and Philip had waved and gone out. Claryce stared at the door in baffled disbelief. *Just what, she wondered in chagrin, is going on here?*

* * *

"You *can* carry it off," Philip assured Augusta as they descended the stairs to the carriage he'd rented for this occasion—a smart, open equipage which seated only two and was known as a *vis-à-vis*. "All you need do is hold your head high and completely ignore your attire." He handed her into the carriage with a flourish, ran round to the other side and jumped up into his place. "Well," he asked as he picked up the reins, "are you ready for the game? I am your new suitor, and I've just presented you with a nosegay. Shall we start from there?"

She nodded. "The flowers are lovely, Mr. . . . er . . ."

"Smith," Philip supplied promptly, but then reconsidered. "No, Smith is not nearly important enough for you. We shall give him a hyphen. Ashton-Smith. Robert Ashton-Smith."

She giggled. "The flowers are lovely, Mr. Ashton-Smith," she said with proper formality, burying her face in the blooms. "It was very thoughtful of—"

"Just a simple thank you will do, you goosecap," he said, already out of character. "No need to become effusive over a little gift."

Impulsively, she too dropped the pretense and responded by lifting her head and sticking her tongue out at him.

He laughed, gave his greys a little nudge, and they started toward the park. After a moment or two of silence, he looked at her challengingly. "What a lovely day for a drive, ma'am, don't you agree?"

"Oh, yes, Mr. Ashton-Smith, quite delightful," she said in her formal voice, adding *sotto voce*, "I hope *that* was not too effusive for you, Sir Pedagogue."

There was another long moment of silence. "It's *your* turn to initiate a subject now, you know," he prodded after a while. "You can't expect the gentleman to keep the conversation flowing all by himself."

"I told you I had no talent at conversation," she muttered.

"Nonsense. During the several afternoons we've spent together, you've never had the least difficulty in expressing yourself."

"Yes, but that was because we had something specific to discuss. I don't have the slightest idea of what to say to a strange gentleman in a carriage."

"But I've *told* you what to say! Do you remember my suggestion?"

"Yes. I'm to find something about my escort to admire and then tell him I admire it."

"That's not too difficult, is it?"

She sighed. "I suppose not. Very well, let's try again. You start."

He sat back, adjusted his hat to a rakish angle and began again. "So good of you to drive out with me, ma'am," he said unhelpfully.

She searched his face for a suggestion, hesitated awkwardly and then brightened. "What remarkable horses you have, sir. So well matched. You must be the envy of your friends."

His eyes gleamed in approval, but he stayed in character. "Yes, indeed, that is quite true. I've had any number of offers for my greys—far beyond what I paid for them— but of course I've refused them all."

"Have you really?" she murmured with patently-exaggerated admiration. "How . . . er . . . *loyal* of you. Mr. Ashton-Smith."

He burst into a guffaw. "Really, Augusta . . . *loyal*? Can one be loyal to one's *horses*?" You're bound to put a fellow quite out of countenance with remarks of that sort."

She giggled. "I couldn't think of anything else. I suppose I should have said something like, 'Of *course* you refused to sell them, sir. What is a *profit* when compared to the pleasures of owning a beautiful pair of animals like that?'"

"Yes," he said approvingly. "That's much better."

"You can't mean it! Must I speak in such . . . platitudes?"

He shook his head helplessly. "You are an incorrigible pupil, my dear. If you are determined to avoid platitudes, I'm afraid the young bucks of the *ton* are going to find you either a very quiet sort or the most disconcerting female they've ever encountered."

Before the game could be resumed, they arrived at the park. Augusta was horrified to see the crowd. The pathways were overflowing with strollers and the roads crammed with carriages of every size and description. Men on horseback and dashing ladies driving high-perch phaetons darted in and out among the slower-moving vehicles, giving the entire scene an air of precarious disorder. In addition, drivers were constantly stopping their carriages to exchange greetings with passers-by.

Augusta was terrified of entering into such a *mêlée*, but Philip maneuvered his equipage very neatly into the park roadway, and they soon were in the very center of the activity. Augusta had all but forgotten about the vulgar color of her dress, but when two horsemen galloped alongside the carriage and greeted Philip warmly, she suddenly became suffused with self-consciousness. However, the two gentlemen, on being made known to her, bowed politely and looked at her with decided approval. So obvious was their admiration that Philip flashed her one of his heart-stopping grins, and she was forced to admit to herself that she was beginning to enjoy herself hugely.

But there was one moment during the drive when she was certain her self-satisfaction was to be short-lived. A carriage drew up alongside them, carrying two formidably-fashionable ladies. *"Philip Denham!"* one of the ladies cried stridently. "I am quite *irked* with you. Why did you not present yourself at my rout-party last week? You are firmly fixed in my black books for that!"

Philip made a light-hearted apology and introduced Miss Glendenning to his cousin, Lady Hortense Lavenham, and to her companion, Lady Jersey. The famous Lady Jersey studied Miss Glendenning frowningly through her lorgnette. "You're the third sister, I believe," she said at last. "Augusta, isn't it?"

"Y—yes, Lady Jersey," Augusta stammered, wishing she could snatch up her salmon-colored skirts and flee into the shrubbery.

Lady Jersey nodded and gave a sudden, completely unexpected smile. "I thought so. Why haven't I seen you at Almack's, my dear child? You must come one evening soon, with your dear mother. I shall send a card." With a pleasant nod and a wave for Philip, she signaled her coachman to proceed.

"That's a lovely gown, my dear," Lady Lavenham called back as they drove off.

Philip flicked the reins and, without a word, drove on. When Augusta took a sidelong glance at his face, she saw that his lips were curled in a very self-satisfied smirk. She would have found his air irritating in the extreme, except that she had to admit he'd been right—it was very agreeable to be admired. She sat back against the cushion and smiled, too. It had turned out, after all, to be a *most satisfactory* outing.

Chapter Twelve

NED LOOKED OUT of his bedroom window at the sunny morning sky and wished that it would rain. If it rained, he could postpone his riding appointment with Lady Lucia Greland—thus postponing the confrontation which would undoubtedly occur when he admitted to her that he'd made an ass of himself. But the October sky was a clear, bright blue, and the brisk wind had nothing but the most insignificant bits of white fluff to blow across the azure expanse. It would not rain today.

He turned from the window and sat down to don his riding boots in stoical submission to his fate. He knew that he could no longer, in good conscience, keep up the pretense that he was trying to arrange a marriage of convenience between Lucy and his friend. When Philip had informed him, a week ago, that his debts were paid, Ned had realized he'd been foolish and hasty in going to Lucy with his plan. As Philip's friend, he should have been delighted to learn that the fellow was free of debt, but the news had certainly placed *him* in a position of considerable embarrassment. If Philip no longer needed—nor wished for—an advantageous marriage, what was he, poor Ned, to tell Lucy Greland?

He'd seen Lucy three times since Philip had told him about paying his debts, and each time he'd tried to explain that his attempt at matchmaking had been—to put it bluntly—premature. But he'd felt so ashamed . . . so foolish . . . so inept. He'd been a meddler, and he'd bungled it badly. He was certain that the lady would react to his confession with a tirade of scorn, and he was too cowardly to face her disdain. During each of his visits, he'd found her so kind—so attentive to his ramblings, so sympathetic to his views of politics and society, so charming in the way she teased him when he grew too serious or pompous—that he couldn't bring himself to cloud those occasions by admitting his humiliating error.

But he would put it off no longer. He promised himself that he would make his confession this very morning during their ride in the park. Before he returned with her to her stables, he would tell her what he'd done. However, as he pulled on his riding coat and reached for his gloves, he couldn't help sighing with regret that the weather was so fair.

On the bridle path, Lucy and Ned held their mounts to a gentle, ambling pace, for the packed earth of the pathway was still soft from the rains of the week before, with patches of mud here and there. The air was brisk, the path free of company, and the atmosphere conducive to peaceful conversation. If ever a moment was appropriate for confessing his transgression, this was the one. "About that . . . er . . . matter we've been discussing all week, ma'am—" he began with awkward bravery.

"Matter? What matter?" the girl asked, throwing him an arch glance which he found very disconcerting and which he was unable to interpret.

"The matter of an . . . *arrangement* . . . with my friend."

"Oh, that." She tossed her head and rode on a few steps ahead of him. "I don't wish to talk about that today," she threw over her shoulder.

He urged his horse to catch up, wishing his conscience would permit him to oblige her by dropping the subject. But his conscience was not as obedient as his horse. "But you see, Lucy, there is—"

"Neddie, my dear boy, why don't you look around you?" she urged, raising her arm in an expansive sweep of enthusiasm. "The air is divinely brisk and smells like wine, the trees are bursting into a riot of color—all *nature* is crying out for your attention! Yet all you want to do is speak of mundane matters of business."

"It's not exactly business, you see, ma'am—"

Her arm fell. "I *said*, my lord, that I don't wish to talk about it." Her face hardened and her voice had a decided rasp.

"Yes, I quite understand. But I shall not feel easy in my mind until—"

"Damnation!" she burst out irritably, using the unladylike epithet with bold disregard for the proprieties. "You, Ned Glendenning, can be the most provoking fellow in the world! I think I've had enough of you!" And, spurring her horse viciously, she galloped off in a sudden, terrifying burst of speed, her mount's hooves throwing up clumps of sod and mud into his face.

"*Lucy!*" he cried, not certain for a moment of what he was expected to do. He watched as her horse raced down the path, horse and rider growing smaller and farther away with every passing second. The horse seemed almost to be flying. *Good God!* he thought in sudden alarm. *Has the horse run away with her?* Spurring his rather sluggish mount to his ultimate effort, he galloped headlong down the path, his heart pounding with fear. Ned was not what was known as a "bruising rider," nor was he given to the performance of daring deeds or heroic actions. He knew he could never catch up with her, especially if her horse had bolted . . . and even if he did, he had no idea of what he would have to do *then*. But he galloped on, trying to ignore the pulse beating in his ears and the terror constricting his throat. *Please, God,* he prayed, *don't let her be thrown*!

There was a bend in the path just ahead of him, but he didn't so much as tug on the reins. He took the turn at a greater speed than he'd ever before attempted. If only he could get to her before . . . before . . .

But there ahead of him, placidly astride her now-unmoving animal, Lucy sat waiting for him. He pulled his horse to and came to a plunging halt beside her. Her hair had blown loose from under her little riding cap, her cheeks were flushed, and her eyes shone with a maddening glint of laughter. She'd done it on *purpose*!

Something inside him snapped. It was irksome enough under normal circumstances to feel her laughing at him behind her eyes (for even during their most pleasant encounters, he would look up and catch that taunting expression lurking deep in her eyes or at the corners of her mouth), but after this wild ride it was just too much. "Have you lost your *wits*?" he demanded furiously, shaken by emotion from his usual, mannerly composure. "Don't you know you could have *killed* yourself?"

"Rubbish!" she said, grinning at him brazenly. "I *told* you, Neddie, that I'm a wild one on horseback. You can't say you weren't warned—"

"*Wild* is the right word! I should not be so proud of wildness if I were you. It means that you are completely heedless of anything but your own uncontrolled impulses. Not only could you have killed yourself, you could have killed *me* as well!"

"Now, really, Neddie—" she began, her eyebrows rising at his unwonted display of temper.

But Ned could not control his tongue. The momentary sense of relief which had struck him the first second he'd seen that she was safe was now completely overwhelmed by the tide of rage which flooded over him. "A wild one!" he repeated with angry scorn. "You say that phrase as if it were something to be admired. You think it sets you above the herd. But in reality, it only shows a selfish, headstrong disregard for conventions, an irresponsible, thoughtless nature, and an immature willfulness that—"

"*Enough*, my lord!" she ordered, drawing herself up in offense. "I told you quite plainly when you first came to call that I was a virago. If you chose to ignore my warning, the consequences are on your own head. You were not *compelled* to seek out my company."

"That much at least is true," he said, still infuriated. "I shall not make that mistake again. And now, permit me to escort you back to your stables, if you please. I've had quite enough riding for today."

"I do *not* please," she said, now thoroughly angered. "I am quite capable of getting to my stables without your escort." Giving him no opportunity for another word, she wheeled her horse about and galloped off the way she'd come, the speed of her horse's flying hooves giving him ample evidence that his ranting scold had not the least effect on her.

Well, he thought, turning his horse around and plodding back slowly, *that is the end of that. I didn't have to apologize about Philip after all.* But the thought gave him no relief, and he returned to his stables feeling as miserably depressed as he'd ever been . . . without the slightest understanding of why he felt that way.

*   *   *

Letty, too, could not enjoy the beautiful day. All during the past week she had felt an unexpected unhappiness creeping over her. She, however, was very much aware of what it was that caused her dejection—for the first time in her four-year marriage, she was keeping a secret from her husband. She hadn't realized, when she'd agreed to keep the knowledge of Philip's gambling debts from her husband, that it would become an invisible impediment inserting itself between Roger and herself. For the first time, she had to guard her tongue with him. For the first time, she had moments of discomfort in conversation. For the first time, she had to lie. She was guiltily aware that Roger took notice of her failure to wear the magnificent emerald he'd given her. As the days passed, she felt more and more strained.

Not until yesterday, however, did Roger actually *remark* on the absence of the pendant around her neck. In response to his casual question about it, she merely said that the jewel was too spectacular to wear on ordinary occasions with ordinary dress. She hoped that her response would end the matter, but at the back of her mind she knew he would ask again.

Today had been her most difficult day since she'd sold the pendant. Roger had not been at home during the afternoon, but when he'd returned and they'd gone up to play with children, he'd seemed strangely silent and remote. She'd told herself that his coolness was only in her mind—that her guilt was making her imagine things. But after dinner they'd gone to see a play at Covent Garden. During the entire performance, she'd felt a terrible constraint between them. Again, she tried to tell herself that she was only imagining it. But she'd stolen a look at his face during the third act; it was set in stony lines, and his eyes were fixed on the stage in a blank, unseeing stare. Letty had felt her heart sink in misery, quite unable to think of a way to bring matters back to the way they were.

Now that they'd returned to the privacy of their home, and Roger was removing her cloak (for they'd ordered the servants not to wait up for them), Letty searched about desperately for something amusing and warm to say to him. But her mind was clogged by guilt, and she couldn't find the words. His voice, coming unexpectedly from behind her, made her jump. "I see, Letty, my dear, that you haven't worn the pendant this evening either," he remarked in a voice that sounded to her ears very stiff and distant.

Her hand flew unwittingly to her throat. "No...
I...didn't think the color would blend with the...the blue
of this gown," she murmured, unable to look at him.

"You know, Letty," he said gently, turning her to face him,
"it occurs to me that perhaps you don't *like* the bauble." He
lifted her chin up, forcing her to look at him. "You mustn't
be afraid to tell me so, my love. I promise I shall not be
offended if you find my taste a bit vulgar. We can always
exchange it for something more to your liking."

She felt a sting of tears constrict her throat. "It is a b-
beautiful jewel, Roger. It's the m-most beautiful thing I've
ever had in my l-life..."

"Then why don't you *wear* it, my love?" His eyes seemed
to burn her face with the intensity of his gaze.

She pulled away from him and turned aside. "I suppose you
will th-think me quite silly," she said, her head lowered but
her voice artificially casual and light, "but I like to s-save
it...for only the most special of occasions, you know." She
cast him a quick, uncomfortable glance over her shoulder.
"I...I think I shall dash up and look in on the children before
we go to bed," she said hastily and ran up the stairs.

Some minutes later, having composed herself sufficiently
to face him again, she came into the bedroom. To her surprise,
Roger wasn't there. Assuming that he was still in his dressing
room, she turned to her dressing table to remove her pearl
earrings and take down her hair. The sight of her face in the
glass caused her to wince. The tension she'd observed in her
husband's face was reflected in her own. Her mouth was set,
her eyes distended and unhappy, and her whole face looked
strained. What was happening to her? No *wonder* Roger was—

She gasped, and her face turned ghastly white, for there on
the dressing table was a familiar jewel-box. She dropped down
on the little chair before the dressing table as if her legs had
melted under her. With trembling fingers she picked up the
box and pried up the lid. There, nestled on its velvet cushion,
was the emerald pendant!

For a long moment she stared at it, frozen into immobility.
What did it *mean*? *Who* could have—? But, of course, it had
to have been Roger who'd recovered it. Mr. Birdwell must
have *told* him! That *horrid* Mr. Birdwell! She snatched the
pendant from its box and turned in the chair. "*Roger*—!"

He stood in the doorway, watching her. Meeting his pained

eyes, she felt her heart race in a kind of frenzied hysteria. That look that *Philip* had never wanted to face again was being focused on *her*! Mutely, she held the pendant out to him in a hand pathetically unsteady.

He crossed the room in three strides and knelt beside her chair. "Letty, my dearest," he said softly, taking her outstretched hand in both of his and closing her fingers around the jewel. "The pendant is yours. If you had a need for nine thousand pounds, why couldn't you ask *me*?"

"I . . . I *couldn't* . . ." she whispered miserably. "I . . . just *couldn't*."

"Letty, I love you! Don't you know that there is nothing you could do . . . no scrape you could fall into . . . no foolish debt . . . nothing in the *world* you could confess to me that could make me stop loving you?"

He looked up at her, waiting. *Oh, God*, she thought, her heart stopping its wild pounding in sudden, frozen alarm, *he wants me to explain*! Her eyes flickered from his face to the hands with which he'd clasped hers. She couldn't find her voice but only shook her head.

"You won't *tell* me?" he asked in pained amazement.

"Roger, don't ask me. It isn't m—my *right* to . . . that is, I simply can *not* explain—"

"Please, my love. I promise to forgive you, whatever it is you think you've done . . . and I shall try to understand . . ."

She merely shook her head again, unable to meet his eye.

He dropped her hands and got to his feet. "Are you quite certain, Letty, that there is nothing you can say to me?"

Something in his tone made her perceive that this was some sort of ultimatum. Her eyes flew to his face, pleading. "Roger, please! I *can't*—!"

His face was stiff, his jaw set tightly and his eyes darkly forbidding. "Then there's no more to say, is there, ma'am?" He made a curt bow, and, with a cold "good night," he strode from the room. She didn't move as she listened to his footsteps recede. It was not until she heard the slam of the door of a guest bedroom, far down the hall, that she burst into inconsolable tears.

Chapter Thirteen

AUGUSTA WAS IN the downstairs sitting room, writing a letter to Mrs. Dolphiner, her elderly friend in Bath, when the sound of angry voices in the corridor outside the room distracted her. "If you insist on making a *scene*, Dennis Wivilscombe," she heard Claryce saying, "at least come in here and do it in *private*. Do you want the whole *household* to—?" The door burst open and Claryce came storming into the room. "Oh! *Gussie*"! She stopped her advance abruptly. "I didn't know anyone was here."

Dennis Wivilscombe came in behind her, his usually good-natured face scowling and red. "Good morning, Miss Glendenning. We didn't mean to disturb you," he said in obvious embarrassment.

Gussie rose hastily. "You are not disturbing me, Mr. Wivilscombe, I assure you. Please come in. I...I was about to leave." She gathered up her writing things and scurried to the door. "I hope you will both excuse my abrupt departure, but I must find Ned and ask him to post this letter for me."

Mr. Wivilscombe looked after her with a smile of approval, his high color receding. "Your sister seems to be in the best of looks lately," he remarked. "One would think she was coming into a late bloom."

"Yes, I suppose it might look that way," Claryce said grudgingly, throwing herself upon the sofa. "It's because of our brother-in-law, Philip Denham. I think Gussie fancies that he's become interested in her, and it has quite turned her head."

"Denham, eh? That reminds me that *he* is *another* of your confounded flirts. Don't you think, my dear, that, if you are truly desirous of my courting you in earnest, you might *try* to refrain from playing the coquette with every fellow who passes by?"

"I do *not* play the coquette! Can I help it if young men like to buzz around me?"

"No, I don't suppose you can." He sat down beside her and looked at her earnestly. "I don't deny that excessive beauty such as yours is like pollen to the bees . . . but you mustn't try to pretend that you don't encourage them. You simper and giggle and flirt outrageously . . . with every one of them!"

"See here, Denny, I don't have to sit here and listen to you insult me. I don't behave any more outrageously than any of the other young women—"

"Yes, you do. You're not content with playing with the hearts of those who seek you out—like Lord Garvey and Neville Trevithen and myself—but you set out your lures quite brazenly for those gentlemen whose interests are aimed in *other* directions. Even *Augusta's* caller, Mr. Denham, has been the object of your wiles. I've seen you try to beguile or entrap him every time the fellow is in your vicinity."

"How *dare* you speak to me in this way!" She drew herself up in angry offense. "What *right* have you—you who are known to all the world as *The Seal* for having slipped out of the net of wedlock so often? You are every bit as bad as I am . . . and perhaps worse!"

His indignation faltered. "Perhaps I am," he admitted, lowering his eyes, "but I had hoped that . . . *this* time . . ."

His words caught her up short, and a measuring gleam took the place of anger in her eyes. "Hoped what, Denny?"

"I had hoped that, this time, matters might be different," he said.

"Well, you haven't said anything to *me* that would lead me to believe your intentions are markedly different from those which caused the other females you've pursued such disappointment."

He sighed. "It's true that I've been fearful of matrimony in the past. However, I am no longer a green boy, you know, and I've been thinking of late that it is time to make a change . . ."

She leaned back against the cushions, her expression softening. "Yes?"

". . . And you *are* the one who's inspired my thinking on these lines."

"Is *that*, Mr. Wivilscombe, supposed to be an *offer*?" she asked, her voice mellow with the return of her feeling of power over him.

He shifted in his place uneasily. "How can I make you an offer when I've no confidence in the steadiness of your feelings? If you would cease your eternal flirtations long enough to permit a sincere attempt at courtship—"

She jumped up from the sofa in a fury. "Do you think me a fool?" she asked, looking down at him with smoldering eyes. "Did you truly expect me to cut myself off from all my beaux merely because it would please *you*? And how long would it be, my dear, before you'd slip away from me as you did from so many others? This may be my first season, sir, but I'm not a babe in the woods. When you've quite made up your mind to offer for me, I *may* be willing to discuss the matter with you, but until then, I'd be obliged if you'd keep your opinions of my behavior to yourself!" And before he had a chance to say another word, she swept out of the room and slammed the door behind her.

* * *

If Philip had overheard the conversation, he might have been less optimistic about Augusta's chances to win his wager for him. But he had no idea how close Wivilscombe had come to declaring himself to Claryce. It seemed to Philip that his pupil, Augusta, was making remarkable progress; whatever doubts he'd had at first about her ability to compete with her spectacular sister were long since dispelled. Augusta might not ever be called spectacular, but she had a quiet loveliness that was more and more beginning to shine through.

Since the day he'd first taken her riding in the park, she'd become more confident of her appearance. Her walk was more assured, she held her shoulders back and her head high. Her gleaming hair, which he'd insisted she continue to wear tied back with one thick curl falling over her shoulder, caught the eye of every passer-by whenever she went out strolling. She'd begun to wear the brighter-colored gowns he'd chosen for her with the assurance and the casual disregard that were necessary for a woman of style. In fact, he felt that she was almost ready to face her first test.

Lord and Lady Trevithen had invited all the Glendennings and all the Denhams to a large ball being held to celebrate the completion of the new wing they'd built at the back of their magnificent house in Berkeley Square. Most of the important members of the *ton* would be present. It would be the perfect occasion for Augusta to burst on the scene in her new identity. They had already chosen the gown that Augusta would wear for the ball. It was a pearl-white Chinese silk, covered over with lilac-and-silver gauze. He could see her in his mind's eye, like a shimmering butterfly emerging from the chrysalis. He had no doubt at all that she would turn every head, catch every eye and make an overwhelming success.

There were still some matters, of course, which needed work. The girl still found it difficult to make conversation with strangers. She still had moments of unaccountable shyness. And she knew nothing of the Art of Dalliance. *That* was to be the subject of their meeting this afternoon. But he had every confidence that, as soon as she'd mastered the tricks he was ready to impart, she would be ready to make her mark.

When Augusta admitted Philip to the house that afternoon, she was relieved to note that Claryce and Wivilscombe were no longer anywhere about. She did not like the family to take notice of Philip's visits. They were wont to make too much of those occasions. Her mother had taken it into her head that Philip was courting her, and Claryce probed and questioned and fussed every time she saw Philip leave the house. Such a to-do over Denham caused Augusta to feel unnerved. It was difficult enough for Augusta to keep in mind that Philip's visits had no significance beyond his brotherly interest and his desire to win his wager—she didn't want to have to endure the additional pain of having to make excuses to the family when he stopped coming.

Augusta had been finding her days both thrilling and painful. Philip's daily presence was heady wine for her. They'd become comfortable in each other's company, laughing and joking as easily as if they were *indeed* brother and sister. She knew he was growing fond of her. But the fondness he felt was a pale, insignificant emotion compared to the passion for him which she kept hidden inside her. His brotherly affection, while she treasured it as being a great deal more satisfying than the indifference he'd felt for her earlier, was agonizingly inadequate when she measured it against the ardor he felt for her in her dreams. It is hard to be warmed by starlight when you want the sun.

But she accepted, as contentedly as she could, whatever of him she could have. She led him into the sitting room with her usual, cheerful eagerness. "You're a bit early today, aren't you?" she asked, closing the door to protect them against interruptions or eavesdroppers.

"We have a great deal to do today, so I didn't want to waste a moment. I've had the most *inspired* idea! It's a complete cure for your problem about making conversation with gentlemen you don't know very well."

"A complete cure?" she asked, smiling at him doubtfully. "It must *indeed* be inspired."

"It is, I tell you. It can't fail. Come here, and I'll demonstrate. Let's say I'm the gentleman, and we're dancing. I'm holding you like this, and I'm looking down at you eagerly. You've got to say something, and—"

"And I haven't an idea in my thick head."

"Ah, but I have one for you. 'My dear fellow,' you say, smiling up at him, 'I've heard the most *enthralling* secret about you.'"

She blinked up at him, baffled. "What secret?"

He laughed. "There *is* no secret, really. It's only a ploy. It will drive the fellow *wild*!"

"But, Philip, I don't understand. Are you saying that you want me to *pretend* to know a secret? Won't he ask me what it is?"

"Of course he will. But you will not reveal it. In fact, you *can't* very well reveal it, because there *is* no secret. But the resulting badinage will be most productive."

"I think you've taken leave of your senses. How can such a foolish pretense be productive?"

He grinned down at her, his eyes brimming with mischief. "There is only one way a fellow can respond to such bait—he will become intensely curious. That curiosity will be all to your advantage. He will keep *at* you for an answer. He will follow you about in fascination, hoping for a clue, a hint, a word. He may even suggest some possible secrets himself, in which case you may or may not (depending on your instincts at the moment) accept his suggestion to be the very secret you'd heard about. In any case, your problem about making conversation will be solved, for the poor fellow will not be able to free his mind enough to speak of anything else!"

Augusta, half appalled and half amused, regarded her tutor with reluctant admiration. "Philip, you are truly dreadful," she said, the twinkle in her eyes belying her words. "How *can* you have concocted so fraudulent a scheme? Why, it's dishonest, it's cruel and so devious as to be positively Machiavellian!"

His grin widened. "Yes, isn't it? And you'll *do* it, won't you?"

She nodded her head. "Yes, I suppose so. You're completely corrupting my character, you know. I hardly recognize myself any more."

"No, I don't think I am," he responded, his expression becoming serious. "I think, underneath all these superficial changes I'm attempting to make, you remain quite *in*corruptible, my dear. It's a quality I've found very . . . disconcerting." He looked at her with a long, steady, contemplative stare until she began to feel uncomfortable. The color rose in her cheeks, and, seeing it, he shook himself from his reverie. "But that is neither here nor there. I must now approach a very important part of today's lesson." He drew her to the sofa, and they sat down side by side. "It is to teach you the most flirtatious ways to *remain* uncorrupted."

"What on earth do you mean, Philip?" she asked, bewildered.

"Let me explain. All these tricks we've been talking about— like using your eyes to advantage—do you remember them?"

"Of course." She turned her face up to him and demonstrated what she'd learned. "Here is the *Innocent Flutter* . . . the *Come-Hither Beckoning* . . . the *Questioning Invitational* . . . the *From-the-Corner-of-the-Eye Challenge* . . . and the . . . oh, dear, I've forgotten the last one."

"The *Lowered-Lash Penitential*," he supplied. "But otherwise, that was very well done, Augusta. If I didn't know better, I would swear you'd been using those techniques since birth. Do you remember the laughs, too?"

"Naturally. I've been quite assiduously practicing them. There is the *Upward Trill* for surprise, the *Short Snicker* for disapproval, the *Gossamer Giggle* for accepting compliments, and the *Outright Exuberant* for sincere amusement. But what have all these artifices to do with remaining uncorrupted?"

"A great deal, I'm afraid. You see, they are specifically-designed techniques to inspire gentlemen with lustful desire. Once having inspired such feelings, you must learn how to control them."

"Come now, Philip," she said disparagingly, "you don't sincerely believe that *I* shall ever 'inspire gentlemen with lustful desire,' do you?"

"I'm quite *certain* you will. And you must learn how to handle them when their desires tempt them to take action."

"I don't need any lessons in *that*, my dear boy," she told him, amused. "I shall simply administer the *Slap Savage*."

He guffawed. "You are becoming a veritable wit, Augusta. I thought that only *I* was proficient at giving titles to the various stratagems in the ignoble Art of Dalliance. However, to return to the subject at hand, I must warn you that a slap, while effectively putting the misbehaving male in his place, will not keep him dangling from your hook. A slap must be avoided except as a last resort. We want to ensure the bounder's continued devotion to you, you know."

"Do we?" She sighed. "Well, how do we do it?"

"We remove ourselves from his attack with one of three basic maneuvers."

She made a face. "I might have known. And the three 'maneuvers' all are appropriately titled by my eminently-talented tutor, is that right?"

"Right," he acknowledged, unabashed by her taunt. "They are called the *Flout Flippant*, the *Affronted Prideful*, and the *Rebuff Regretful*."

"Oh, very *good*, Philip," she said in mocking admiration. "I think you've outdone yourself this time. Your epithets are almost poetic."

"Thank you, ma'am, but I'm not likely to be distracted from my object by your barbs," he said with professorial disdain. "We shall now demonstrate each one. Are you ready?"

"Quite ready, sir."

"Good. Now, suppose you've just finished dancing with a volatile young man who has been attracted by your *From-the-Corner-of-the-Eye Challenge* and smitten by your *Gossamer Giggle*. He has led you, tired and breathless, to a shadowy corner in one of the side rooms, he has slipped an arm around

your shoulders . . . like this . . . and has tilted up your face, like
this . . ."

Augusta, her face much too close to his for comfort, began
to feel distinctly uneasy. This game with Philip had been great
fun, but was she now about to play with fire?

"His intention is obvious," Philip went on. "He's about to
kiss you, is he not?"

"Is h–he?" She wondered if she were pretending to *naiveté*
only to prolong the moment.

"Yes, my little innocent, he is. But he is a boyish, cheerful
fellow and not likely to turn brutish. So you will choose—?"

"The *Flout Flippant*?"

"Exactly. You will, as soon as his face is close, giggle
loudly—"

"Giggle?"

"Yes. A giggle is most disconcerting to a fellow with seriously romantic intentions. He will jump away as if shot. Then
all you need do is to give some reason for laughing at him,
and the danger will have passed. Shall we try it?"

"I don't think," she demurred shyly, "that it will be necessary to try it. I seem to have grasped the idea adequately—"

"But a short rehearsal will not be amiss," he insisted. He
put an arm about her and drew her toward him, tilting her face
up with skilled assurance. "Oh, Miss Glendenning," he whispered with exaggerated fervor, "you are so lovely you take my
breath away—" And he lowered his face to hers.

Obediently, she giggled. He dropped his hold abruptly and
drew back. "Miss Glendenning!" he said in sham offense.
"What—?"

"I'm sorry, Mr. Ashton-Smith," she said, performing an
excellent demonstration of the *Innocent Flutter*, "but your neckcloth was tickling my chin. Shall we return to the ballroom
now? I feel quite rested."

He beamed at her with pride. "You're a very quick study,
I must say, Augusta. You'd have completely outshone me at
Cambridge. But let's go on. Suppose the fellow is more insis-
tent. Suppose his hold is too tight, his manner too intense.
Then, what?"

"Then, I suppose, I must try the *Affronted Prideful*."

"Exactly. You thrust his arms away, jump to your feet and
declare that he's offended you beyond repair. Here, let's try

it." And before she could object, he seized her in an iron grip, pulling her tightly against him.

Her heart beat so wildly that she, in terror that he would hear it, wrenched herself from his arms and jumped up. Philip, believing that she was merely following his instructions, nodded approvingly. "Very good, girl, very good. Now make your declaration."

"Declaration?"

"Yes. You've been affronted, haven't you? *Tell* the bounder so!"

"Really, Philip, I *couldn't*. 'You, Mr. Ashton-Smith, have offended me beyond repair!' It sounds like a lurid melodrama at Drury Lane."

He shrugged. "The entire business of flirtation depends on acting, I'm afraid. It's *all* a sort of performance. But sit down again, girl, and let's try the *Rebuff Regretful*. That one is the most effective of the lot."

Feeling quite weak in the knees, she sat down beside him once more, "Very well, *maestro*," she said, trying to maintain an atmosphere of easy raillery, "what next?"

"The object of the *Rebuff Regretful* is neither to embarrass the fellow nor to chastise him. You want him to believe that you would really prefer to *succumb* to his advances if it were proper to do so. This technique has the advantage of keeping you safe while at the same time giving the gentleman the very flattering impression that you have some feeling for him."

"Wonderful," she murmured with a touch of irony. "And how is this paradoxical feat to be accomplished?"

"Quite simply. The gentleman has you in his arms, like this, and is looking down at you soulfully. His face draws nearer. His arms shake and his breath quickens. You sway toward him, as if you, too, are quite carried away. Then, at the last moment, you put your fingers up to his lips. 'Mr. Ashton-Smith,' you murmur, your lips trembling, 'we mustn't . . . !' He will release you, reluctant, miserable and regretful, but completely noble."

As he released her, she moved imperceptibly away from him. With her eyes averted, she shook her head. "I don't think I'm capable of . . . of performing such a . . . a tender scene."

"Dash it, Augusta, of *course* you are. If you keep reminding yourself that it's all a game, you'll find it quite easy."

"Are there no . . . *genuine* emotions to be found in this world of games and artifices?" she asked, her eyes fixed on the hands clenched in her lap.

He stared at her. It amazed him how frequently in their encounters she made him aware of the depth of her character... and the shallowness of his. "How is it, my dear," he asked, humiliated, "that you always manage to make me feel small? I don't know the answer to your question, I admit. I'm not as familiar with *genuine* emotions as I am with pretense. I'm... sorry."

She put a hand on his arm. "I didn't *mean* to make you feel small," she said quietly. "You've been very patient with me, and I'm truly grateful. Come, let's try the *Rebuff Regretful*. I suppose I can manage it if you think it necessary."

He hesitated for a moment and then nodded. "Yes, I think it may be useful. And it's the very last trick in my repertoire. After this, we shall go to the Trevithen ball, and I shall sit back and watch as you capture every male heart in London and tuck them all in your pocket. But now, here we go. I have just brought you to this secluded spot and taken you in my arms. I stare down at you soulfully... like this... and you sway toward me..."

She held back for an imperceptible beat of time. It was the very last trick in his repertoire, he'd said. This, then, was the last afternoon they would spend in this way, the last time they'd sit together in this intoxicating intimacy. She wanted to prolong the moment forever. She closed her eyes and let herself melt against him. She felt his arms tighten and his breath quicken. She tried to remind herself that he was only acting his role. But was he so gifted an actor that he could actually tremble like this? Or was it only her *own* tremors that she felt?

His face was close to hers now—she could feel his breath on her cheek. She knew that now was the time to put her fingers up against his lips—to stop him. But instead, her hands were moving, quite of their own accord, up along his shoulders and round his neck. She wondered dazedly what would happen if she *ignored* the moves of the *Rebuff Regretful*!

What happened was something she *almost* expected, yet did not *quite* expect. She knew that if she didn't stop him, his lips would meet hers. What she *didn't* expect was that the touch would set off a charge of electricity coursing through her entire body. It made her shiver and cling to him, her hands locking together at the back of his neck. His arms tightened about her, and his lips pressed against hers with an intensity of feeling that seemed as genuine as her own.

When he let her go, she opened her eyes. He was staring at her in complete astonishment. "I . . . b—beg your pardon," he stammered breathlessly. "I can't *imagine* what I was thinking of!"

"It was *my* fault, Philip," she said, equally short of breath and blushing a fiery red. "I . . . er . . . completely forgot the details of the *Rebuff Regretful*."

He shook his head in denial and got unsteadily to his feet. Her kiss had shaken him to unexpected depths, and he didn't fully understand why. Whatever feelings the embrace had stirred up, they were certainly not *brotherly*. What did it mean? If she had the same effect on any *other* man who embraced her, she might have a greater success at the game than he wished! Had he gone too far—taught her too much? He had better take his leave and think this matter through. "I think, Augusta," he said awkwardly, moving hastily to the door, "that I should eliminate the *Rebuff Regretful* completely from the repertoire, if I were you. You do very well without it. Very well indeed. In fact, from here on, it might be advisable for me to let you follow your own instincts. Your *Slap Savage*, for instance. A very useful technique, I think . . . or at least it seems so to me after due consideration. Your instincts, I'm convinced, make a better teacher than I could ever be."

Chapter Fourteen

THE MEMBERS OF the Glendenning household set out for the Trevithen ball with high expectations and varying degrees of high spirits. The most euphoric of the group was Lady Glendenning herself. As she permitted Philip to hand her into his barouche at the start of the evening, she was almost beside herself with happy anticipation. She had come down the stairs in her new ball gown (a magnificent silk creation in Bishop's purple), with the feathers of her turban waving jauntily, and had been filled with pride to see her two younger daughters standing waiting in the hallway. Claryce, as usual, was breathtaking in a gown of Brunswick green and Augusta was—this time—quite her equal in shimmering white. Lady Glendenning had high hopes for both of them.

Mr. Wivilscombe had arrived to take Claryce up in *his* carriage, and he'd escorted her out with an air of excitement that made Lady Glendenning feel certain he'd decided to make her an offer. A few weeks earlier, she might not have enjoyed that realization. But now that Augusta seemed to have a most attractive suitor of her own—the very likeable Philip Denham—Lady Glendenning was pleased to see Claryce attach Mr. Wivilscombe for herself. The prospect of both girls making such excellent matches—and quite soon, from the look of it—

was more than enough to make a mother's heart dance like a girl's.

Her two daughters, however, were not as blithe of spirit as their mother. Claryce, full of confidence that she looked as ravishing as ever this evening, was nevertheless discomposed by the appearance of her hitherto-dowdy sister. It wasn't that Augusta had suddenly become spectacularly beautiful—for Gussie was still Gussie—but there *had* been a change in her. In her pallid way, Augusta seemed, somehow, to glow. Her gown, while it lacked the daring of Claryce's bare-bosomed, clinging creation, had a subdued elegance; her hair, despite its simple style, shone with a pale-gold richness; and she carried herself with a new confidence. Claryce suspected that everyone would soon be whispering about the change in her—and *that* would detract from the attention normally paid to *herself*. Claryce knew quite well that her feelings were selfish and petty—they she should, if she possessed any character, wish her sister success. For even if Gussie did manage to win for herself a little attention, it would not greatly affect Claryce's popularity. Claryce would have liked to show some generosity of spirit. But somehow she couldn't. As she went off on Dennis's arm, she found herself hoping that her sister would have a disagreeable evening.

Neither was Augusta in high spirits. When she'd dressed, earlier that evening, she'd begun to feel a pleasant glow. The soft, silk underdress had a way of rippling when she moved that made her feel graceful, and when Katie had helped her slip the gauzy lilac-and-silver robe over it, she'd felt like a fairy-tale princess. Katie and she had whirled round the bedroom in a spontaneous outburst of rapture at the way she looked. And later, when Augusta had seen Philip's face at his first glimpse of her, she'd felt her skin prickle with delight. But once they'd climbed into the carriage, she began to feel an increasing trepidation. No matter how she looked, no matter how well-trained she'd been, she could not be happy at the expectation of trying to make herself the center of attention. The closer the carriage came to their destination, the lower her feelings plummeted.

Ned, sitting opposite her in the carriage, was himself feeling strained and tense. He'd learned on very good authority (from Neville, the son of Lord and Lady Trevithen) that Lady Lucia Greland had been invited to the ball and was expected to attend. He'd not laid eyes on Lucy since their altercation in the park, even though he'd found himself thinking of her constantly. He did not understand why she so persistently filled his thoughts and why he so often tried to find an excuse to visit her. One would have thought—since it was plain that Philip had no interest in the lady—that Ned would feel *relief* at not having to face her again. But Ned was *not* relieved. He wanted *very much* to see her again . . . to try to return to a friendly footing, to explain, to apologize. Well, he would see her this evening. Would she smile? Would she speak to him? Or would she cut him completely?

When the Glendenning party arrived at the ball, Claryce was already surrounded by a number of swains, and Dennis Wivilscombe was looking angry. Lady Glendenning took due note of the situation, felt a wave of dismay and, seeing her eldest daughter in the crowd, drew Letty aside to confide her feelings. "I don't know what to make of Claryce," she muttered irritably. "I was certain that Wivilscombe could be brought to the point, but your sister seems determined to throw away her chances. Can't you *say* something to her?"

Letty, who had not been able to find a way to overcome her husband's disaffection, was living through a nightmare of her own. So deep in misery had she sunk that she hadn't the capacity to concern herself with Claryce's foolish indulgences. "Really, Mama," she said impatiently, "I thought you wanted Wivilscombe for *Gussie!*"

"Not any longer. Gussie has *Philip Denham* now," Lady Glendenning replied with some satisfaction.

This remark caught Letty's full attention. "*Philip?*" she asked with a gasp. "Whatever makes you believe that?"

"He's been calling almost every day for more than a fortnight. And, Letty dearest, you'll never credit it, but the fellow positively *ignores* Claryce whenever she tries to interfere. I must admit I find it entirely satisfying."

Letty stared at her mother askance. It hadn't occurrred to her that her mother might mistake Philip's attentions to Gussie for *courtship*. She herself had dreamed of an alliance between Gussie and Philip, but she'd lost her confidence that it would ever come to pass. In fact, she'd lost her confidence in *everything*. "Mama," she cautioned worriedly, "you mustn't refine on Philip Denham's visits too much. I don't believe he has serious intentions."

"Nonsense. Why would he bother to call so often if—?"

She peered at her daughter with sudden intensity, caught by the young woman's unusual pallor and an unmistakable shadow deep in her eyes. "Letty, my dear, are you feeling well?" she asked in sharp concern. "It seems to me you are not in quite your usual looks this evening."

"I'm fine, Mama," Letty said curtly, her eyes dropping away from her mother's intent stare. "Let us not stand here gossiping. I see Lady Sanderson over there trying to catch your attention, so do go along and speak to her. I only hope you will take my advice and not set too much store by Philip Denham's attentions. They may not signify anything at all."

Her mother frowned dubiously, took one more worried look at her daughter and turned away. A crowded ballroom was not the place in which to discuss intimate family matters. But something was decidedly wrong with Letty... and her hint about Philip Denham was disturbing as well. Lady Glendenning's happy mood was rapidly disintegrating. She wondered, as she took a seat beside her crony, Lady Sanderson, where *Prue* was keeping herself. There was no sign of *her* here tonight. It would be too much for her to bear if things were not well in *that* direction either.

At first it seemed that Augusta was truly embarked on an evening of social success. Her hand was sought the moment she entered the ballroom. Neville Trevithen, son of the hosts, claimed her hand as soon as she'd stepped through the door, his eyes gleaming in appreciation of her appearance. Philip released her arm and turned her over to her first conquest with a proud grin and conspiratorial wink. He was certain the evening would turn out to be a triumph for them both.

Neville was a cheerful, open-faced young man who was talkative to the point of loquacity. Augusta had no need at all to search for topics of conversation, and the dance passed more pleasantly than she'd imagined it could. As soon as it ended, however, Neville introduced her to a young friend of his. The young man, whose name she didn't catch, looked to be a mere boy, certainly not above nineteen years. He had an unruly thatch of red hair, a round face spattered with freckles and a smile that revealed both a vulnerable sweetness and a painful shyness. It was obvious that, by the time he'd taken his place next to her on the dance floor, the experience of standing up with a lovely young woman was almost too much for him. Feeling keenly sympathetic to his plight, she racked her brain to think of things to say to him. She could think of nothing but Philip's suggestion about pretending to know a secret about him. However, she was convinced that such a trick would only deepen the poor fellow's discomfort. As a result she lapsed into silence, and the dance proceeded quite awkwardly for both of them. When it ended, he led her off the floor looking acutely unhappy.

She headed for an empty chair on the sidelines, but before she could reach it, her hand was claimed by none other than the worldly Lord Garvey. Garvey was one of Claryce's most persistent cavaliers, and it was quite flattering to hear him murmur a number of extravagant compliments on her appearance as he led her to the dance floor. As they took their places in the set, Augusta realized that this was just the sort of situation for which Philip had prepared her. Lord Garvey was one of the leaders in Corinthian circles, and a sign of approval from *him* would ensure the attention of many others.

This realization made Augusta quake. If she were to win Philip's wager for him, this dance with Garvey might well be decisive. She had to sparkle. She had to entice him with speaking looks, entrance him with spirited laughs, impress him with witty jibes, but she felt completely unequal to the task. To add to her uneasiness, she noticed that the red-headed boy who'd danced with her previously now stood on the sidelines observing her fixedly with the most lugubrious expression on his face. Could she embark on her first real attempt at flirtation while being so closely observed by a third party?

The partners in the dance were facing each other for the allemande, and Lord Garvey was smiling at her expectantly. Desperately, she tried the *Innocent Flutter*. "Have you something in your eye?" Lord Garvey asked in concern.

She shook her head, too flustered to permit the laugh that burst inside her to find its way out. "I ... I've heard the most ... er ... *enthralling secret* about you, Lord Garvey," she offered next.

"Really?" Lord Garvey raised his eyebrows in decided offense. "What has Claryce been saying to you?"

"Oh, it wasn't Claryce," she said in hasty denial, coloring to her ears. She had never intended to involve Claryce in any awkwardness.

"You needn't defend her," Lord Garvey muttered irritably. "She's told almost everyone that I accosted her in the Cranshaws' library, which is the grossest calumny! She completely misinterprited my actions, and—"

"But, my lord, that is *not* the—"

The figure of the dance separated them at that moment, and when they came together again, he refused to permit her to explain further. His mouth was set in a tight, angry line, and she had no doubt he would promptly seek out Claryce and berate her soundly. And before long, *she* would have to face *Claryce*'s retributive wrath. How had she gotten herself into such a coil?

Since there was no hope of setting the matter to rights, and since she and Lord Garvey were still trapped together in this wretched dance, she made a last-ditch effort to make a mark on him. She attempted to lure him with the *Lowered-Lash Penitential*. But he'd been so disconcerted by their earlier conversation that he didn't even seem to notice. The dance ended without their having exchanged another word and, his brows knit darkly, he escorted her to the sidelines, made a brief bow and stalked off to find Claryce. Augusta looked after him, her feelings wavering somewhere between despair and laughter. *And that*, she said to herself ruefully, *concludes my first, dazzling attempt to become a reigning belle*.

She found herself a small gilt chair partially hidden behind a potted palm and sank gratefully into it. Slowly, a wave of dejection flowed over her. She had let Philip down. She deeply regretted having failed him, but he should have believed her when she'd tried to tell him that she was not suited for the role he'd tried to impose on her. It was not in her nature to succeed in what he called the Art of Dalliance. It would take more than gowns and *Gossamer Giggles* to make her a belle. She didn't have the talent.

When at last she'd recovered her composure sufficiently to take an interest in the activity around her, she noticed with surprise that the red-headed boy who'd danced with her earlier was leaning against the wall at her right—not twenty feet away—staring at her again. What was the matter with the fellow? The expression on his face suggested nothing so much as a puppy who'd been taken from its mother. Good heavens, had he formed an *attachment* for her? It *was* possible, she supposed, for a nineteen-year-old boy at his first ball to fall top-over-tail for the first girl he takes on the dance floor. She almost smiled to think that she'd made *one* conquest at least.

The fellow was a very small fish, but it was comforting to realize that she'd not cast out her lures completely in vain.

Her comfort was short-lived. Before long, an irate Philip loomed up before her. "What are you *doing* hiding here?" he demanded. "I expected to find you busily engaged on the dance floor."

She lowered her head in shame. "No one has asked me," she admitted.

He blinked. "But I saw you stand up for *every dance* before I went to the card room. What happened?"

She made a helpless little gesture. "I wasn't very successful, I'm afraid. I have no talent for this sort of thing, Philip. Please forgive me."

He frowned at her, perplexed. "I don't believe *that* for a moment. When we rehearsed the other day, you were as captivating as any female I've ever known. I can't understand—"

"Perhaps you've permitted your wishes to outstrip your judgment in this case," she suggested gently.

"I have *not!*" he declared angrily. "You've merely given up too soon. Come and dance with me right now. We'll soon have them lining up to sign your card."

She shook her head. "Not now, Philip, please. I'm . . . rather tired. Perhaps a little later . . ."

He eyed her in puzzled anxiety. "Very well, if you wish it. I'll return in a short while."

She looked after him feeling very close to tears. He would soon come back again and urge her to make another try . . . and then, she was certain, the tears would spill over, and she'd make a fool of herself indeed. She had to find a way to prevent it. If she could tempt a gentleman to sit with her—someone who could be induced to appear completely engrossed in conversation with her—Philip, when he returned, would not be able to approach and interrupt. She lifted her head and looked to her right. The red-headed boy was still there. She sighed in thankful relief. That boy could well be her salvation.

Suppressing a wave of manic amusement, she turned her head in the boy's direction and gave him a strong dose of the *Come-Hither Beckoning*. The boy stiffened, reddened and stared. Then, swallowing bravely and squaring his shoulders, he came toward her. She looked up at him with an encouraging smile. "Would you like to sit down and talk to me, sir?" she asked pleasantly.

"W—why, *yes*, I would I—like it above *anything*," he stammered.

She beckoned to a chair right beside her. "I'm afraid I didn't catch your name when we were introduced," she told him frankly.

"I'm Robin Walcott, Miss Glendenning."

"How do you do, Mr. Walcott? I want you to know that I'm not engaged at all until supper, so that you may chat with me as long as you like. And if you should notice any . . . er . . . gentlemen who may come along and seem to wish to interrupt, you may quite properly ignore them. I am completely at your disposal."

The boy was not sophisticated enough to perceive that this invitation was quite unusal. "Thank you, but . . ." He turned almost as red as his hair. "I . . . I'm not sure what you'd like me to talk to you *about*."

"You are to talk about *yourself*, of course, Mr. Walcott." She leaned back in her chair and, feeling, for the first time that evening, quite pleased with herself, favored him with the *Outright Exuberant* laugh. "You must tell me everything about yourself. Start from the time you were a tiny babe and do not stop at all until you've covered absolutely everything!"

*   *   *

Philip, unable to speak to Augusta alone, tried to interest Letty in his predicament. "She has barricaded herself from me by holding a *tête-à-tête* with Colby Walcott's little brother, Robin. For some strange reason which I cannot fathom, she seems to have given up the game. Do you think *you* might approach her and see if you can separate them?"

"No, Philip, I don't. Perhaps I should never have instigated this little experiment." She sighed mournfully and patted Philip on the shoulder. "You did your best, my dear. Don't refine on it too much."

"But . . . you're not suggesting that *I* give up, are you?" he asked, appalled. "We've only been at it a short while. Surely you'll allow me more time to win the wager than this! This evening was only the first test, you know."

Letty put a weary hand to her forehead. "Don't ask me to think about it now, Philip. I have the most dreadful headache and can't seem to concentrate on anything. I don't think I can

endure any more of this noisy crush. Will you find Roger for
me and tell him that I've gone home?"

Philip stared after his retreating sister-in-law with a brow
knit worriedly. What was *wrong* with Letty? Never in all the
years he'd known her had he seen her in such low spirits. Was
it Augusta's lack of success that was upsetting her? He could
hardly believe it; Augusta's performance this evening was not
as discouraging as all that! No, it must be something else
troubling her. He made up his mind to try to find out what it
was. If Letty was in some sort of trouble, he would like very
much to help. That, more than anything else, would be a way
to show her how grateful he was for what she'd done for him.
But in the meantime, he would go back to Augusta. She had
promised to go down to supper under his escort. At least for
the supper hour the girl would not be able to evade him.

By the time the late supper was over, every member of the
Glendenning family was unhappy. Claryce and Dennis had
quarreled in hissing whispers over their plates of lobster patties
and truffles, and they'd gone home in his carriage in frozen
silence. Also in the carriage with them were Ned and Lady
Glendenning, neither of whom had any desire to remain longer
at the ball. Lady Glendenning, worried sick about *all* her daughters (for Letty was unwontedly moody and pale; Prue had never
appeared; Claryce had evidently lost Wivilscombe for good;
and Gussie had not stood up *once* with Denham) was fit only
for bed. Ned, too, was quite miserable. Lucy had not put in
an appearance at the ball, and Ned had the uncomfortable
feeling that she might be trying to avoid him. He told himself
that he was, perhaps, flattering himself to think so; it was more
likely that she didn't think of him at all. But he'd looked
forward to seeing her and found himself unable to dismiss a
pervasive feeling of keen disappointment.

The three Glendennings—her ladyship, Claryce and Ned—
disembarked from Wivilscombe's carriage at their door and
watched gloomily as the carriage disappeared down the street.
Then, entering the house and handing their wraps to Hinson,
they nodded in glum agreement as Claryce voiced their
thoughts. "Well, I'm glad that's over," she said testily. "If you
ask me, the Trevithen ball was the very worst I've ever at-
tended."

Chapter Fifteen

PHILIP'S BAROUCHE, returning from the ball, arrived in Argyle Street only minutes after Wivilscombe's carriage had departed. Philip jumped out and ran quickly round to help Augusta down. She offered her hand for his assistance, giving him a thankful but rather wan smile. Neither of them was feeling very cheerful. During the late supper, Augusta had begged him to refrain from discussing the evening's fizzle until another day, and Philip had grudgingly agreed. Therefore, the drive homeward had been depressingly silent, and the mood still clung to both of them.

Her foot had hardly touched the pavement when their attention was attracted to a curricle racing madly down the street toward them. They exchanged puzzled looks, realizing that the driver was pulling up alongside. "Augusta, is that you?" came a distracted voice.

"*Brandon*?" She ran toward the curricle in alarm. "What's wrong? Has Prue—?"

He leaned out of the carriage dangerously. "Thank *God* you're not abed. The *baby's* coming, and I don't know what to *do*!"

"What do you mean?" she asked in confusion. "Isn't the midwife with her?"

"You mean Mrs. Miles? Yes, she's there, but the wretch

is as drunk as a lord." Even in the darkness of the night street, Augusta could discern his dishevelment and agitation. "The housekeeper's almost hysterical, and the entire household is in complete chaos. Do you think you can—?"

"Yes, of course. I'll come at once." She ran up the steps and hammered on the door. "Hinson," she cried as soon as he opened it, "get Katie at once. Tell her we must go to Prue immediately. The baby is on the way. And see what you can find in the way of cloths and towels—" She looked back over her shoulder. "Don't sit there waiting for me, Brandon. Go back at once and tell Prue we're coming directly."

"But how will you—?"

"I'll take them round to your place, Mr. Peake, if that's what's worrying you," Philip offered promptly.

Brandon nodded, flicked at the reins and wheeled his carriage about so hastily it almost overturned. As soon as it careened out of sight, Augusta turned a grateful face to Philip. "I don't know how to thank—"

"Don't be a goose," he said flatly. "Go and get whatever it is you'll need. I'll be ready whenever you are."

The sight that met their eyes when they opened the door of the Peake residence was one they would never forget. The floor of the modest entrance hall was awash in water spilled from a large kettle which lay on its side at the bottom of the stairs. The housekeeper, waving a mop, was begging a young housemaid, who sat on the stairs bitterly weeping into her hands, to stop her bawling. On the first floor landing a large, florid-faced woman enveloped in a voluminous apron, with her mob-cap askew and her hair wild, was shouting curses at the maid in drunken abandon. And from upstairs, punctuating the scene with pathetic regularity, came cries of pain from the laboring mother. Katie, ignoring every impediment in her path, dashed up the stairs and disappeared from sight. Augusta, after a moment's horrified pause, took a deep breath and stepped over the threshold. "Mrs. Miles, be silent!" she ordered the drunken midwife. "And you, Mrs. Woods, get busy with your mopping. And you, girl, stop that whimpering at once. Take the kettle to the kitchen, fetch some more hot water, and bring it upstairs. Perhaps it you don't fill it quite so full, you won't have so much difficulty with it this time."

She turned to Philip, who still stood in the doorway watching the scene aghast. "Do you think, Philip, that you could take Mrs. Miles to the kitchen and find someone there to pour coffee into her? I believe I've heard that coffee can sometimes reduce the effect of strong drink."

"I think it can," he said, shaking himself into action. "Just go on about your duties and leave Mrs. Miles to me."

An hour later, the atmosphere was completely transformed. The stairway and hall had been mopped up, the little maid was running up and down stairs with calm efficiency, Mrs. Miles had managed to shake off the worst effects of intoxication and, having straightened her hair and her cap, had gone up to her post. Even the screams, which still issued from the upstairs bedroom with alarming frequency, seemed somehow less agonized and fearful.

Philip sat tensely in Brandon's study, an untouched glass of brandy in his hand, watching the father-to-be pace about in nervous agitation.

"Do you think it will take much longer?" Brandon asked with discouraged anxiety, biting his lip and wringing his hands.

"I haven't the foggiest idea," Philip was forced to admit, not knowing what else to say. "Don't take on so, old man. Everything seems to be proceeding calmly now. I know nothing of these matters, of course, but I would guess from the sound of things that your wife is experiencing a normal birth."

Neither one of them had yet been able to shake off the terror of the earlier confusion. Brandon sighed and resumed pacing. It struck Philip forcibly as the night progressed that Brandon did not, even once, resort to a quotation. It was as if the fellow was experiencing something so unique and special that all the philosophizing of his heroes from the past did not appear any longer to be relevant.

The clock had just struck four when Katie came in, smiling wearily. "Miss Augusta sended me down, Mr. Peake, to tell you 'twill not be much longer now. An' Mrs. Peake's doin' fine."

But it was almost dawn before they heard the sound of a baby's cry. The sound sent a shudder right through Brandon's body. "Oh, thank *God*!" he whispered fervently, a tear slipping down his cheek. He threw Philip a look of ineffable joy and made for the door. But Philip jumped up and blocked his way. "Don't you think you should wait until one of the women says it's all right to go up?" he asked gently.

Brandon blinked in indecision. "Do you think so?" he asked, brushing a trembling hand across his forehead.

Philip poured out two glasses of brandy. "Here. Let's drink to the new life."

A moment later, the study door opened. Augusta stood framed in the doorway, a swaddled infant in her arms. She beamed at Brandon, her face glowing. "Here's your *son*, Brandon," she said in quiet elation.

Brandon seemed to freeze. He stood rooted to the spot, staring across the room at the bundle in her arms, the hand holding the brandy glass raised halfway to his lips. "My *son*—?" he asked in a disbelieving whisper.

"Aren't you going to come and have a look at him?" Augusta suggested with a tender smile.

Dazed, Brandon put the glass down on his desk and walked unsteadily across the room. While he stared in rapt stupefaction at the tiny red face of the infant that squinted up at him in unseeing intensity, Philip gazed in wonder at a transformed Augusta. The girl had not taken the time to remove her ball gown, which was now crushed and soiled beyond recognition. The long, tight-fitting sheer sleeves of the gauze overdress had been pushed up above the elbows, the white silk underdress had been badly soiled and ripped at the hem, and the entire costume showed signs that its fragile delicacy had been completely ignored. Pinned to the front was a large towel (probably intended to protect the baby against being scratched by the silver threads rather than to protect the dress itself) which was smeared with blood. Her face was pale with weariness, and strands of her fine hair had escaped their bonds and were hanging, damp and limp, over her forehead and about her face. She was dirty, weary and disheveled—and he thought he'd never before seen *anyone* so beautiful.

"Would you like to hold him?" Augusta asked Brandon, her smile widening at his awed expression. Carefully she transfered her burden to his awkwardly eager hold. While Brandon stared down, enraptured, at his miraculous firstborn, Augusta turned her glowing face to Philip. Whatever it was that she read in his expression startled her, for she blushed and her eyes flickered down as if she couldn't bear the urgency in his. Philip had a sudden and almost overpowering urge to take her in his arms. He wanted to hold her, to soothe the weary lines from her face and let her tired body sag against his own. He moved toward her, his arms reaching out . . .

"Some words of Horace come to me," Brandon announced proudly, his eyes fixed on the baby's face. *"'He will through life be master of himself.'"*

Philip stopped short, the sound of Brandon's voice bringing him sharply to his senses. Dropping his arms to his sides with inward frustration, he laughed aloud, as much in amusement at himself as at Brandon. "If you are quoting Horace," he said, grinning at the proud father, "you must have recovered your equilibrium."

Brandon looked up at him with a self-deprecating smile. "I *do* tend to spout quotations at the most inopportune moments. Prue is always teasing me about it. But the quotation is quite apt, I think. In fact, I shall name this little fellow Horace, if Prue agrees."

"Would you like to ask her about it now?" Augusta put in. "I believe she's waiting to see you."

"Oh, may I?" Brandon asked eagerly, returning the mewling babe to her more secure hold. "I shall tell her that Horace also said, *'O, fair son of a fairer mother.'* It will be a pleasing phrase for Prue's ears, don't you think?—even though it's a completely inaccurate rendering. Horace Brandon Peake. The name has an imposing sound, has it not?"

The sun had fully risen by the time Philip had delivered Augusta and Katie to their door, stabled his horses and dropped, still half clothed, onto his bed. He was suddenly feeling unexplainably depressed and weary to the bone. But even though he'd drawn the draperies across the windows, removed his boots and coat and loosened his neckcloth, sleep eluded him. He couldn't wrench his mind from thoughts of Augusta. He reviewed the events of the evening over and over, each particular returning to his mind's eye in clear, carefully-etched detail. He saw her again as she'd looked coming down the stairs at the beginning of the evening. He saw her smiling pleasantly up at Neville Trevithen as she made her bow to him at the start of the minuet. And he saw her as she sat listening to young Walcott, leaning toward him with such interest in his words that Philip had felt his fists clench in rage.

He'd been very angry with her then, but *now* he felt more

dismayed by his own behavior than by Augusta's. He'd taken a young woman of unique, distinctive quality and tried to mold her into something conventional and false. He had once said to Letty (it seemd to have been eons ago, when he'd been a stupid and callow youth) that he couldn't make a silk purse from a sow's ear. What a fool he'd been! All this while, he'd *really* been attempting to do the exact opposite—to make Gussie into something *less* than she was.

What right had he to think he could teach a girl of her quality how to behave? She was gentle, kind and innately high-minded. She was honest and sincere in all her dealings with others, both men and women. Her lucidly-clear instincts made her uncomfortable with the superficial and tawdry tricks and wiles he'd attempted to instill in her. Her natural pride made her disdain an easy, dishonestly-won popularity. Why couldn't he have seen it before? One had only to see her as she'd appeared early this morning, holding her sister's baby in her arm, to realize that she was a woman of rare beauty—the beauty that comes from something inside.

He groaned and threw an arm over his throbbing forehead. How could he have been so presumptious? And so *blind*? In a world of simpering, artificial, vain and pleasure-seeking females, he'd come face-to-face with one girl whose inner worth made her stand high above the rest—and anyone with half an eye could have seen it, for it shone out of her clear eyes and set an unmistakable mark on her serene brow—but he'd failed to recognize her. Time and again her words, her glances and her silences had pricked his mind with signals . . . and he'd ignored them. Instead, he'd shown her, over and over again, the side of himself that was shallow, self-seeking, unprincipled and crafty. How she must despise him!

Yes, it was clear that she despised him. Why else would she have kept the freckle-faced young Walcott at her side for half the evening except to keep *him* from returning to her as he'd told her he would? Well, it was nothing more than he deserved. He'd tried to make her into something other than she was . . . he'd as much as *told* her that she was unsatisfactory in her own person. Why *shouldn't* she despise him now? Now that he, Philip Denham, who'd sworn only recently to avoid any attachments to females—had fallen so desperately in love with her, Augusta had decided to avoid him!

Good Lord! He sat up abruptly, breathing as rapidly as if

he'd wakened with a start from a nightmare. He *was* desperately in love with her! Why hadn't he recognized that blazing truth before? He *loved* her . . . just exactly the way she was, with her pale hair and shy eyes, her modest walk, her way of listening without intruding, her tendency to hide in corners, her surprised blush when anyone paid her a compliment, her flashes of humor which popped out at the most unexpected times, the quiet allure of her that might not be noticed—that *he* hadn't noticed until he'd held her in his arms and had been struck by it with a force that had shaken him to the core. He *loved* her, and yet he'd never even uttered the words to himself until this moment . . . the same moment when he'd understood, with a sinking heart, that he'd probably lost her.

He couldn't blame her if she despised him, but he would no longer continue in a manner which would cause him to despise himself. He would no longer go on with the farce of 'tutoring' her. To make her the toast of the *ton* was no longer a goal he wished to achieve. The role was unworthy of her. He would tell her, the very next time he saw her, that he no longer wished her to win his wager for him. And as far as his debt to *Letty* was concerned, he would find *another* way to repay her.

He lay back against the pillows, feeling suddenly at peace with himself. Perhaps all was not lost. Perhaps, after he'd apologized to Augusta for his arrogant presumption . . . after he'd described the complete turn-about his feelings for her had taken . . . perhaps, then, she might be able to view him with less revulsion. But no matter what her reaction would be, he knew with a calming certainty that he was on the right path at last.

Chapter Sixteen

LATE THAT AFTERNOON, after Ned had brought his ecstatic mother to Prue's bedside and had stayed long enough to congratulate his sister and brother-in-law on the birth of their yowling, red-faced son-and-heir, he came out of the Peake domicile and hesitated. It was only a short walk from Prue's house to Upper Berkley Street where Lucy Greland lived. Did he dare to stroll over there to inquire after the lady's health?

His mind answered the question in the negative. In the first place, the wind was biting, the day blustery cold, and it would undoubtedly rain. And besides, what was the point of going to see Lucy? Sooner or later the conversation would turn to the marriage plot he'd attempted to arrange for her and Philip, and he'd have to suffer the embarrassment of admitting his stupidity in approaching her with too-hasty eagerness and making a mull of the matter. No, it would be better to forget the entire matter and never look Lucy in the face again.

But he wanted to see Lucy again. *That* was the truth that was becoming more obvious with each passing day. He no longer wished for Lucy to make a *mariage de convenance* with Philip. He wanted her to make a *love-match*—with *him*! It was difficult for him to face the fact that he'd somehow slipped into love, but there seemed to be little question about it now. He'd thought of nothing and no one else for days. He'd searched for her through all the crowded rooms of the Trevithen house last night with trembling eagerness, only to be tumbled into the doldrums by her absence. If only he hadn't begun his relationship with her so *idiotically*, he might have been able to court Lucy with proper dignity . . . and with some hope of success. But as it was . . .

So deep was he in his thoughts that he failed to realize he'd already walked some distance in her direction. His feet were bearing him to Upper Berkeley Street in spite of his mind's firm decision to keep away. Throwing caution to the winds— and with an uncharacteristic surrender to impulse—he strode rapidly on in the direction his feet had taken.

The elderly butler, quite shabby again in his everyday coat, seemed reluctant to admit him. But before he could succeed in shutting the door in Ned's face, the lady herself appeared on the stairway, her hounds bounding down ahead of her. "Well, Lord Glendenning," she said with a distinct tone of derision, "what an honor to see you at my door again! I would have thought that your time was much too precious to waste on a thoughtless, selfish, headstrong, irresponsible, immature creature like myself."

Even if Ned had been able to think of a suitable rejoinder, he would not have been able to utter it, for the dogs were upon him, licking his face, barking in his ears and leaping up and down in eager greeting. The butler, feeling that all this was too much for him, tottered off to the nether regions, muttering under his breath about the changeable moods of females in general and his mistress' in particular. Ned, interpreting the butler's mutterings to mean that Lucy had signaled permission for him to enter, crossed the threshold and closed the door behind him, while at the same time trying to keep the hounds from knocking him over. But it was not until the lady called her dogs to heel that he was able to take a good look at her.

She looked very much the same as she had the day he'd first come to see her. Her hair was loose and wild, her clothes were chosen more for their utility than for their effect on observers, and her expression was suspicious, wary and distant. Her appearance, so different from what it had been during their recent meetings, made him realize with satisfaction that she'd taken some pains with her *toilette* during those days when his calls had been prearranged. Nevertheless, he found her present, careless, unruly air quite enthralling. From that very first day, he'd sensed in himself a shocking attraction toward her in this wild, unkempt state. Her untamed look was very stimulating to his senses, despite an ingrained feeling of vague disapproval that added a confusing ambivalence to his emotions.

Her eyes caught his, and a spark of amusement seemed to light up deep within them. She tossed her head at him scornfully, as if in some uncanny way she'd been able to read his thoughts. Without a word, she turned and led the way to the library. "Well, my lord," she said as soon as she'd closed the door, "what is it you want with me *this* time?"

"I . . . er . . . came to inquire after your health, ma'am," he said awkwardly.

"My health? Why?"

"I had understood that you were to attend the Trevithen ball last evening, and when you didn't appear, I became concerned."

She uttered a derisive snort. "I didn't attend because I don't care for those horrid social squeezes, that's all. My health is quite as robust as it was when I outraced you on my horse."

"I see. I'm delighted to hear it, of course." He paused, completely at a loss as to how to proceed.

"I suppose I ought to thank you for being sufficiently disquieted about me to make this call."

"It is not at all necessary to thank me," he responded with stiff pomposity. "I've done nothing specific for you, after all . . ."

"Speaking of doing things for me, my lord," she said, dropping down on a nearby chair, "I have a confession to make to you."

"A confession?"

"Yes. My conscience has been troubling me, you see . . . and now that you've appeared at my door to inquire after my health with such solicitude, you make me feel even more guilt-ridden. So if you'll sit down, I'd like to unburden myself to you."

Puzzled, he took a chair opposite hers and looked at her inquiringly. "I can't imagine why your conscience should be troubling you in any matter which involves *me*, ma'am."

"I have been lying to you, Ned," she said with sudden and brusque directness. "Lying quite shamelessly, and almost from the first."

"*Lying*? But I don't see—?"

"Let me explain. When you first came and told me about your little marriage proposal, I was enormously entertained. I know it was very irresponsible and immature of me to have done so, but I succumbed to temptation and permitted you to think I was seriously considering the possibility of such an arrangement—"

"When in truth you were *not*?"

"Of *course* I was not," she sneered impatiently. "What a poor sort of creature you must think me! Am I so pathetic a female—such an *ape-leader*, in fact?—that I have need of *buying* myself a husband?"

He blinked at her in outraged bafflement. "I *never* thought that! Good *Lord*, Lucy, I told you *repeatedly* that the suggestion was made in admiration—!"

"Yes, I know. That's why I permitted you to return so often. I realized that your suggestion was more *naive* than insulting. But the truth is that I never for a *moment* seriously considered entering into such an arrangement. I merely *pretended* to be interested."

"But . . . *why*?" He leaned forward, agonizingly intent.

She turned her head away. "I don't intend to tell you why. If you can't guess the answer for yourself, then you're too thick-headed to understand . . . even if I tried to explain it to you."

He rose slowly from the chair, a tide of anger rising in his throat. "Thick-headed, am I, ma'am?"

"Quite."

He stalked angrily to her chair. "And during all our . . . meetings . . . you were only playing a cat-and-mouse game with me?"

"Yes, I was," she answered, looking up at him with teasing derision.

"And you kept me dangling at your side for *nothing*?" he asked, seething. "Only to *laugh* at me?"

"Well, you must admit you *were* amusing in your ridiculous attempt at matchmaking."

"Oh? Ridiculous, was I?" he queried, his mouth tight.

She could feel his anger striking out at her like a palpable emanation. "Quite ridiculous," she taunted spitefully.

A black fury seemed to break out somewhere right behind his eyes. It didn't matter that he himself had recognized how foolish and ridiculous his matchmaking attempt had been. It didn't matter that her scorn was really quite justified. It only mattered that she was mocking him, the irritating, insolent gleam winking contemptuously at the back of her eyes. He wanted only to shake her—to pry her loose the derisive leer. He leaned down, grasped her shoulders and pulled her to her feet. "Confound you!" he muttered insanely, "I'd like to shake the laugh right out of you. You *enjoy* making a fool of me!"

But there was no longer a laugh in her eyes. She was staring up at him with an arrested expression, as if she were waiting for . . . for what? Her wild, curly hair fell over his fingers that were clutching her shoulders with cruel pressure. Her suntanned skin, a feature held in disdain by most of the ladies of society, seemed to glow, sending out waves of intoxicating warmth and the aroma of wind and rain. And her lips, full and pink and very slightly curved in an expression that was not quite a smile . . . all these combined to make him dizzy with desire. It was a feeling so strong, so unexpected and so frightening that his anger left him. Horrified at himself, he let her go so abruptly that she fell back into her chair. "I'm . . . sorry . . ." he mumbled, reddening painfully.

She looked up at him, her expression enigmatic, and rubbed her shoulders while they stared at each other wordlessly. Finally, realizing that he'd come close to making a fool of himself *again*, he made a stilted bow and, his knees shaking, walked stiffly to the door. "I believe there's nothing more for us to say to each other," he said bitterly. "I'm glad that this futile and fruitless exercise at least provided *you* with some amusement. For me, it has been nothing but a painful waste of time. Good day, ma'am."

"Ned? Please . . . wait . . ." Her voice was breathless.

He paused. "Yes, ma'am?"

"Is that *all* you want to . . . to say to me?"

He looked at her over his shoulder, his brow knit suspiciously. "What is there left to say?"

She stared at him again with eyes that held scorn, disappointment and something else that was completely unfathomable. "You're the greatest fool I've ever met in my life," she said in disgust. "Goodbye, Ned. If ever your sluggish brain manages to comprehend some of the import of this conversation, feel free to return and tell me what you've grasped. Until then, however, I have no wish to lay eyes on you."

Stung by her contempt, he clamped his mouth shut, made

another stiff bow and walked angrily from the room, slamming the door behind him. The noise brought the dogs barking to the door and the butler from below stairs. He took his hat from the butler's hand and clapped it on his head, hoping the library door would open and the lady would emerge. The weakness of the wish made him disgusted with himself, but he hated to take his leave with the sound of her insults ringing in his ears. If only she would repent . . . run out and stop him . . . and apologize. . . .

But his hat was on his head, and the butler was holding the door open. There was no reason to delay any longer. He walked unhappily out the door, inwardly cursing his phenomenal stupidity, her headstrong moodiness, and the arbitrariness of the fate which had led him to her door in the first place. The fact that a driving, icy rain was now falling—and that he would have to walk all the way to Argyle Street with the knife-like drops beating at his face—did not surprise him at all. It was all-of-a-piece with the rest of his luck, and no more than he deserved.

Chapter Seventeen

THE RED-HEADED young Robin Walcott knocked at the door of the Glendenning house in Argyle Street, the biting rain not in the least dampening his glowing optimism and bouyant spirits. He'd come to call on Miss Augusta Glendenning, his new-found inamorata, with the highest expectations. All the previous night, after he'd returned from the Trevithen ball, he'd been unable to sleep, so stimulated and delighted had he been at the signs of interest Miss Glendenning had shown in him. She'd signaled that interest—or so he believed—in several ways: for one thing, she'd granted him a dance; secondly, she'd beckoned him to her side a short while later; and lastly, she'd urged him to talk about himself at great length. It was therefore, to his mind, unmistakably obvious that she was taken with him. And since he'd lost his head over *her* from the first moment that Neville Trevithen had brought him to her side, his happiness knew no bounds.

The butler took his calling card upstairs, and after what seemed to him an endless wait, a surprised-looking Miss Glendenning appeared at the top of the stairs. If the boy had been in his right mind, he would have noticed that the girl was really not the exquisite, ethereal creature she had seemed the night before. Her hair was tied up in a neat knot, her brown-and-white striped muslin round-gown, with its high collar and long sleeves, could be described by no adjective more fitting than *drab*, and her manner was not in the least flirtatious. But in Robin's eyes, Miss Glendenning could not be anything but the embodiment of gossamer loveliness. His eyes were misted by the illusory veil of first love. "M–Miss Glendenning , . . !" he breathed, awe-struck.

"How kind of you to call, Mr. Walcott," she said in a voice that even Robin's besotted brain had to recognize was lacking in the delight and eagerness he'd hoped for. The young lady was plainly not filled with joy at his unexpected appearance on her threshold. If he'd had any sense, he would have made a hasty withdrawal.

But Robin was young and very inexperienced, and—this being the very first call he'd ever made on a girl—he didn't know enough to retreat with his pride intact. He foolhardily plunged ahead. "I . . . I couldn't wait to see you again, Miss Glendenning," he declared with unrestrained fervor.

Augusta was nonplussed. She was fully aware that she'd led the boy on during their secluded conversation of the night before, but she hadn't anticipated that his obvious infatuation would outlast the night. She had no wish to hurt the boy's feelings, but neither did she desire to have him hanging about the premises. "*See* me again, Mr. Walcott?" she asked, trying desperately to think of what to say that would make him understand—in the kindest way, of course—that his infatuation was quite hopeless. "Whatever for?"

"What *f–for*?" he echoed, dumbfounded, having not the slightest notion of how to reply to so unexpected a question. "Well, you know . . . to *call* on you."

"Yes, I quite see *that*. But why?"

"Why? *Why*? To . . . er . . . further our acquaintance, of course. Didn't you wish me to—?"

"No, I'm afraid I didn't," she answered with frank gentleness.

"But I thought . . . that is, I assumed . . ." he mumbled in embarrassment.

"I'm sorry, Mr. Walcott, if I misled you last evening. I thought you'd have understood that a closer acquaintanceship between us would not be . . . er . . . suitable."

"No, I *don't* understand. *Why* would it not be suitable?"

"Oh, for many reasons. I'm much older than you, for one thing."

He frowned, chagrined. "It's this freckled face of mine," he said in despair. "It makes me look like a mere boy. Everyone teases me about it. But Miss Glendenning, I'm *not* a mere boy!"

The look on her face was kind but unconvinced. "Mr. Walcott, surely you——?"

He didn't listen to her words. It was enough to see her eyes, to perceive that she remained unpersuaded. He could think of only one way to convince her of his manhood. He drew himself up to his full height, took in a deep, desperate breath—and *lunged* at her.

* * *

Behind the closed door of the sitting room just beyond the front hallway, Dennis Wivilscombe and Claryce were having the most serious altercation of their brief but stormy association. Dennis, pushed beyond his endurance, had found the evening at the Trevithens' his last straw. "Not only did you refuse me a second dance, but you disappeared when I expected to escort you to supper," he'd accused her angrily. "And then, when I found you at last, there you sat in intimate discourse with *Garvey*, your eyes aswim in tears and his hands clutching yours!"

"Really, Denny, you are making a mull over nothing," Claryce declared in earnest defense. "I've already *told* you how it was. Gussie had *maligned* me to him, and I was trying to set things right."

Dennis rose from the sofa in disgust. "It is bad enough, ma'am, for you to play Garvey against me in the coquettish fashion you've indulged in all these weeks . . . but to drag your *sister* into it is the outside of enough! If you expect me to believe that Augusta is even *capable* of telling lies about you, then you take me for a simpleton. I may be many ways a fool, but I'm not such a bobbing-block as that!"

Claryce felt impossibly thwarted. Gussie was so universally thought of as above reproach that no one could believe her to be guilty of *any* transgression. "It's *true*, I tell you! I know it doesn't *sound* like Gussie to have done so, but she really *did*! She has been behaving very strangely of late, ever since Philip Denham——"

"Stop it, ma'am!" Dennis ordered, appalled. "You only lower *yourself* when you persist in such disparagement of your sister. She's worth *ten* of you, and if I had a grain remaining of the sense I was born with . . ." But he stopped himself before he could say more.

Claryce was unaccustomed to such strong criticism (especially from a gentleman who'd been so persistent a suitor), and she burst into unwilling tears. "Why d-does everyone think *me* so d-dreadful and Gussie so *p-perfect*?" she muttered jealously through her sobs.

"You needn't think that a show of tears will soften me, my dear," he said, stroking his walrus-like moustache with nonchalant indifference. "I'm not a green boy, you know."

"N-no, you're not," she agreed, dashing the tears from her cheeks with the back of her hand and looking up at him angrily. "Th-this is the way you've avoided commitments in the p-past, *isn't* it, Mr. Wivilscombe?" Her shoulders shook, and her eyes narrowed accusingly. "You find some trumpery reason to stage a quarrel, and then make a slippery escape. *That's* your g-game, isn't it?"

He sneered. "You may think so, if you like. But I'll admit this much to you, my dear. *You* almost had this *Seal* right in your net. It was only your desire to catch so many *other* fish that caused you to lose this one."

She drew herself up proudly. "Then why do you stay? If I am so w-worthless in your eyes, why don't you g-go!"

"That is *exactly* what I intend to do, ma'am. And if you think you'll be able to wiggle your finger and draw me back, I suggest that you disabuse yourself of that notion. Good day, my dear. Please accept my best wishes for your future happiness." With a curt bow, he stalked out of the room.

He entered the hallway just in time to see Robin Walcott lunge at Augusta. The poor girl was thrown off balance by the force of the boy's intended embrace, and she fell against the wall with a cry of alarm. Robin, determined to prove his adulthood, pressed himself against her and attempted with clumsy persistence to plant a kiss on her face which she turned and twisted out of his reach. "What on earth's going on here?" Wivilscombe demanded, seizing the boy by the collar of his coat.

"Oh, Mr. Wivilscombe!" Augusta breathed in relief. "Thank *goodness*!"

"Have you lost your *mind*?" Dennis demanded of the red-faced boy.

"Well, I only . . ." the miserable lad mumbled, ". . . that is, she thinks I—"

"Never mind the excuses," Dennis said impatiently, propelling Robin inexorably toward the door. "If you can't be trusted to behave like a gentleman, you shouldn't be permitted to enter the abodes of gently-nurtured ladies." And without permitting Robin to utter another word, he thrust him out into the unfeeling rain and slammed the door on him.

Augusta had by this time regained her balance, but she found herself trembling from shock and alarm. She'd sustained a painful bump at the back of her head from her contact with the wall and a painful blow from her conscience for having encouraged Mr. Walcott's fantasies for her own selfish pur- poses. Dennis, seeing her perturbation and believing it to be caused by a tender-hearted, delicate sensibility, approached her with affecting gentleness. "Are you very upset, my dear?" he asked softly, putting an arm about her shoulders and leading her into the open drawing-room. "Come in here and sit down. I should not refine on the incident too much if I were you. May I bring you a glass of sherry?"

"No, no, thank you," Augusta said, still breathless but un- willing to be fussed over. She let him lead her to the sofa. "I'm quite recovered, *truly*."

"You look distressingly pale. Damnation, I should have *thrashed* the fellow! I let him off too easily."

Augusta shook her head. "On the contrary, Mr. Wivil- scombe, I'm glad you *didn't* thrash him. The incident was more *my* fault than his."

But Dennis wouldn't believe it. He spent the next few min- utes soundly berating, with strong verbal abuse, the members of the younger generation for their wildness, ill-manners and lack of self-control. Augusta, too perturbed to wish to argue the matter, sat silently and let him sermonize, her hands folded in her lap and her eyes downcast. Dennis eyed the girl in approval. He liked her sensitivity, her quietness, her sweet, becoming modesty. *Why*, he asked himself, *couldn't I have fallen in love with a paragon like this*?

He fell silent, studying her speculatively. "I must admit, Miss Glendenning," he remarked after a while, "that I've been struck with the realization that I've been taking quite the wrong path in my calls at this house."

"The wrong path? I don't know what you mean."

"It means that I've suddenly begun to wonder if you and I might suit."

"Suit?"

"Yes. In a marital way, I mean."

Augusta turned and blinked at him. "Mr. Wivilscombe, I can't have understood you," she exclaimed in astonishment. "Are you making me an *offer*?"

Dennis was rather astonished himself. He burst into a rueful laugh. "Yes, I think I *am*!"

Augusta was almost bereft of speech. A proposal of marriage from Dennis Wivilscombe was the *goal* Philip had set for her! Had she achieved it so soon—and so *easily*? The situation was beyond belief!

"Don't look at me so incredulously, Miss Glendenning," he said, smiling warmly at her. "I know I have the reputation for not coming to the point, but this time I'm quite sincere. I find you a most admirable young woman in every respect, and I think we might deal famously together. Will you not *consider* the matter?"

"But . . . we don't even *know*—"

A tap at the door interrupted her. At her response, Hinson put his head in. "Mr. Philip Denham is here, Miss Augusta. Shall I send him in?"

A gurgle of irrepressible laughter bubbled up from Augusta's chest. "What an *appropriate* time for him to have arrived!" she said, grinning. "Yes, Hinson, tell him to come in." She turned to Dennis with a blush. "I hope you will understand, Mr. Wivilscombe, when I say that this has been much too confusing and chaotic an afternoon for me to think about your unexpected offer with any semblance of seriousness. Perhaps we had *both* better wait and discuss this at another time. It will give *me* an opportunity to accustom myself to the surprise . . . and *you* to reconsider what I suspect was too impulsive a declaration."

"It was the most *sensible* declaration I've ever made in my life, my dear," he said, rising and taking her hand, "but I shall be happy to give you all the time you need to consider my proposal." With that, he lifted her hand to his lips in farewell. The gesture was executed with an air that was both courtly and sincere, and Augusta couldn't help but be touched by it.

When she looked up, she found that Philip was standing in the doorway, his eyes wide and his expression not at all the guarded one of the experienced gambler. He was clearly suffering from acute dismay.

Dennis, aware that Augusta's next caller had arrived, dropped her hand, bowed and went quickly to the door. He gave Denham a friendly nod and made his exit.

"Augusta, what on *earth*—?" Philip said as soon as the door had closed.

She giggled. "Philip, I have the most amazing news. I think I've *won* you your *wager*!"

"*What*? Do you mean that Wivilscombe . . . ? Just*now* . . . ?"

She nodded. "I'm not at all certain he was serious, but—"

Philip's face flushed an angry red. "*Serious!* I should hope he wasn't! How *dared* he make such a proposal? He barely *knows* you!"

"But . . . *Philip* . . ." Augusta's face fell, and she gaped at him, startled. "I thought you'd be so *pleased*—!"

"Pleased? *Pleased?* That a skirter-jilter of the first magnitude had the temerity to add *you* to his list of conquests?"

Augusta's head began to throb in confusion. First Robin Walcott had behaved in that terrible way, then Wivilscombe had made his completely unexpected offer, and now Philip was reacting in a quite irrational way. Had the world gone *mad*? She put a hand to her forehead and tried to rub away the confusion. "Philip, I don't understand you. Didn't you tell me that an offer from Mr. Wivilscombe would be the *symbolic moment* which would indicate that you'd won your wager?"

"Yes, perhaps I *did* say that. But I've changed my mind. I don't *wish* any longer to win that blasted wager."

"I don't understand any of this. For almost a month we've been expending *every effort* in that direction. And now that we've achieved—"

"*What* have we achieved?" Philip cut in bitterly. "A precipitate offer from a notorious jilter who isn't worth a moment's attention?"

"But he's *not* a jilter, Philip. As I understand it, he never came to the *point* with all the others."

"Oh, I *see*! Quite *proud* of yourself, are you?" he sneered, completely aware that he was wild with jealousy and behaving quite illogically, but unable to stop himself.

"Yes, I am," she said, drawing herself up in offense. "And I thought *you* would be proud of me, too."

Shamed, he turned away from her and walked to the window. He stared out at the rain beating down on the panes with unseeing eyes. "I'm not behaving at all well, I know. But I've been reconsidering matters ever since I left you this morning, and I've decided that I'd been an idiot to have agreed to that fatuous wager in the first place. It was a selfish, inconsiderate and shallow-witted thing to have done, and I'm sorry I ever embarked on the enterprise..."

Augusta felt herself grow cold all over. Painfully aware that she had made a mull of her first test as a 'belle' during the Trevithen ball, she interpreted Philip's remarks as a confession of defeat. He had evidently given up hope that he could succeed at making her the toast of London. And of course he was quite right. It had been an impossible task from the first...she'd tried, *herself*, to warn him that the project would fail. But his unquenchable optimism had so greatly affected her that she'd been carried aloft by it. She'd begun to believe, in some deep recess of her spirit, that his confidence in her would be the magic to make her succeed. In the few weeks of their association, she had felt herself flowering. His faith in her had been the next-best thing to love, and she'd permitted herself to float in a euphoric fog of unwarranted happiness. But one small failure had shattered his faith completely—or so his words seemed to indicate—and without *his* faith in her, her own bouyant self-image collapsed like a punctured balloon.

It was all too painfully clear. He had realized, last night, that there was no hope of her ever succeeding in becoming a reigning belle, and he had come today to break the news to her. He was trying to be kind, but the import of his words was unmistakable. Even her announcement of an offer from Wivilscombe had not made a significant difference to him. Wivilscombe's proposal was to have been the symbol of a *greater* victory; without that victory, the *symbol* was meaningless.

She looked at him as he stood, tired and discouraged, in the window embrasure. She couldn't see his face, but his tousled hair, the raindrops which still dotted the shoulders of his coat and his bent head all added to his air of defeat. She felt a stab of pain in her chest so strong that she was certain her heart had cracked. The game was over between them...all over. The emptiness that stretched ahead of her seemed bleaker than it had ever been before. Why had she not recognized in the beginning that *this* would be the inevitable end?

He turned from the window and faced her. "I'm...sorry, Augusta. You didn't deserve—"

"There's no n—need to say anything more, Philip," she said, trying desperately to keep hold of herself. She would try to be as kind as he. There was no purpose to be served in allowing him to see any signs of her abject misery. She pulled herself to her feet. "You tried your best to make me a b—belle. It's not your fault if you couldn't m—make a silk purse from a sow's ear."

He turned ashen-white. Whatever had brought that horrid phrase to her mind? The mere recollection of his ever having said something so blatantly arrogant and untrue made him sick. And, worse, she seemed to believe that he'd been trying to tell her she'd *failed*! "*Augusta*!" he gasped. "Surely you don't think I meant—!"

She put up a restraining hand and walked with firm purpose to the door. "Let's not talk about it any more, Philip. It's . . . not important. I never really believed . . . that is, I only entered into this g—game to help you win your wager. And I do believe that, with Wivilscombe's offer, you can quite justifiably claim to have done so. As for the rest—"

"I don't *care* about the wager, Augusta, don't you understand? I only wish to try to make up for—"

"Please, Philip, don't go on. I've had a very difficult day . . . and I don't feel capable of . . . of going on with this. Forgive me if I'm behaving rudely, but I m—must ask you to excuse me."

He could do nothing but bow his head in acquiescence. She pressed her lips together and fled from the room. She had just reached the second step of the stairway when his voice stopped her. "Augusta, wait! You're not . . . not . . . ?"

She did not turn. "Not what?"

"Not going to *accept* Wivilscombe, are you?"

"*Accept Wivilscombe*?" came a voice from the hallway. Claryce, her eyes red-rimmed and her mouth swollen from a long bout of tears, came up alongside Philip and stared up at Augusta with an expression of horror. "You don't mean that Dennis offered for *you*! He *couldn't* have!"

Augusta had stood all she could bear. "He *could* and he *did*!" she declared, trembling. "And . . . And I *shall* accept him if I ch—choose . . . no matter *what* you think—*either* of you!" And, clapping her hand to her mouth, she turned abruptly, ran up the stairs and disappeared from their view.

Chapter Eighteen

KATIE, SOFTLY OPENING the door of Miss Augusta's bedroom, could not at first see anyone in the dark of the room. But just at that moment, a carriage rolled by on the street below, and its lamp threw a moving beam of light through the window, briefly lighting the girl's face as she sat on the window seat staring out into the rain. The raindrops on the pane refracted the light and seemed to etch their outlines on Augusta's still face. "Miss Augusta, you're cryin'!" Katie gasped, entering the room hurriedly and lighting a candle.

But the light of the candle revealed clearly that Augusta was *not* crying. To Katie's knowing eyes, the truth was worse. The girl looked *stricken*... as if she were beyond the solace of tears. Something had happened, and Katie had no doubt that Mr. Philip Denham had been the cause of Augusta's obvious unhappiness. From the look on the girl's face, Katie knew that she could neither tease nor chatter the pain away. The abigail sighed silently. She would not question Miss Augusta, nor would she press her to speak. *Least said, soonest mended*, she reminded herself as she knelt to light the fire.

After several minutes of absolute silence, during which Augusta did not move or show any awareness that Katie was there, the abigail spoke up. "Ain't you goin' t' dress fer dinner, love?" she asked, crossing the room and placing a gentle hand on Augusta's shoulder. "It's growin' late."

At the touch Augusta started violently. Then, blinking, she

tried to bring the abigail into focus. "Oh . . . Katie! Is it dinner time already?" She rose from the window seat, wavered and almost fell. Katie caught her in a pair of strong arms. "Miss Augusta, you're not *ill*?" she asked, alarmed.

Augusta shook her head. "No . . . just dizzy. Oh, Katie, I'm so *tired*! Do you think you could tell the family that I've decided to miss dinner and go to bed early?"

Katie nodded and led the girl to the bed, but her brow wrinkled worriedly. It was too bad that Miss Augusta would not be going down tonight. There was something about the mood of the household that was bleak and foreboding, and Katie felt that Augusta's presence at the dinner table would have held things together. But it was plain that the girl needed sleep. Her face was strangely benumbed, her eyes deeply pained, and her body suddenly began to tremble uncontrollably. Katie was well aware that Augusta had had very little sleep during the last twenty-four hours (as little as Katie had had herself)—but weariness was only part of the problem. Miss Augusta had suffered a blow, and she was still reverberating from the shock of it. "Yes, Missy," Katie said firmly as she set about undressing the girl, "bed it'll be fer you."

With gentle efficiency, she pulled the gown over Augusta's listless, unresisting arms and head, helped her to lie back against the pillows, and removed her slippers. The gentle handling seemed to melt the remnant of strength that had sustained Augusta until that moment, and her eyes filled with tears. "Oh, K–Katie," she murmured brokenly.

"There, there, my poppet," Katie whispered, brushing the girl's tears away with loving fingers, "don't you cry. Just close yer eyes and go to sleep."

Augusta, feeling completely drained of spirit, obediently closed her eyes, although tears continued to squeeze themselves out from beneath the lids. Katie tucked the coverlet all around her and sat down at the edge of the bed. "There, there," she whispered again, picking up the girl's hand and squeezing it comfortingly, "you'll feel a sight better by mornin', see if you don't."

"Nothing will be b–better by morning, Katie," Augusta sighed hopelessly, "nothing at all."

* * *

But the weather, if nothing else, had improved by morning, although the house remained as gloomy as it had been the night before. No one came down to breakfast, and the servants moved about on tiptoe, as if dire illness had fallen upon the house. The first noise of life was heard a little after ten, when Letty's carriage drew up at the door. There was the usual bustle to admit her, but Hinson, seeing her pale cheeks and drawn expression, refrained from his usual welcoming chatter. "Good morning, Lady Denham," he said in a low voice. "Her ladyship is in the upstairs sitting—"

"Yes, I know," Letty said brusquely and ran up the stairs. As she expected, she found her mother stretched on the sofa with the usual cloth over her eyes and both Katie and Miss Dorrimore hovering over her. "Oh, Mama, not again!" Letty exclaimed in spite of herself, her usual patience having deserted her of late.

"I can't help it," her mother moaned, lifting a corner of the wet cloth from one eye and peeping up at her eldest daughter dolefully. "Gussie has taken to her bed, Claryce is locked in her room and not seeing a soul, and even *Neddie* is mooning about the house as if he's lost his last friend. If it weren't for Prue's darling little baby having been born hale and hearty, I should be quite at my wit's end!"

"Good Lord, what's happened to everyone?" Letty asked, dropping into a chair. "When I saw you at Prue's house yesterday, everything seemed to be in order. How could a series of crises have descended on all of you so *suddenly?*"

Lady Glendenning launched into a tearful and barely-coherent account of the events at the dinner table the previous evening, during which Claryce had accused the absent Gussie of maligning her to Lord Garvey and stealing Wivilscombe from under her nose. Her accusations had disturbed Neddie, who'd fired up in the most unusual way and stormed at everyone quite violently. All this had done much to overset Lady Glendenning's nerves, and when she'd learned that Augusta had taken to her bed because of what seemed to have been a quarrel with Philip, it was more than a high-strung mother could be expected to bear. "I have *never* been strong," she said, sniffling into her handkerchief in self-pity, "and having to *agonize* over the indiscretions of th–three of my children all at *once* has completely undone me!"

Letty was more bewildered than enlightened by her mother's account, but she knew better than to pursue the subject further with her distraught parent. She got up from her chair and offered to talk to all three of her troublesome siblings. This seemed to give some comfort to her mother and, with a speaking look at Katie, Letty left the room. Katie quietly followed her out. "What is going *on*, Katie?" Letty asked her bluntly when they'd closed the door behind them. "I can't make head nor tail of my mother's story."

Katie studied Letty's face shrewdly. "I might ask the same o' you, m' lady. Seems to me that *you* ain't lookin' too sharp yerself."

"Never mind about me. What's wrong with Gussie?"

Katie shrugged. "It ain't fer me t' say, but I'd go bail she's 'ad a nasty shock."

Letty frowned worriedly. "Was it Philip? I thought it was only *Mama* who was foolish enough to raise her expectations in that direction. I *told* Mama it was only friendship. Perhaps I should have warned Gussie, too, that—"

"I never 'eard o' no words what could keep a 'eart from goin' where it pleased," Katie said flatly.

Letty gave the little abigail a piercing, appreciative stare. "Yes, you're quite right, as always. What do you think we can do?"

"If I knowed the answer to that, I'd a done it. But it won't 'urt fer you t' speak to 'er. She always set the 'ighest store by 'er sister Letty."

Letty nodded and set off down the hall. When she entered her sister's room, however, she found Augusta fully dressed and quite in control of herself.

"*Letty*," Augusta said with an eager smile, "I didn't know you were here! Have you breakfasted?"

"Yes, I have. I've come to have a talk with you, Gussie. What's this about taking to your bed?"

"Oh, it was nothing. I had a most eventful day yesterday, after being up all night with Prue, and it wearied me. But, as Katie predicted, I'm feeling much better this morning."

Letty looked at her sister suspiciously. "Are you *sure*? You look a little peaked, if you—"

Before she could pursue the subject with her sister, the door burst open and Claryce stormed in, wrapped in a morning robe, her hair disheveled and deep circles under her eyes. "Ah, *Letty*," she exclaimed with restrained fury, "I'm glad *you're* here, too! I want you to hear what I have to say to Gussie. Perhaps, if *you're* a witness, *someone* will believe me!"

"Good heavens, Claryce, calm yourself," Letty said placatingly. "I've not seen you in such a state since you were a child of thirteen and you'd discovered that Prue had eaten your sweets."

"Well, this is a bit more important than sweets! *Tell* her, Gussie, what you said to Garvey about me!"

Augusta gaped in surprise. "I didn't say *anything* to Lord Garvey about—"

"You *see*? Everyone thinks Gussie is such a *paragon*, but she's as much a liar as—"

"Come now, Claryce," Letty cautioned, urging Claryce to sit down on the bed, "you know Gussie doesn't lie."

Claryce shook off Letty's hand, refusing to be seated. "But she *is* lying! She hinted to Garvey that I'd been telling the world he'd made shocking advances to me at the Cranshaws' ball. You *did*, didn't you, you liar! *Admit* it!"

"I didn't even *know* Lord Garvey had made shocking advances," Augusta assured her. "But . . . wait . . . I *did* say something to him which may have—"

Claryce hooted in triumph. "See? I *told* you!"

"All I said," Augusta explained calmly, "was that I knew a secret about him. I had no *idea* that he would assume I was referring to such an intimate incident as that."

Claryce put her hands on her hips in an attitude of decided belligerence. "What secret *were* you referring to?" she demanded.

Augusta blushed. "Well, there *was* no secret, actually . . ."

Letty was bewildered. "No secret? Then why did you say you *knew* one?"

Claryce dropped down on the bed in disgust. "It's just as I said. Anyone can tell this is all a hum. Why would anyone say she had a secret if she had *none*?"

"It was only a bit of stratagem," Augusta explained, "though I must admit it seems quite silly now."

"A stratagem?" Letty asked.

"Yes. To give me something as a subject for conversation when I was at a loss. It was intended only as a harmless bit of flirtation, which Philip suggested as a means to—"

"Philip?" Claryce echoed with disdain, jumping up from the bed and striding about the room angrily. "I might have guessed. Ever since that man has been calling on Gussie, she's been behaving completely unlike herself. I blame him for this entire—"

"It wasn't Philip's fault," Augusta said in his defense. "He was only trying to help me to make easy conversation."

"And I suppose it wasn't his fault that Denny made you an offer!" Claryce said sullenly, throwing herself upon the window seat and staring out in chagrin. "He's been pushing you in *that* direction from the first."

"Good Lord!" Letty exclaimed, her eyes widening. "*Did* Wivilscombe make you an offer?"

"Well, it was only on an impulse. I don't refine on it—"

"*I* refine on it!" Claryce muttered glumly. "He never behaved the least bit impulsively toward *me*."

Letty stared at Claryce in surprise. "Did *you* wish for an offer from him, Claryce?"

Claryce glared at her and then seemed to collapse. With a pathetic tremor, she covered her face with her hands. "I've been waiting for *weeks* for him to . . . to . . ."

Augusta felt a surge of sympathy. She went up to her sister and pulled her hands away from her face. Large tears were running down the younger girl's cheeks. "Do you *love* him then?" she asked intently.

Claryce merely nodded and turned her head away.

Letty could hardly believe her ears. "But I thought you wanted only to collect swains and play the coquette!"

"Yes, that's wh—what *everyone* thinks of m—me!" Claryce said bitterly, turning away and staring out of the window again. "Glassheart Glendenning—I've heard that name used behind my back! Well, everyone is quite wrong. I *do* have a heart . . . and Augusta and her Philip have schemed so well that they've . . . b—broken it!"

"Oh, dear!" Letty, appalled, looked from one sister to the other. "Do you *both* want to marry Wivilscombe?" she asked in horror.

Augusta sat down beside Claryce and put an arm across her shoulder. "I don't love Mr. Wivilscombe, my dear. I'm sure that you and he can—"

Claryce turned a chastened face to her sister. "He doesn't want me any m—more," she said morosely. "It's *you* he wants. He talks about you all the time. Ever since Philip turned you into a *femme fatale*, Dennis has been noticing you. It's all Philip Denham's fault! Why couldn't he have left you the way you were? I liked you a great deal better before."

Her anger again aroused, she got up and stalked to the door. Throwing it open, she declared, "I blame Philip Denham for this whole muddle!"

She turned to leave and came face-to-face with Ned, who'd just come along the corridor with the intention of knocking at Augusta's door. "*What* muddle do you blame Philip for?" he asked curiously, looking at each of his sisters in surprise. "What's amiss here?"

"Ask your precious Gussie!" Claryce snapped, brushing by him. She dashed off down the corridor to her room and slammed the door.

Ned shook his head as he looked after her and then entered Augusta's room. In a very few moments he learned the reason for Claryce's emotional outburst. And while he had to agree with Augusta that Claryce had exaggerated Philip's responsibility for the problem, he *did* feel that *part* of the blame could be placed at his friend's door. "It was an unwitting result of your little game, Gussie, but it *does* stem directly from Philip's gambling and his need to pay off his debts." He lowered his head and added in a glum undertone, "Even *my* heartache can be traced to the same source."

"*Your* heartache?" Letty's head came up sharply, and the two sisters exchanged puzzled glances. "What's happened to *you*?"

Ned had come upstairs to seek sisterly advice and did not need a great deal of urging to unfold his tale of his confrontations with the wild and unpredictable Lucy Greland. His sisters listened to him in stunned fascination, for neither of them had had an inkling of his recent adventures. It was quite astounding to realize that their conventional, meticulous brother could have experienced so romantic an encounter with a young woman who was apparently his exact opposite in temperament.

"I find the experience most puzzling to contemplate," Ned said when he'd concluded his narration. "What do you think Lucy meant when she asked me to return after I could understand the import of our conversation?"

"I'm not certain," Letty said thoughtfully. "What do *you* make of it, Gussie?"

Augusta studied her brother's face. "Have you fallen in love with her, Neddie?" she asked softly.

Ned stuffed his hands in his pockets and reddened. "Yes, I think I have," he admitted.

"And did she, in all your conversations, ever ask who the gentleman was for whom you were making the proposal?"

"No, never."

"Then I think you should go to her, Neddie, and tell her

how you feel," she suggested. To Augusta, Lady Lucia's enigmatic remark was not at all mysterious. It was *Ned himself* who'd interested her. But she had evidently believed that Ned should perceive this fact for himself.

"I *couldn't* go to her," Ned said unhappily, wandering about the room in moody abstraction. "If I tell her that I continued to see her on my *own* account, while hiding behind the ruse of arranging a marriage for Philip, she will think me an even greater idiot than she now believes I am."

"Well, you know best, of course," Letty said with tender sympathy. "If you believe that you started off with the lady on the wrong footing, and it is too late now to correct matters—"

He nodded despairingly. "I'm afraid it is." He began to chew his moustache nervously—a mannerism his sisters knew he indulged in only when he was in the lowest of spirits—and wandered to the door. "If only I had let Philip solve his *own* problems, I wouldn't be in this fix," he muttered bitterly.

If only Philip had been man enough to deal with his problems by himself, Augusta realized with a painful shock, *a number of the Glendennings would be better off this morning!*

When Ned had taken his disconsolate leave, Letty sank down on the window seat, stared out at the windswept blue of the sky and sighed deeply. "I seem to have heard nothing but insoluble problems all morning. For all the good I've done, I might have saved myself the trip." She looked across the room at Augusta, who had dropped down on the bed and was resting her head wearily against the bedpost. "And I have yet to hear what it is that's troubling *you*."

"I've told you, Letty, my love," Augusta responded, attempting without much success to give her a reassuring smile, "that I'm only a bit tired. If you ask me, I'd say that *you* look more peaked than I do."

"Do I?" She turned back to the window uneasily, feeling unequal to facing her sister's steady gaze. "You're only saying that to try to shift attention away from yourself."

But Letty's unease was not lost on Augusta. She rose from the bed and crossed the room in quick strides. "I may have intended to do so," she admitted, grasping Letty's shoulders and turning her face up, "but I think I've stumbled on the truth." Her brows drew together in sudden concern. "There *is* something wrong with you, *isn't* there! Look at me, Letty! What *is* it?"

Letty tried bravely to meet her eyes. "*Nothing*, I tell..." But her throat seemed suddenly to burn her, and her eyes filled with tears. "Oh, Gussie," she cried, sagging against her sister in surrender, "I'm so utterly *miserable*."

Augusta knelt on the floor beside Letty and put her arms around her. "Letty, it *can't* be as dreadful as that. *Tell* me, my dearest!"

Slowly, trying vainly to keep her voice steady, Letty revealed to her sister the story of Roger's separation from her. Aware that Gussie knew all about Philip's debt, she was able to confide the entire tale without feeling that she was betraying a confidence. She poured out every detail, from the hatching of her matchmaking scheme to Roger's withdrawal from their former, blissful intimacy. "He barely even *speaks* to me any more," she admitted despairingly, "and I don't know what to do to win him back."

Augusta rose and sat down beside her sister, her eyes clouded. "It's *Philip's* fault," she said after a moment of silence. "It was thoughtless and selfish of him to ask you to keep his secret from Roger."

"It was thoughtless of *both* of us, I suppose," Letty sighed, "but I can readily sympathize with Philip's reluctance to face Roger with the truth. There's something so ... so *upright* about Roger, you know, that makes one utterly shamed to face him with one's own transgressions." She gave a deep, trembling sigh and took her sister's hand. "I feel better for having told you, Gussie. Thank you for lending an ear, my love ... especially when you obviously have troubles of your own."

After Letty had left, Augusta remained on the window seat, her head whirling with all that she'd heard. Everyone in her family (except Prue, of course, who was too absorbed with the bliss and cares of new motherhood to be aware of the chaotic adventures of the rest of the family) was sunk in misery, and somewhere at the bottom of each tragic circumstance was *Philip Denham!*

Yesterday she'd believed she'd sunk to the lowest point it was possible to reach, but now she found that she was more deeply shocked and tormented than she'd been before. Until this moment, Philip had remained in her imagination as the most charming, the most attractive, the most *perfect* of mortals. She'd idealized him beyond human capacity ... but now it was plain that her idol had feet of clay. Claryce was suffering from a blighted romance, Ned had made a fool of himself before the first woman he'd ever loved, and—worst of all!—Letty's perfect marriage had been badly damaged . . . and all because Philip had not been able to solve his gambling problems for himself! She still loved him with a futile fervor—despite what he'd done or how flawed his character—but she couldn't blind herself to the fact that the flaws were there.

A slow tear trickled down her cheek at the recognition that her idealized Philip no longer existed . . . and could never exist again. The man she loved was thoughtless, selfish, weak, addicted to gambling and not in the least in love with her. And she was further depressed by the sudden knowledge that in spite of all, she loved him anyway . . . perhaps even more than before. The human, flawed Philip was even more deeply imbedded in her soul than the idealized one had been.

Even more troubling to her spirit was the awareness that it had been she, Letty and Ned—all of them—who'd aided and abetted Philip in his weaknesses of character. Instead of helping him to grow, to mature, to strengthen his character, they had merely made it easy for him to continue as he was. Because of his charm and natural attractiveness, they had all unwittingly excused or ignored his flaws and tried to smooth the path for him. And in the end, it had not been Philip who had paid the price for his weakness of character—the price had been paid by all the rest of them!

This could not go on! She couldn't bear to think that Philip might grow even worse with the years. She couldn't really love him and permit him to go on in this self-indulgent way. His flaws had, directly or indirectly, caused a number of painful consequences to a number of people, and something had to be done about them.

She wiped her cheek with the back of her hand, her back stiffening in strong resolve. *Some* of those consequences could be corrected or repaired. Although she didn't know how those repairs could be contrived, she did know *one* thing—she had to see to it that *Philip himself* would be the one to set things right.

Chapter Nineteen

LETTY ENTERED HER home with a firm, purposeful swing to her step. Something had happened to her since she'd given Augusta the account of her dire circumstances: she'd become angry. She'd spoken those words aloud, and her misdeeds had not sounded so very dreadful to her ears. True, she had attempted to sell the emerald pendant. And true, she'd kept the secret from Roger. But she'd not done either of those things for selfish benefit. They had been done for a good cause—Roger's own brother's welfare had been at stake! So why was she skulking about the house in shamed silence, as if she'd commited some heinous crime like bedding the second footman or dissipating the money on smuggled rum?

She pulled off her bonnet, threw it impatiently on the hall table and strode directly to the library, where she knew she would find Roger reading his newspaper. "Good afternoon, my love," she greeted him cheerily.

Roger couldn't hide his surprise. He and his wife had, of late, been avoiding each other as much as possible and speaking to each other in only the most low-voiced and necessary monosyllables. He raised his eyebrows and looked up at her questioningly.

"I wish to speak to you, Roger, and I'd be obliged if you'd

put down the *Times* in order to favor me with your full attention," she announced briskly.

"Oh?" he queried, lowering the paper. "Don't tell me that you've decided to confide in me at last." The dryness of his tone did not completely hide a distinct tinge of hopeful anticipation in his voice.

"No, I won't tell you that, for, as I've said before, I *cannot* confide in you on this matter."

His face darkened. "Then I don't see what there is to speak about, ma'am," he said and lifted the paper again.

"There is a *great deal* to speak about," she countered firmly, snatching the newspaper from his grasp and flinging it aside. "I've been playing the role of *guilty little mouse* for much too long. Look at me, Roger! I am, and always have been, a faithful, loving wife to you. I know I did a dreadful thing in trying to come by a large sum of money without discussing it with you, but I give you my word that I did not use the funds for anything reprehensible. I am very sorry that I cannot tell you more, but—"

"There is no *but*, my dear. As I've told *you* before, it is not the money which troubles me. It is the fact that you cannot trust me enough to share with me your secret needs."

She knelt beside his chair and looked up at him earnestly. "I *haven't* any secret needs, Roger. There is *nothing* about me you don't know! I swear it!"

"Then, why—?"

"It is not *my* secret to share," she answered simply.

He stared at her for a moment, the look in his eyes telling her how much he wished things could be otherwise, but his mouth was set and adamant. "We have gone round this path before. I don't see that there is anything more to be said. If you cannot *trust* me, then our marriage has been a sham from the first."

She stood up in angry defiance. "If you intend to maintain that stubborn intractability, Roger, then *indeed* there is no more to be said. But I warn you that I can no longer live this way. Each day the crack in my heart grows wider. If you'll not change your mind, I shall take the children and return to my mother's house."

She put her chin up and walked proudly to the door. There she paused and, with her pulse racing in trepidation, made a last attempt to win him back. "You speak of my trust in *you*," she said, unable to keep the tremor from her voice, "but should trust not flow in *both* directions? Why should you demand trust from me when you are obviously unwilling to give any to *me*? If our four years together had any meaning at all, they should have made it clear to you that I am as deserving of your trust as you are of mine."

He shut his eyes in pain and couldn't seem to answer.

"Roger!" she cried, agonized. "Do you *wish* me to leave you?"

"Oh, God, Letty," he muttered, his voice choked with emotion, "I couldn't *bear* it if you left me." He rose slowly from his chair and held out his arms to her.

That admission was all she needed. Flying across the room, she threw herself into his arms. "Oh, my dearest, does this mean you *will* trust me, then?"

"Yes," he murmured, his arms tightening around her and his lips in her hair. "Yes, yes, *yes*! *Nothing* can be worth another day without you."

He held her against him for a long while, letting himself grow accustomed to a new, ambivalent sort of joy. She was sobbing in his arms, her happiness and relief providing ample evidence of the depth of her affection. He knew he had made a surrender . . . that there had been a battle which *he* had lost. But no victory would have given him this heart-wrenching consolation, this intense feeling of joyful deliverance. Their marriage might never again be the unscarred diamond it had been before—he'd always be aware that there was some part of her which was closed to him—but their love had survived. Perhaps the knowledge that it *could* survive the darkness of suspicion and separation was a better reality than the precarious perfection of the earlier time. As her arms stole up about his neck, he lifted her face to his, banished all misgivings from his mind, and permitted himself to yield to the very considerable delights of complete surrender.

*   *   *

Philip wanted very much to have a talk with Augusta, but he was almost afraid to attempt it. He'd always been considered a fellow of remarkable daring, but this time, when it meant so much to him, his tendency toward swashbuckling behavior seemed to have deserted him. He'd really made a mull of it

during his last interview with the girl. He'd tried to tell her
how she'd grown in his esteem . . . how wrong he'd been to try
to change the lovely creature she was . . . but his words had not
seemed to convey those thoughts to her. He'd made her believe,
somehow, that she'd *failed* him—and that was the very last
thing in the world he'd meant to do.

He spent most of the day following that interview in wandering about his rooms in unhappy restlessness, not wishing
to go out to his usual haunts or indulge in his usual pursuits.
By late afternoon, however, the rooms seemed like a prison.
He would go and face her, he decided. He could no longer bear
this self-imposed inaction.

He arrived at the Glendenning house in a chaotic state of
mind. His feelings had, all day, been alternating between high
hopes and bleak despair. His usually rational mind had been
unable to control the extreme swing of his ambivalent expectations. One moment he convinced himself that his dreams
would come true—that she would fall into his arms as soon
as he declared his love for her; the next moment he was certain
that she would refuse even to *see* him. He was soon to learn
that neither his dreams nor his fears would prove to be pro-
phetic.

She *did* agree to see him. She joined him in the downstairs
sitting room where so many of their previous encounters had
taken place. "I'm glad you've come, Philip. There's something
I must say to you," she said as soon as she'd closed the door.

Her face was pale and her tone quite serious, and he found
himself gripped with the same fear that had overwhelmed him
the day before. "You're not going to wed *Wivilscombe*?" he
asked, aghast.

"No, I'm not," she responded flatly, sitting down on the
sofa, "but that is not the subject I wish to discuss."

"Good," he said in relief, taking a seat beside her. "There's
something I've been wanting to say to you, too, Augusta. I
tried to explain yesterday, but—"

"If what you want to say has anything to do with that confounded wager, Philip, I don't want to hear it. It has been the
cause of more difficulty for me and my family than you can
imagine."

"Difficulty? I don't understand."

"That's what I've come down to tell you." She glanced at
him with a mixture of apprehension and determination. "But

before I do, I want you to know that I say these things with the greatest reluctance. I don't wish to give you the impression that I'm ungrateful for all your efforts in my behalf . . ."

Philip found himself growing tense. This preamble was making him feel decidedly uneasy. "There's no need for reluctance," he said, attempting to reassure her with a smile that he knew was lacking in conviction. "Please feel free to say whatever you like."

"Thank you. I'll be as brief and blunt as possible. It's the damnable wager, you see. Because of it, almost everyone in my family has had to pay a price. Did you know, for example, that Letty and Roger have had a very serious falling out because you made her promise not to tell your brother a word about your debts?"

Her words struck him like a blow. "No, I had no *idea*—"

"It's quite true, however. And although I believe *that* to be the *worst* consequence of the events leading from your falling into debt, there are others. Ned, in trying to arrange an advantageous marriage for you, has incurred the lasting enmity of a young lady for whom he seems to care a great deal."

"He tried to arrange a *marriage*? For *me*? But *I* never—!"

"And even *Claryce* has been affected. Did you realize that, in trying to play our little game with Dennis Wivilscombe's affections, we've managed to break Claryce's heart?"

"Are you saying she really *cares* for him? But I thought—"

"I know. None of us suspected that Claryce's heart was truly engaged."

Philip stared at her. Her words were swirling around in his brain in a confusion of inchoate but stinging significances. What was the *meaning* of all this? "Are you trying to say, Augusta, that *I* am to blame for *all these*—?"

"I'm not speaking of blame." She clenched her hands, trying to keep them from trembling. It was very painful to try to tell the man she loved that he was not a very admirable person. "I'm merely trying to say that this little scheme of ours was ill-considered and thoughtless from the start."

The muscles in his face tensed tightly. "It is kind of you to say 'our' scheme. But the wager was never *your* idea." He stood up and looked down at her. "What you're really saying is that it is *I* who am thoughtless and inconsiderate, isn't that it?"

She could feel her underlip begin to tremble. If she tried

to answer, she knew her voice would choke, so she merely shook her head in woebegone assent.

"I see." Philip was stunned. None of what she was saying was quite clear to him. Only *one* impression was making itself felt in the fog of emotions which were muddling his brain—she despised him! "You *are* blaming me, then?" he said, his face whitening.

"It . . . it's not a question of blame, Philip," she repeated, her voice as choked as she feared it would be. "I only want you to see the consequences of your acts . . ."

He felt a rush of anger. He knew it was an irrational, almost deranged reaction to the confusion of his feelings, but he couldn't seem to help himself. His dreams of declaring his love for her and gathering her into his arms in a jubilant embrace had come crashing down about his ears like a destructive avalanche. She *did* despise him—she had just said it! Nothing else of what she'd said was clear. How could he think of Claryce, or Ned . . . or even Letty . . . when he seemed to be standing, bewildered and bruised, amid the wreckage of his own life? His anger was the instinctive reaction of the wounded man for self-protection.

He glared down at her, a red flush replacing the pallor of his cheeks and his hands tightening into fists. "The consequences of *my* acts, ma'am? Does that analysis seem like a fair one to you? I admit to being a bit muddled about the details, but it seems to me that blame can be placed at *other* doors more easily than at mine. If Ned has made a muddle of an encounter with a female whose identity *I* don't even *know*, it was certainly not at *my* instigation. If Claryce's flirtations caused her to lose a man she'd come to care for, I don't see how the blame is *mine*. And even Letty's situation, no matter how closely it touches me, would not have come about if Letty had not *insisted*— But I speak to no purpose. It is plain that you've already assigned the blame where you find it appropriate. If that is your assessment of my character, so be it. Now that I know what you think of me, you may be assured that I shall not inflict my presence on you again! Good day, ma'am."

"B–but, Philip, wait—! I didn't mean—"

He hardly heard her, so great was the angry roaring in his ears. He strode to the door and slammed it behind him before the words left her lips. She stared at the door, appalled. She had not expected to win any *love* for her attempt to criticize his character, but she'd not anticipated a response like *that*. She'd infuriated him without having achieved any benefit to his character or to the various situations she was hoping he'd try to correct.

Slowly, the surprise she felt at his anger and abrupt departure gave way to an all-enveloping misery. She'd lost him. *I shall not inflict my presence on you again!* he'd said. His daily visits, their shared laughter, the comfortable companionship, the heady nearness, the exhilaration of the game—all were gone. She wanted to run after him. She wanted to throw herself down full length on the sofa and weep. She wanted to run away somewhere . . . far, far away from London, far from society and far from her suffering family . . . and hide.

But she didn't move. She sat absolutely still, staring at the closed door with wide, dry eyes. Nothing in her face revealed her inner devastation. If anyone had seen her, he would have likened her appearance to that of a marble statue—white, cold and totally devoid of feeling.

Chapter Twenty

TWO DAYS PASSED before Philip was able to think clearly about his conversation with Augusta, but by that time he began to see that there was some justice in her accusation. It had been *he* who'd fallen into debt, and that debt had embroiled her entire family—as well as Augusta herself—in his affairs. If he'd kept his own counsel and had attempted to work out his own solution, none of the problems which now faced them would have occurred. He was, at least in part, responsible for their present dilemmas.

The more he thought about it, the more he realized that Augusta was right to have found him weak and selfish. He had let *his* problem become *theirs*. If he had any character at all, he should now make *their* problems his. After all, what was done could sometimes be undone. And if he could straighten out the situations in which they now found themselves, perhaps Augusta would despise him less. Before he would attempt to see her again—and he knew, in spite of what he'd said to her, that he *had* to see her again, no matter what it would cost him—he'd do what he could to mend matters.

There were many details he still had to learn about their various situations, and he'd have to do some careful thinking and planning, but he was sure that he could set *some* of the matters aright. Before another day went by, he'd made his plans. Then he washed, dressed and made for his stables. He had a great deal to do, and he wanted to do it in the shortest time possible.

The first call he made was on Dennis Wivilscombe. Dennis lived in a luxurious suite of rooms just off St. James, and the butler who admitted Philip to the apartments was attired in a manner which bespoke a household of considerable affluence. After delivering Philip's card to his master, the butler returned and informed Philip that Mr. Wivilscombe was dressing to go out but was willing to see Mr. Denham in his dressing room if Mr. Denham would not object to so informal a meeting. Mr. Denham did not object and was therefore ushered into the richly-paneled room in which Dennis readied himself for the world.

Dennis was sitting in a chair having his moustache trimmed by a small, efficient and energetic valet. "How do, Denham?" Wivilscombe said in greeting. "Hope you don't mind my not getting up, but Wagnall, here, is engaged in a most delicate operation. If he becomes perturbed, he may make one side of my moustache shorter than the other."

"Well, I'd hoped we might speak privately," Philip suggested awkwardly.

"I'm quite finished, sir," the valet said, whipping away the towel that he'd placed around Dennis's neck and holding up a mirror for his employer's approval.

"This isn't going to take long, is it, old fellow? I'm due to dine at White's at nine."

"Not very long," Philip assured him.

The valet bowed himself out. "Now, then, Denham, out with it. You look as if you're about to announce the demise of the King."

Philip threw him a quick grin. "No, nothing at all like that. I've come to make a confession to you. But first, I hope you won't take it amiss if I ask you frankly if you've lost your heart to Augusta Glendenning."

Wivilscombe looked at him in shocked abhorrence. "Yes, I *do* take it amiss. None of your affair, as far as I can see."

"It *is* my affair in a way. She told me that you'd made her an offer."

"Did she? Well, since you know that much, shouldn't it be *obvious* that I've lost my heart to her?"

"No, not necessarily. Augusta seems to have the impression that it's her sister *Claryce* whom you care for."

Dennis, who'd busied himself tying his neckcloth while they spoke, spun around from the mirror and stared at Philip in red-faced irritation. "Did Augusta tell you *that*, too? I hadn't thought of you as a gossip, Denham."

"I'm sorry, Wivilscombe. This is deucedly awkward. But it may be my fault that you offered for Augusta, you see, and I thought it only right that I come to set things straight."

"Your fault?" Wivilscombe's eyebrows rose disdainfully. "It seems to me that you're touched in your upper works. How could *you* have had anything to do with that? I made the offer on an impulse of my own."

Philip put a hand to his forehead. It wasn't easy trying to be a Good Samaritan. "Yes, of course you did . . . but you see, I'd made a wager that you *would* offer for Augusta, and she was helping me to win it . . ."

"Are you trying to say . . . and I can't believe you're serious about this . . . that I was *tricked* into it? You know, Denham, that I've been dealing with female trickery for more years than I care to count—before *you* were free of leading-strings, I dare say. It isn't very likely that—"

"No, it isn't *likely*. Augusta was completely taken aback by your proposal, so your offer may not have *anything at all* to do with the tricks I taught her, but—"

"Taught her tricks, did you?" Dennis regarded Philip with a combination of bewilderment and amusement. "Wish I could follow what it is you're trying to say, old man. If she didn't trick me, then what is it you're trying so maladroitly to confess?"

"I *am* bungling this, I know. But, dash it all, Wivilscombe, it's not easy to speak to you on a subject of such intimacy."

Wivilscombe, affected by Philip's ingenuous outburst, dropped his antagonistic air. "Sorry, old fellow, I didn't mean to make you uncomfortable. I'm quite fascinated. Do go on and make your confession."

"Well, then, to put it simply, Augusta is disturbed about the incident. Even though she hadn't put our plan concerning you into effect, she nevertheless had *intended* to do so. Therefore, she is quite guilt-ridden about having received your offer. And since *I* was the instigator of the plot, I felt that I should come and explain."

"But I still don't understand. If she's won you your wager

without using her trickeries, why should she feel guilty?"

"Because of her sister, you see."

"Her sister? *Claryce*?" Dennis, about to pull on his coat, seemed to freeze. "What has *she* to do with this?"

"It seems she's quite beside herself over what she calls Augusta's treachery," Philip explained.

Dennis let the coat slip from his fingers to the floor. "*Beside* herself? *Claryce*?"

"So I've been given to understand."

Dennis gawked. "You don't mean it!"

Philip knelt and picked up the coat. "We . . . Augusta and I . . . didn't feel we could face ourselves—or you—without explaining—"

"Claryce is *beside* herself? I can't believe it!"

Philip didn't answer but merely helped the gaping Wivilscombe into his coat.

"So the little coquette really cares for me after all, does she?" Wivilscombe chortled, his eyes gleaming in triumph.

"I wouldn't like to say anything more in *that* regard, Wivilscombe, but it would be a very great relief to Augusta and to me if you would ask Claryce that question yourself."

Dennis peered intently into Philip's face. "Are you saying that Augusta doesn't wish to hold me to my offer?"

"I don't believe she took it very seriously. It was my impression that she would be happy to see you and Claryce make a match of it."

Dennis patted his moustache in decided satisfaction. "Well, thank you very much for telling me all this, Denham. You don't know how obliged to you I am!"

Philip grinned. "I'm equally obliged to you, I assure you. But I think I'd better not try to explain the reason for *that*. Good evening, Wivilscombe."

*   *   *

Philip next called at the house in Upper Berkeley Street, but there he was less fortunate than he'd been before—the butler informed him that Lady Lucia was not at home. It had taken a great deal of patient questioning to elicit the lady's name from Ned, and now it took more patience to elicit from the butler the information that her ladyship had gone to the opera with her aunt. Philip left the premises deep in thought, but then he broke into a smile. Jumping into his carriage, he made straight for Argyle Street. There he told Hinson to announce him, not to Augusta, but to Ned. "Put on your evening garb,

Neddie," he ordered as soon as Ned appeared on the stairs. "Hurry!"

"But why?" a bewildered Ned asked.

"Because we're going to the Haymarket. Catalani's singing *Semiramide*."

Ned shook his head and made a listless gesture with his hand. "I'm not in the mood for Catalani tonight. Philip . . . or any other diversion for that matter. Please excuse me."

But Philip would brook no objection. With a combination of cajolery, contention and command, he managed to urge his friend into the appropriate dress and pull him out the door.

When they arrived at the King's Theater, the second act was already in progress. The five tiers of boxes were filled to capacity, but there was always room in the pit for two more dandies. Philip and Ned milled about with the others until the lights went up for the intermission. "Do you see anyone here that you know?" Philip asked his friend, letting his eyes roam over the boxes.

Ned looked up and, after a brief, bored examination of the many faces looking down from the boxes, was about to shake his head when his eye fell on a familiar face in the second tier. Reddening to the ears, he turned quickly away, but not before Philip had followed his glance and had recognized Lady Lucia's distinctive face. "Ah," he remarked with elaborately casual unconcern, "there's someone *I* recognize."

"Who is it?" Ned asked, alarmed. He didn't wish to turn his head around, even though the chance of being recognized from a second-tier box among the press of people around him was quite unlikely. He had no wish to be recognized by Lucy tonight. He was not mentally or emotionally prepared to face her. What would he say? How would he behave? The best thing to do would be to hide himself behind a pillar until he could convince Philip to leave.

"It's only my . . . er . . . cousin, "Philip lied. "Do you wish to go up with me and meet her?"

"Why don't you go by yourself, Philip? I'd rather wait here."

Philip nodded. "Very well. But don't move away from this post, or I shall have difficulty in finding you again."

Philip pushed his way up the wide but overcrowded stairway and knocked at the door of Lady Lucia's box with trepidation. It had been difficult enough to speak to a gentleman like Dennis Wivilscombe about intimate matters, but to attempt such conversation with a lady whom he barely knew might be almost impossible. Nevertheless, he pushed the door open as soon as he heard a "Come in," and entered the box with apparent ease and self-confidence. Lady Lucia and her elderly aunt watched his approach with puzzled expressions. "Lady Lucia," he said, bowing over her hand, "I hope you remember me. We met at the Revingtons' ball."

The young lady looked at him blankly. "No, I'm afraid I—"

"Young Denham, isn't it?" the elderly lady interjected. "I knew your mother very well. I'm Charlotte Greland."

Philip gave her a broad smile, feeling quite relieved that *someone* had recognized him. "Yes, Lady Greland. I've heard my mother speak of you."

"Do you wish to see me about something, Mr. Denham?" Lucy asked curiously.

"Well, yes," Philip hesitated, realizing that he could not ask to see Lucy alone and that it would be very awkward to broach his subject under the aunt's interested scrutiny. "There's something I'd like very much to . . . er . . . tell you."

The two ladies exchanged glances. Neither one of them knew Philip Denham at all well, but they had both heard of him. His reputation was not that of a shy, hesitant fellow, yet that is how he appeared at this moment. "Well, out with it, boy," the aunt urged impatiently.

It seemed to Philip that, having gone this far, there was nothing for it but to plunge in. "I wish to inform you, ma'am, that it is *I* in whose interest Ned Glendenning came to see you."

Lady Lucia stiffened. "Is that so?" she said, her eyebrows raised and her expression growing cold. "How very interesting." She looked him over in icy appraisal. "I hope you're not under the impression, Mr. Denham, that I have any intention of even *considering* Lord Glendenning's ridiculous suggestion."

"What suggestion?" her aunt inquired, her bright, bird-like eyes flitting from one to the other. "What are you two talking about?"

"Nothing important, Aunt Charlotte. Mr. Denham's friend had once made a foolish suggestion that Mr. Denham and I might make a match of it. I told Lord Glendenning *then*, as I tell you *now*, Mr. Denham, that a more ludicrous proposal I've never heard."

"Oh, I don't know about that," Charlotte Greland murmured, casting an approving glance over the attractive young man standing beside her. "He seems a personable-enough candidate. Good family and all that."

Philip colored but managed a grin. "Thank you, your ladyship, but I haven't come to push *my* suit. You see, my friend changed his mind as soon as he came to know Lady Lucia. He realized that I was not nearly good enough for a lady of her quality—"

Lucy peered at him intently. "Is *that* what Ned told you?"

"Yes, ma'am. The more he learned about you, the more he realized he'd made a dreadful mistake."

"Then why didn't he *tell* me that?" the girl demanded irritably.

"Well, having made the proposal, you see, he didn't know how to retract it without giving you offense."

"Your friend Ned is a fool. And so I told him," Lucy said in disgust.

"Not usually, ma'am, if I may take the liberty of contradicting you. I have always found him the very best of fellows, and one of the most sensible men I've ever met. Sometimes, when a man very much admires a lady, he behaves in uncharacteristic ways, you know."

"Did Ned tell you he very much admires me?" Lady Lucia asked, a little light flickering up in her eyes.

"Yes, he did. And you can ask him yourself, if you wish. He's right downstairs at this very moment."

"What? *Here?*" For the first time since the conversation began, the young woman seemed to lose some of her composure.

"How delightful," the aunt declared, watching her niece with her shrewd, bird-like eyes. "Bring him up here at once, Denham. I want to have a look at the fellow who can discompose this niece of mine."

"Don't be silly, Aunt Charlotte," Lucy said, a blush tinging her cheek under its tan. "The third act will begin in a moment."

"Then you can speak to your Ned in the corridor, while *this* charming young buck keeps me company. Does that plan meet with your approval, Denham?"

He grinned at the crusty old lady warmly. "It certainly does, your ladyship. I'll bring him back in a moment."

But it was more than a moment before he was able to drag a white-faced, uneasy Ned to the door of the box. It took all of Philip's powers of persuasion to convince Ned that he had no choice but to make his greetings to the ladies in the box. The third act of *Semiramide* was well under way by the time Philip took Lucy's seat beside Lady Greland and Lucy left the box to confront Ned in the corridor.

"I . . . I never meant to disturb you like this," Ned said in awkward embarrassment.

"I'm not disturbed. I don't much care for Catalani anyway." She glanced at Ned's face with the disconcerting glimmmer of amusement back in her eyes. "So it was Philip Denham you'd picked out for me. I suppose I can't feel great offense at that. My Aunt Charlotte thinks he's a perfectly adequate candidate."

Ned chewed his moustache nervously. "Do you think so, too? Is *that* why you wished to see me . . . to tell me you've changed your mind?"

"No. I'd rather choose my *own* suitors, if you don't mind."

"Yes, you're quite right. I never should have tried to—"

"At least you finally understand *that*." She cocked her head and grinned at him. "Mr. Denham tells me that you're usually a man of very good sense."

"I'm glad that *someone* finds me so," Ned said ruefully.

"He says that you may have seemed foolish because you . . . as he put it . . . very much admire me."

Ned took a deep breath. "I don't admire you, Lucy. I love you."

Lucy's eyes flew to his face, all their teasing glint gone. "*Do* you, Neddie? Then why were you trying so hard to push me into the arms of someone else?"

"Only because . . . I was afraid you . . . thought so little of me."

She put a hand on his arm. "Oh, you *gudgeon*, are you *still* so thick-headed? I only became interested in your proposal in the first place because I thought you were speaking for *yourself*!"

For a moment, all Ned could do was gape at her. Then the import of her words swept over him, and, like a man in a dream, he took her slowly in his arms. "Oh, Lucy, my dearest," he whispered into her hair, "if only you knew how long . . . how *very* long it's been . . . that I've *wanted* to speak for myself!"

Chapter Twenty-One

WITH A NOTICE on its way to the *Times* announcing the forth-coming nuptials of Lady Lucia Greland to Edward Lord Glen-denning, and with Claryce happily revealing to all the world that she'd captured Dennis Wivilscombe, the elusive Seal him-self, Philip had but one task left before he could present himself to Augusta with his conscience clear: he had to repay Letty the full amount of the wager he'd failed to win.

Philip knew that his most important task of all was to mend the rift in Letty's and Roger's marriage. The only way he could think of to accomplish that task was to present Letty with the entire sum she'd given him, thus enabling her to give the full amount to Roger. Philip still couldn't bring himself to admit to Roger that he'd gambled away so huge a sum, but he was convinced that the mere act of repayment was all that was needed to solve Letty's problem.

Of course, *his* problem was to find the money, and for that he turned to the very method he'd used for so long to accumulate funds—the gaming table. He sold his last asset—the diamond ring his mother had given him—and arranged to meet Shackle-ford for a long-delayed return match of piquet. He'd felt severe misgivings about selling the ring, for it had been held dear by both his parents, but he'd not permitted himself to dwell on that. He could not permit Letty and Roger to suffer on his account. The loss of the ring would be made bearable if the money it had brought re-stimulated his luck at the gaming table. Only by gambling could he increase the sum the ring had brought sufficiently to make it possible to repay Letty, and only by repaying Letty would it be possible to face Augusta again.

The word spread throughout Watier's that Shackleford and Denham were about to resume their long-standing battle at the card table, and, by the time the two sat down opposite each other, a large crowd had gathered to watch. Although the sentiment was almost completely in Denham's favor, the side bets were quite evenly divided. The bettors may have *wished* to see Denham give Shackleford a trouncing, but many of them didn't dare put their put their money on a man who'd been, when he last played, on a losing streak of enormous proportions.

The stakes were high, and as the first hand was dealt, the crowd watched with hushed suspense. No one could tell, from Denham's relaxed, smiling expression, that his entire future hung on the outcome of this match. Shackleford, too, seemed confident and cheerful. It was only after an hour of play that his fingers began their nervous drumming on the table, for by that time it was becoming obvious to everyone that Philip Denham's phenomenal luck had returned.

By the end of the second rubber, Philip had won more than a third of the amount he needed. Marmaduke Shackleford was showing signs of strain; his forehead was wet with perspiration and his neckcloth wrinkled and loose. He'd already indulged in his most effective ploys (like slowing down the game to a snail's pace and demanding a new deck after each hand—both ruses designed to irritate his opponent enough to unsettle his judgment), but none of his stratagems had the slightest effect on Philip's even temper or his good luck. The onlookers were gleeful. Even the side bets were now running high in Denham's favor.

But something strange was happening within Philip himself. He was not enjoying himself. For the first time in his life, he was finding the game boring. He began to wonder what he'd ever found so attractive about card-playing. Had he really spent so many hours of his life in these smoky, drab surroundings, expending his cunning, his concentration and his emotions on the turn of a card?

What am I doing in this place? he wondered. He'd sold his father's ring and risked the gains thereof on *luck*! If that luck had deserted him, as it had done so often in the past, he'd have sacrificed the ring for nothing. Was *this* the way he'd intended to make things up to Letty? Had he gambled her happiness on so flimsy a thing as *chance*? What would Augusta think of him if she knew what he was doing? Would she approve of his solving the problem of Letty in this way? Was *this* the way to win her admiration or approval?

In the attempt to see himself through her eyes, he was suddenly filled with sharp self-disgust. He was nothing but a wastrel and a gambler, and both Ned and Roger had tried to warn him of it. If he continued in this way, he would never be worthy of a woman of Augusta's character. If he was to be the kind of man whom Roger could respect and Augusta could love, he had to find a better way to solve his problems.

Abruptly, he pushed his chair back from the table. "Let's finish this hand, Shackleford, and call it quits. I've had enough of this."

The sudden end of the game caused a puzzled ripple in the crowd, but Philip pushed his way out of the room without really noticing. "Losing your nerve, old boy?" someone asked.

"Not like you to stop in mid-play, Denham," said another.

"Never mind, Philip," old Lord Lytton said comfortingly, patting his shoulder. "No need to keep the game going for *their* benefit."

Philip stared at Lord Lytton with a sudden, speculative gleam. "Have you a moment to spare, sir?" he asked. "I'd appreciate the chance to have a word with you."

The two men went into the lounge where they sat down and spoke together in low voices for a quarter of an hour. When they stood up again, they shook hands in the friendly way that indicated that a bargain had been struck that was a satisfaction to them both.

Philip left the club without a backward look. The sharp, cold air of the street struck him with an invigorating blast, and he breathed it in with real pleasure. He was aware of an enormous sense of relief, and he realized that the fear of the taint of gambling had been lodged inside him for a long time. But now he felt braced, cleansed and free. He was *not* a gamester after all.

The jeweler to whom he'd sold the ring would not sell it

back without making a sizeable profit, but Philip didn't mind. By the time he'd replaced the ring on his finger, he'd made up his mind about what to do about repaying Letty. It was really the only thing to do... and he should have known it from the first.

It was quite late at night when he arrived at Arneau House; to his chagrin, he learned that his brother had already retired for the night. But Philip could not wait for morning. He insisted that the butler wake his brother at once. Roger, pulling on a robe, came hurrying down the stairs with a look of perturbation quite plain on his face. Letty, her hair hanging down in a long plait and tying her dressing gown, was trailing anxiously behind him. "Philip! What on earth's the matter?" Roger asked worriedly.

"I must talk to you, Roger. Do you think there might still be a fire in the library? I'm chilled to the bone."

"If there isn't, we shall soon have one," his brother answered shortly and went off to catch the butler.

Letty, pausing on the last stair, looked at her brother-in-law with apprehension. "Has anything dreadful occurred?" she asked quietly.

"No, not really. It's just that I hadn't realized what I was doing to you by forcing you to keep my secret," he admitted. "I couldn't wait another day to try to set things right between you."

She sighed in relief. "Is *that* all? You needn't have troubled. Things are nicely mended between us now, you know." She gave him a tremulous smile that spoke more clearly than her words of her renewed happiness. "And without my having to give you away."

"I'm glad to hear it, truly. But—"

"No buts. If you still wish to keep your secret, it is not necessary to reveal it for my sake," she assured him.

"It is necessary for *mine*. I was a thoughtless *cur* to have waited so long."

After a silent pause, she nodded. "I've always suspected that it would have been best to confess to Roger openly. I'm glad you've decided to do it. But perhaps I should let you speak to him in private. Tell Roger I've gone back to bed." She reached up, kissed his cheek with encouraging affection and ran upstairs.

When the fire had been lit and the two brothers supplied

with glasses of brandy, they sat down near the library fireplace
and faced each other. "Do you remember, several weeks ago,
when you sent me three thousand pounds to pay my gambling
debts, Roger?" Philip asked without preamble.

"Yes, of course I remember." He studied his brother
shrewdly. "Have you incurred some *additional*—?"

"It's worse than that." Philip put down his glass and got up
restlessly. He went to the fire and stared down into it, unable
to meet his brother's eyes. I'm afraid I . . . misled you that day."

"Misled me?"

"Yes." Squaring his shoulders, he turned around bravely.
"My debts at that time amounted to twelve thousand pounds."

Roger paled. "Good God!"

Philip, reading the pain in his eyes, winced. "I'm . . . sorry."

Roger stared up at him. "I can hardly believe it of you,
Philip. I know that you have a tendency to indulge in too-deep
play, but—"

"But you didn't think of me as an incorrigible gamester . . . is
that what you want to say?"

Roger took a large gulp of his brandy. "Yes. I can't believe
that you have gaming in the blood. But twelve thousand
pounds—!"

"It isn't in the blood, Roger, I assure you. I found that out
tonight. I don't care if I never see a card or a gaming table
again. But until I could say those words—and really believe
them—I found it impossible to face you to . . . tell you the rest."

"The *rest*?" Roger looked up at his brother with knit brows.
"Perhaps I'd better take another swig first." He took another
generous drink. "All right, then, go on."

"I don't know how to say this in a way which would make
it sound less reprehensible," Philip murmured, deeply ashamed.
"I couldn't face you with my debts, you see. You'd been so
good to me . . . so often . . . that I felt unable to bring myself
to ask you for another nine thousand pounds—"

"*Nine thousand*?" The number reverberated in Roger's
brain. "Good Lord! *Letty!*"

"Yes." Philip turned back to the fire, staring down into the
flames in humiliation. "I let her pay the debts for me."

"Of *course*! What an *idiot* I was not to have *suspected*!" His
brow cleared as the last vestige of suspicion and resentment
which he'd harbored against his wife melted away.

"No, how *could* you have suspected that your own brother could have behaved so cravenly?"

"Don't be too hard on yourself, Philip. If it was so difficult for you to come to me, there must be something in *me* which prevented you. Perhaps I've been too stern with you . . . too unfeeling . . . or too self-righteous."

"Nonsense." Philip turned around in quick disagreement. "You've been the best of brothers . . . always. I don't want you to make excuses for me."

Roger looked down into his glass. "Very well, I won't. But we've both learned something from all this, I think. Perhaps we can do better from now on."

"Then . . . you forgive me?"

Roger got up and stood beside his brother, placing an arm about his shoulders. "Let's forgive *each other*, Philip. We've *all* behaved badly in this matter. Don't look so miserable about it. I thank you for coming to tell me. You've no idea what a difference it makes to my state of mind."

They walked slowly from the room. "I'll repay the entire amount one of these days," Philip promised earnestly.

"Don't think about that damned money any more," Roger ordered firmly. "So long as you are serious in your intention to refrain from throwing away your blunt at the gaming tables, I intend to see to it that your resources are increased."

"No need for that," Philip announced with a sudden look of pride. "I spoke to Lord Lytton today. He's offered me a post under him in the Civil Service."

Roger stared at his brother in pleased surprise but demurred nevertheless. "There's no need for that, you know. I never meant to force you to scratch for an income."

"I know that, Roger. But I think I shall like myself better if I can stand on my own two feet."

Roger felt a wave of admiration for his brother. He smiled and clapped the younger man on the back. "Good for you, Philip," he said proudly. "But we'll speak of these matters of income and finance at a more propitious time. Right now, if you have no objection, I have more pressing business to attend to."

"Oh?" Philip eyed him curiously. "What business?"

"I am most eager to make a long and very humble apology—"

"Don't be a clunch," Philip cut in. "I don't want—"

"Not to you, you mooncalf," Roger laughed, urging him to the door. "The humble apology is to my noble, foolish, irritating and very adorable wife."

Chapter Twenty-Two

HIS CONSCIENCE CLEAR and his prospects bright, Philip appeared the next day on the Glendenning doorstep and demanded to see Augusta. All night he had rehearsed what he would say. He would tell her that she was—and had always been—more of a reigning belle than the fools of the *ton* deserved. He would tell her that he was bitterly ashamed of ever having tried to remake her into something less than she was. He would tell her that, whether she chose to become a toast of London or live in quiet obscurity, he would always find her the embodiment of his dreams of womanly perfection.

He had never been particularly adept at putting his feelings into words, but the last phrase pleased him. She could not misunderstand this time—not if he succeeded in expressing his feelings in just that way. All night long and during the endless morning before he arrived at the Glendenning house, he repeated the phrase to himself. The waiting was so interminable that he had become, by the time he was admitted into her front hallway, a fearful hulk of nervous anticipation.

So concerned was he to avoid making a mull of the forthcoming interview that Hinson's words had no immediate effect on him. For a full minute he stared blankly at the butler's face, not comprehending. "Gone?" he croaked when the meaning of the butler's words sank into his brain. "Gone where?"

"No one knows, sir. She left the house last Tuesday morning without an explanation to anybody . . . except for the note."

"Note?" Philip felt as if the ground had been pulled from under him and he was falling into a black abyss.

"Yes, to her mother. She told her ladyship not to worry . . . that she would be quite safe. She only wanted to go to a quiet, out-of-the-way place she knew of—she wouldn't say where—for a bit of rest. She'll return in a month or so."

"A *month*!" The black abyss now seemed to have no *bottom*. One could not fall through an abyss for a *month* and expect to find ones' way back to the light again. All his hopes, all his cheerful dreams of the future, were extinguished with that one word. "Does *no one* know where . . .? Can no one in the family *guess* where she might have gone?"

"No, sir. Lady Glendenning summoned all of them, but no one has the slightest notion."

Numbed by his overwhelming disappointment, Philip turned and stumbled to the door. There was little point in remaining. Gussie had put herself beyond his reach; there was nothing he could do. He had to go home, to think, to try to find some way to come to terms with the fact that she despised him so much that she'd gone away without a word to him.

But he couldn't come to terms with that abhorrent fact. He had to find her. For the next few days he spoke to everyone in the family. He questioned them with such urgency that they all began to feel sincere pity for him. He asked them about her habits, the details of her past, the clues that might suggest where she'd gone. But none of them had anything of substance to suggest. Prue told him that Gussie had gone to Bath a few years before but hadn't liked it very much. Lady Glendenning said that she'd visited a distant cousin in Devon when she was a child but that the cousin had since passed on. Letty said that Augusta had always liked the sea, but there was no *specific* place she could fix on where the girl might have fled. Even Claryce tried to be helpful, suggesting that Augusta couldn't have gone very far, for she hadn't taken much money with her, but the suggestion only gave Philip an additional and particularly nightmarish fear—that Augusta might be living in some shabby hole, alone, hungry, sick or destitute.

He was on his way out of the Glendenning house when he thought of Katie. If anyone in the household would be privy to Augusta's secrets, it would be she. But when Hinson fetched the abigail and brought her to Philip, the maid had nothing of use to tell him. "If Miss Augusta 'ad wished us t' know, she'd 'ave tole us somethin'," Katie said bluntly. "Leave 'er be, Mr. Denham. She knows what she's about."

Philip returned home sunk in misery. He had no appetitie for food and was too restless to sleep. He wished only to pack a bag and set out in search of her, but he didn't even know in which direction to turn the horses. Ned came to his door with an offer of companionship and sympathy, but Philip turned him away. He had no stomach for idle conversation, and sympathy only made him feel worse.

Ned had been gone only a few minutes when there was a tapping at his door again. Believing that Ned had returned, he answered the knock with a feeling of rising irritation. Why couldn't he be left alone? But it was not Ned standing in the dimly-lit corridor outside his door—it was Katie. "Might I speak t' you, Mr. Denham?" she asked.

"Of course, Katie." He stood aside and let her enter.

She waited while he lit the branch of candles on his dining table, but she refused to sit down. "I c'n on'y stay a moment...don't want Mr. Hinson t' ask me where I been," she explained. "I just comed t' tell you I...found somethin' in Miss Augusta's bedroom."

Philip's heart began to pound. "Found something?"

She nodded but seemed to hesitate before proceeding. She turned her knowing eyes on his face and asked worriedly, "If I tell you...an' you go t' seek 'er...you ain't goin' t' cause 'er any *pain*, are you?"

"Pain?" He peered at her shadowed face intently. "What makes you ask that? Have I caused her pain in the past?"

She shrugged. "I ain't no tattlin' ol' whiffler, I ain't. An' Miss Augusta wouldn't wish me t' say nothin' private-like, but it seems t' me that you could 'urt 'er more'n most."

The words struck Philip like a barb and a balm at the same time. That he'd ever wounded Augusta was a tormenting thought, but the perception that she'd *cared* enough to be wounded by him more than by others—well, it was the first and only ray of hope he'd had in days. "I won't hurt her, Katie. I *swear* it."

Katie, after another searching look at his face, nodded and held out a crumpled sheet of paper. "I found this on the floor . . . under the writin' desk, y'see . . ."

Philip smoothed the sheet with unsteady hands and held the paper close to the candles. *Dear Mrs. Dolphiner*, he read, *I thank you for your very kind invitation. It could not have come at a more propitious time, for I have been feeling very depressed of late and*— There the writing had been stopped and the paper evidently crumpled and tossed aside. Philip studied the fragment carefully. The word *depressed* had been scratched out, and *propitious* was smudged as if by a tear. He felt his throat constrict. "Who is Mrs. Dolphiner?" he asked, his breath suspended.

"She's a lady what writes t' Miss Augusta regular. She lives in Bath."

"*Bath*? Then you think—?"

"She *invited* Miss Augusta, didn't she? So ain't it likely that there's where she's gone?"

"It's the *likeliest* theory I've yet heard." He took a turn round the table in growing excitement. "I don't know how to thank you! I'm off to Bath at once!" He came up beside the little abigail and grinned down at her gratefully. "I could *kiss* you, Katie!"

"Huh!" she snorted, tossing her head scornfully. "Keep yer kisses fcr them as wants 'em!" Pulling her shawl about her shoulders, she marched, chin up, to the door. "If you bring my poppet back 'appy, that'll be thanks enough fer me."

Augusta had run off to Bath for good and sufficient reasons. The first of these, and the one which she gave to herself and to Mrs. Dolphiner, was that she was tired, run-down and needed a change of scene. But when she was truly honest with herself, she knew that there was a deeper, more fundamental reason for her secret and abrupt departure from London. Before she decided to leave, she'd heard that Philip was attempting to set to rights the problems she'd brought to his attention, and she knew that, one day after he'd solved them, he'd appear on her doorstep. She would have to face him, to express her gratitude for what he'd done. While she *was* grateful, she knew she was unequal to the strain of facing him again. Until she learned to control the emotions which lay trembling and tender just under the surface, she had to stay away from him. She was too vulnerable, too thin-skinned, too easily moved to tears these days; her feelings for him, which had been buried and hidden from the world for so long, had in the days of their association come too dangerously close to the surface. She couldn't trust herself to remain in his company without revealing something of her secret yearnings. The only solution that had presented itself to her was to go away until she'd regained her usual self-control.

Mrs. Dolphiner had welcomed her with open arms and apt quotations from Thomas Gray. "The Bath waters and my company shall soon restore the bloom to your cheeks," the angular, energetic old lady had declared. "Here you shall live

> *'The thoughtless day, the easy night,*
> *Your spirits pure, your slumbers light...'* "

Augusta had gratefully accepted Mrs. Dolphiner's embraces and poetic declamations. Although winter in Bath was not the most salubrious of seasons, Mrs. Dolphiner encouraged the girl to take long, invigorating walks, to drink the waters in the Pump Room, to spend afternoons quietly reading or napping and to go to the Assembly Rooms for entertainment in the evenings. In these activities, Mrs. Dolphiner was happy to act as chaperone. It soon became clear to the observant old lady that her young friend was suffering from more than weariness, but she asked no questions. She merely offered nourishment and companionship, and she recited huge sections of *The Progress of Poesy* aloud—with extravagant gestures and spirited enthusiasm—whenever the silences caused by Augusta's abstractedness threatened to become embarrassing.

The society of Bath was thin in November, so it was not long before the male residents noticed the arrival of a quietly-pretty young woman in their midst. As one after another of them arranged to be introduced to her, it dawned on Augusta that the tricks Philip had taught her were quite useful in helping her to endure the strain of dealing with the attentions of these gentlemen. Before she quite realized what had happened, she had attracted a couple of persistent admirers. And not long after the middle-aged bachelor, Mr. Courtney, and the tall, attractive Mr. Pratt began to court her, one or two others followed suit. Before a week had gone by, she found herself surrounded by a group of eager young gentlemen every time she entered the Pump Room. "You've become known as the

Belle of Bath, my dear," Mrs. Dolphiner informed her one day.

Augusta couldn't help but be amused. If she persisted in her employment of all Philip's little devices and ploys, she might easily become sufficiently proficient at the game to make use of them when she returned to London. Perhaps the attainment of these skills in the Art of Dalliance had come too late to win Philip's wager for him, but she might yet manage to make him proud of her.

To that end, she set about becoming the Belle of Bath in earnest. At the end of a fortnight she'd acquired four steady admirers and had attracted the attention of several other gentlemen. And when she overheard one of Mrs. Dolphiner's acquaintances remark that "the young Miss Glendenning is quite a shameless flirt" Augusta was hard-pressed not to laugh aloud.

Only Mrs. Dolphiner was aware that an abiding sorrow lurked under Augusta's frivolous facade. She explained to her critical acquaintance that she suspected that her young friend harbored a secret sorrow. She had the perfect passage from one of Mr. Gray's sonnets to illustrate her point, which she paraphrased to suit her purpose:

> " '*In vain,*' " she recited to her friend, " '*to her the
>   smiling mornings shine,
> And reddening Phoebus lifts his golden fire;
> The birds in vain their amorous descant join
> Or cheerful fields resume their green attire;
> Her ears, alas! for other notes repine,
> A different object do those eyes require!*' "

Philip Denham arrived in Bath late in the afternoon of a mild November day. It took him several hours to discover the exact location of the domicile of Mrs. Dolphiner, and he therefore did not appear on her doorstep until the evening was well advanced. A prim housemaid answered his knock and informed him—to his intense frustration—that Miss Glendenning was not at home. Mrs. Dolphiner, who had followed the maid into the hallway, curious to see who had called at so late an hour, invited him in. "Are you Augusta's brother?" she asked, looking him over with interest.

"No, ma'am. I'm her ... er ... her brother-*in-law*. My name is Philip Denham."

"I hope, Mr. Denham, that you've not come to bring Augusta bad news. Is all her family well?"

"Yes, quite well. I've brought no news at all. I merely wish to make a ... a *personal* call," Philip explained awkwardly.

"A *personal* call?" She examined him in frank disapproval. "I trust, sir, that you are not the gentleman who has caused her the severe anguish from which she seems to suffer."

Philip was startled. "*Anguish*, ma'am? *Is* she suffering anguish?"

"I believe so, in spite of the gaiety and activity of Bath society. To paraphrase Mr. Gray's beautiful verse:

> '*The fields to all their wonted tribute bear;*
> *To warm their little loves the birds complain:*
> *She fruitless mourns to him that cannot hear,*
> *And weeps the more, because she weeps in vain.*' "

Philip had not been prepared for Mrs. Dolphiner's eccentricities, and he didn't quite know what to make of her. He blinked at her in bewilderment. "Where is Miss Glendenning now?" he asked abruptly.

"She's attending a concert at the Assembly Rooms. I found the soloist not to my liking, but I insisted that Augusta remain."

"Then, if you'll excuse me, ma'am, I shall go there at once."

"You may just as well wait here," Mrs. Dolphiner advised. "I think the concert will be over soon."

But Philip's patience had completely deserted him. With polite firmness, he asked Mrs. Dolphiner for the direction of the Assembly Rooms, took his leave of her and set off up Milsom Street, urging his horses at breakneck speed. He arrived to find that the concert was just ending. A number of people were already emerging from the wide doorway as Philip pushed his way in. He'd not gone more than a step inside the door when he caught sight of her, and his breath caught in his throat in astonishment.

If Augusta was suffering anguish, it was the strangest sort of anguish he'd ever seen. She was smiling coyly at one of several gentlemen who were surrounding her, and she'd evidently said something witty, for they were all laughing. "But my dear girl," a dignified middle-aged man was saying, "you cannot make so light of a drive with my chestnuts. Besides, you went home on Mr. Pratt's arm on Saturday. It *must* be my turn by now!"

With intense chagrin, Philip watched her turn to the speaker with an unmistakable and practiced version of the *Innocent Flutter*. "Oh, *la*, Mr. Courtney, I don't take *turns*!" she said, concluding with a musical *Upward Trill*.

The gentleman who evidently was Mr. Pratt—the tallest and most prepossessing of the group—reached for her arm, shouldering Mr. Courtney firmly out of the way. "Whatever your claims, Courtney," he said with what Philip found to be maddening self-confidence, "you shall not have her tonight. The wench has been teasing me concerning a *secret* she's heard about me, and I shall not rest until I've wormed it out of her."

Philip felt his fingers tighten into fists as a wave of unexpected fury swept over him. Suffering *anguish*, indeed! Augusta looked as if she were enjoying every bit of this abominable male attention. Her cheeks were glowing, her air was confident and her smile seemed to light up the room. In fact, if Philip knew anything of the matter, the girl was behaving like the most heartless of London *coquettes*! He ground his teeth wrathfully. If he could have followed his instincts, he would have broken through the crowd like a raging animal, seized her in his arms and *wrung her neck*! As it was, however, he could only stand, immobile and impotent, staring aghast at the laughing, alluring, capricious, flirtatious creation that he himself had wrought.

Chapter Twenty-Three

PHILIP HAD SEEN and heard all he could bear. He pushed through the milling crowd in the lobby of the Assembly and came up to the group surrounding Augusta. "If you will excuse me, gentlemen," he said with a stiff bow, "I think *I* shall claim the lady's arm."

"*Philip*!" Augusta gasped, whitening.

Several voices rose in objection to this interruption. "Who are *you*, sir?" Mr. Pratt demanded, stepping forward aggressively. "And by *what right*—?"

"By right of the length of my acquaintance with the lady," Philip said curtly, pushing the fellow aside.

Mr. Pratt looked very much annoyed, and he came forward again, lifting an angry fist. "See here—" he said threateningly.

But Augusta, pale and breathless, put a restraining hand on Mr. Pratt's arms. "Forgive us, sir, but I m—must ask you to excuse us. This gentleman, you see, is m—my brother-in-law."

Without further explanation, and ignoring the puzzled looks being exchanged by the men she was leaving behind, she took Philip's arm. They walked quickly and silently from the lobby, leaving the circle of admirers staring after them in considerable bafflement.

Philip led her so quickly through the crowd to his carriage that he gave her no time to breathe or speak. Her breast was heaving and her head spinning by the time she was seated beside him. "Philip, how . . . ? I mean, what*ever* are you doing here? I didn't know you cared to visit places like Bath."

"I don't," he muttered through clenched teeth, whipping up the horses. "I came to find *you*."

"To find *me*?" She was utterly confounded. "But *why*? There's nothing wrong at home, is there? *Mama*? Prue's *baby*?"

"Nothing's wrong, except that their Augusta has disappeared. Didn't you think we'd find your mysterious absence *worrisome*?"

"*We*?" She turned to stare at his frozen profile. "Did *you* find my absence worrisome, Philip?" she asked, her pulse beginning to race crazily.

He threw her a furious glance and turned back to glare at the horses and the dark road ahead. "That's a featherbrained question! I've been completely *unhinged* with worrying! And now I find you brazenly flirting with half the male population of this benighted district as if you hadn't a care in the world for those you left behind!"

She clenched her hands in her lap. *I mustn't refine on this too much*, she warned herself. While it *did* appear that he was showing signs of a deep affection for her, she might very well be mistaking his intentions. She had wished so long for him to care that perhaps her imagination was playing tricks on her. "I was only practicing," she said in a small, embarrassed voice.

"*Practicing*?" He ground his teeth in fury. "For what purpose?"

"Well, I . . . I thought that when I . . . returned to London, I could try again, you see—"

"Try *again*?"

"To make a mark on the *ton*. I hoped to . . . make you proud of me."

"Oh, my *Lord*!" With an agonized groan, he threw down the reins and, turning to her, grasped her shoulders. "Please, Augusta, listen to me! I don't care *what* the *ton* thinks of you! I don't want you to make a mark on *anyone*. I was a fool to believe for a moment that you could be in any way improved. Don't you understand? I want nothing more of you than that you be *yourself*!"

"*Myself*?" She looked at him wide-eyed. "You mean the

little shiver-mouse I was *before*?"

He winced in pain. "I never meant—! Damnation, girl, what can I say to make you understand?" In desperate earnestness, not quite realizing what he was doing, he pulled her into his arms. "Don't you know by this time that I love you?" he asked, his voice husky with emotion. He stared down at her upturned face, his heart hammering loudly in his chest. In the dim light of the night-time streets of Bath, he could hardly read her expression. Her eyes seemed to shine with a brilliant, inner light, and her breath came in short, almost frightened gasps, but she said nothing. He didn't wish to frighten her more than he already had, but was struck with an overwhelming urge to kiss her. He bent his head close to hers.

She could hardly believe what was happening. Had she heard his words correctly? Had she understood their meaning? Was he about to *kiss* her, as he had so many times in her dreams? Terrified that there was some mistake—that she'd somehow misinterpreted his intention—she put a shaking hand against his chest. "Is th—this the time for me to use the *Rebuff Regretful*?" she asked breathlessly.

He shut his eyes in pain and let her go. Numbly, he reached for the reins and turned the aimlessly-plodding horses back along Milsom Street in the direction of Mrs. Dolphiner's abode. "I suppose I deserved that," he said bitterly, his jaw clenched tightly and a muscle in his cheek throbbing in evidence of his inner turmoil. "I've done my task very well. You've put me in my place with consummate skill."

She couldn't mistake the pain in his voice. "I didn't m—mean to put you in your place, Philip," she said shyly.

His eyebrows rose, and he turned to look at her, a gleam of hope leaping into flame in his chest. "Then . . . what *did* you mean?"

She was not sure how to answer. Her head was swimming with all sorts of new and startling emotions, and the overwhelming joy which had seized her when he'd declared his love was almost buried by the confusion. "There's Mrs. Dolphiner's house on your left," she said in some relief, too frightened to grasp the happiness that seemed suddenly—amazingly—within reach. "Perhaps we should speak of this tomorrow . . . when we both are calmer." She brushed his hand with a light touch of farewell, slipped down from the carriage and ran to the door.

"*Gussie!*" It was a cry of despair. He flung himself down from his seat and ran after her. Snatching her hands in a tight clasp, he peered down at her in urgent appeal. "Don't put me off to face another endless night...not when I—"

"You called me *Gussie!*" she breathed, her face alight.

He dropped her hands, took a backward step and lowered his head. "That's what I call you in my mind," he admitted shamefacedly. "I'm sorry I *ever* thought of you as Augusta."

With a little, joyful gurgle, she threw her arms around his neck. "Oh, Philip, I *do* love you so! I've said the words to myself so often and for so long a time that I almost can't believe I've never said them aloud before."

Mrs. Dolphiner, hearing voices on her doorstep, opened the door to find her young friend being quite passionately kissed by the fellow who'd called earlier. The two were so blissfully absorbed that they seemed completely unaware that their activity could be easily observed by anyone who chanced to look out of any one of dozens of windows in nearby houses or who passed by on this very public thoroughfare. "Augusta, *really!*" she exclaimed. "To be the Belle of Bath is all very well, but to dally in this way out there on the street is beyond the permissable! As my friend Thomas Gray has said,

> '*From hence, ye beauties, undeceived,*
> *Know, one false step is ne'er retrieved,*
> *And be with caution bold.*
> *Not all that tempts your wandering eyes*
> *And heedless hearts, is lawful prize;*
> *Nor all that glisters, gold.*'"

"You're quite right, Mrs. Dolphiner," Gussie said in a choked voice, lifting her head. "I've been behaving quite shamelessly."

"Yes, she has," Philip agreed, grinning down at the girl he still held in his arms. "But you have our word, ma'am, that her days of dalliance are over."

Gussie looked up at him, blinking her eyes in an *Innocent Flutter* and giving a distinctly *Gossamer Giggle*. "Do you mean I'm never again to be a reigning belle?"

"Never!" Philip said firmly, lifting her off the ground in a crushing embrace.

"Be that as it may, young man," Mrs. Dolphiner said in her finest elocutionary tone, "if you're going to continue to kiss the girl in that *over-zealous* way, I suggest that you come inside at once and permit me to shut the door!"

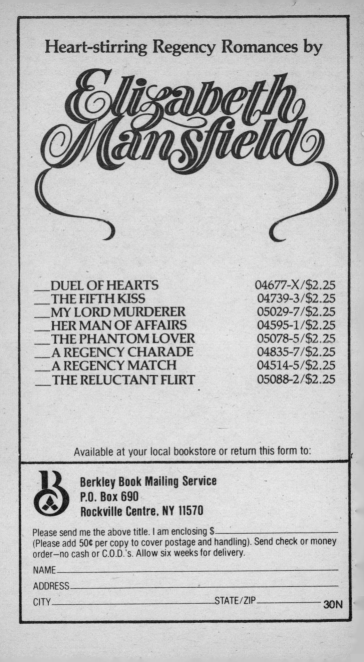